DRAGONLORDS OF DUMNONIA

Dragon Heart

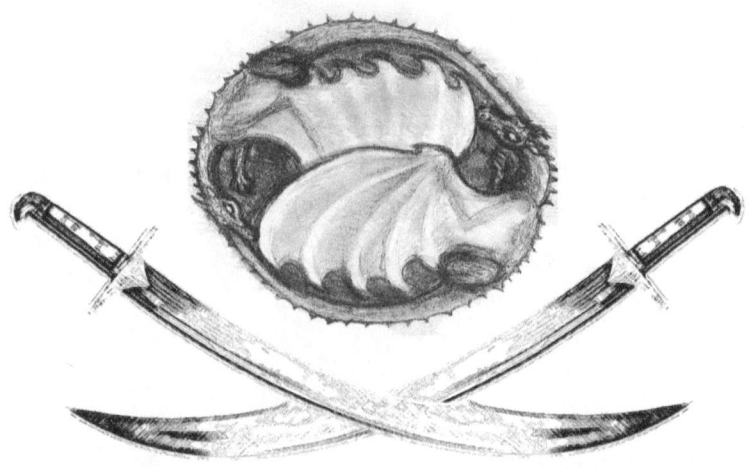

LINDA A. MALCOR

STORY MERCHANT BOOKS
LOS ANGELES
2015

THE STORY MERCHANT

ISBN: 978-0-9963689-4-0

Story Merchant Books
400 S. Burnside Avenue #11B
Los Angeles, CA 90036
http://www.storymerchant.com/books.html

Cover & interior formatting by IndieDesignz.com
Dragon Cover Illustration & interior illustrations © 2015 Laura Cameron
www.lauracameron.net

Dragon Heart

For the Third Foundation

Contents

Shashtah

Chapter 1:

Revelation

War arose in the Land of Light, Criton and his loyal siblings fighting against the Dark One and his brothers, who betrayed the Light. The Dark One and his supporters fought Criton and his followers; but the rebels were defeated, and there was no longer any place for them in the Lord of Light's realm. The Dark One was thrown out onto Centuria, and his supporters were exiled with him. And I heard a voice saying in the Land of Light, "Woe to you, O Centuria, for the Dark One has come to you!"

When the Dark One saw that he was on Centuria, he pursued Daethian women who would bear him male children. But by the magic of Corin some of the women were given the two wings of the Bronze Dragon that they might fly from the Dark One into the wilderness of Dumnonia, to the place where they would nourish the warriors who will end the Dark One's reign.

—from The Book of Light

SHASHTAH'S DESERT BOOTS POUNDED against the algae-covered stone in time to the wild hammering of his heart. The magically-sustained plants that clung to the tunnel floor, roof and walls, gave off a faint glow to his light-sensitive eyes. Using the diaphanous gleam as a guide, he ducked, twisted sidewise, broad-jumped and hurdled through the tomb-dark maze in the heart of Mount Cinnamar. Half by memory, half by faith, he fled through corridor after corridor, praying he would not collide with unforgiving stone. The certainty that his body would be torn into unrecognizable shreds and his soul scattered to the desert winds if he fell drove him as a prong-horned skympsam flees before a ten-winter storm. He ran as though all the demons of Cinnamar were after him.

Which they were.

Except for the one that was in front of him.

Half a heartbeat too late, Shashtah sensed the slight shift in the darkness. He tried to stop, but his boots were better adapted to climbing dunes than to scrabbling down prison halls. He lost traction and skidded directly toward his enemy. He accepted his fate with a philosophical shrug and held onto his turban with his right hand. He crouched and slid toward what he hoped were the demon's legs.

A massive weight, more oppressive than the presence of the mountain above him, brushed past his arms and over his head. The reek of decayed flesh filled his lungs, causing him to gag.

Shashtah spun out of his skid.

The horde at his heels suddenly came horn to claw with the monstrosity that was now at his back. Squeals of pain and fury lanced through the dank air as the demons tore at each other in their eagerness to pursue their prey, only making the tangle of limbs and body parts worse.

Shashtah didn't wait for them to sort themselves out. He fled blindly down tunnel after tunnel until he felt the stone floor level out. His lungs screamed for air as he bore sharply to his left. He took a deep breath—and immediately regretted the action as he choked on the prison's stench. *Down, right, down, down, right, up, left, down, and out!* He forced himself to concentrate on his escape route, silently chanting the path through the maze in time to his throbbing pulse.

Somewhere behind him, the demons finally disentangled themselves and renewed the chase.

Not that Shashtah could blame them. He did, after all, have the black pulsing jewel that contained the heart of the Dark One clutched tightly in his left fist.

Stairs heading down appeared out of nowhere in front of him. He half-jumped, half-plummeted to the next floor, holding his desert cloak tight against his body to keep the fabric from billowing within reach of the claws that slashed at him out of the darkness. Pain shocked through his ankles as he landed at the bottom of the steps, but his bones failed to break. The howls and gibbering of a squabble at the top of the stairs gave him the incentive he needed to limp on.

The horde of demons, prevented by the cramped space of the corridor from taking their true forms and using their most powerful magical abilities, shaped themselves into wind and mist in one final effort to catch him.

Shashtah heard the inhuman cries change to the lonely howl of the North Wind just as his straining eyes located the one spot on the tunnel wall that was not glistening with algae. He closed his eyes and dove head-first toward solid rock. He grinned at the demons' screams of frustration as he passed through the illusion and vanished beyond their grasp.

Shashtah emerged into glaring sunlight that would have blinded anyone except a Dumnonian. He landed in a tuck on the rocky outcropping that jutted out of the sand below him. He tumbled down the barren slope in an undignified tangle of cloth and sand, saying a private prayer of thanks to Leot, Lord of Light, whose merciless orb burned down on the blistering dunes. *Full daylight!* he congratulated himself. *Excellent timing! Now if the legends of Lord Criton's binding spells are true, most of the demons won't be able to emerge until nightfall and the worst ones will remain trapped in the mountain, unable to follow me at all!*

Shashtah drew lungful after lungful of the fresh, desert air into his aching chest as he waited for his solid amber eyes to darken against the glare. Those eyes were the only major thing about his appearance that marked him as closer kin to the elves of the Great Woods than to the Daethians. The elves had the same, otherworldly eyes, ones with neither pupils nor whites. But elven eyes tended more toward greens and violets in color. Plus, Shashtah had yet to meet any elf whose eyes would naturally shield him from the brightness of the desert in full sunlight.

As soon as Shashtah's vision adjusted, he stood up and dusted himself off. Runnels of sweat poured down his deeply tanned face and onto his linen shirt. He wiped his dirt-smudged, beardless chin with his right hand and licked at the moisture out of habit. He had tried to teach a Daethian trader that trick of survival once, but the man's fluids proved too salty to slake his own thirst. Apparently the Dumnonian ability to reclaim water from their own bodies was yet another adaptation to their hostile homeland for which they could thank the Lord of Light.

Shashtah combed his damp, layer-cut, blue-black hair into place with his fingers, revealing his slightly pointed ears. While trading in the shadow of the Dragon's Back Mountains, he tended to keep his hair carefully combed over his ear tips to hide the one other feature that truly differentiated him from the Daethians. He had found that his ears rather than his eyes bothered his customers most for some reason he could not understand. In the deep desert, though, he had no need to hide the strange feature. In fact, at the moment he had great need of it.

Shashtah stood about a third of the way up the peak on the only mountain in the immense wasteland that was Cinnamar. The desert winds whistled around him as they sliced across the mouth of the canyon that sheltered the secret entrance. He listened intently with his superior hearing. No sounds of pursuit mixed with the soul-chilling howl of the winds.

The jet-black stone in Shashtah's left fist throbbed wildly, demanding his attention.

Shashtah stared in disbelief at the obscene gem. *Did I really do it? A lowly desert nomad who is still unworthy of a Dragon? Did I really do what countless Krills and other thieves have died—or worse—trying to accomplish?*

His only answer was the unholy pulsing of the stone.

Shashtah's fingers absently brushed against the brightly-colored patterns that danced across his leather belt as he stuffed his prize into his pouch. The belt was the one piece of Dumnonian flamboyance that he allowed himself. He'd chosen camouflaging, sand-colored cloth and leather for the rest of his garb, but the belt had been a gift from his parents when he had departed on his first mission for the Dumnonian king, Shaharadesh. That was the last time he had been truly happy, the last time he had seen either of his parents alive. The tales of long-dead heroes and their foes paraded around his waist in a glorious swirl of jewel-tone dyes: ruby, topaz, emerald, sapphire and amethyst. *Foes no longer*, he corrected himself. *Now we all have but one foe.* Shashtah felt himself shiver in the desert heat, more at the irony of the alliance between the Dumnonian Dragonriders and the Daethian Dragonslayers, than at the chill of the sweat drying on his golden brown skin.

All his life Shashtah had wanted to be a Dragonrider. The Bronze Dragons of Dumnonia, with their armored hides, fearsome breaths and gem-like eyes had fascinated him since he had seen his first dragonette, Tphah, at the court of Dameth, Dragonlord of Dumnonia. For some reason he still could not understand, his father, Garesh, who usually avoided Dragons like a simoom, had taken the entire caravan to watch Dameth receive the Fledgling Tphah at his basecamp after Shaharadesh assigned her to him. Shashtah still bristled at the way Dameth had stared completely through Garesh and his followers—centaurs, Galantites, Krills, sprites, and even a giant who could use weather magic. Granted, the Dragonlord must have survived at least ten solo missions into Cinnamar to earn his Dragon, Tlee, but Garesh had survived almost seven times that many. The only difference between the two Dumnonians was that Dameth had foresworn all followers in exchange for his Dragon, and Garesh had given up the chance to ride a Dragon in exchange for his caravan of powerful misfits. Every Dumnonian warrior faced that same choice, and, growing up as he had in a dragonless camp, Shashtah could not favor either side. He only knew that from the moment he saw Tphah's glistening eyes, the life of the Dragonrider was the only life for him. Shashtah had undertaken nine missions for the Dumnonian king in the hope of reaching that goal. Nine times he had succeeded beyond even the fantasies of his admittedly irrepressible imagination and had been able to shower Shaharadesh with marvelous gifts. His efforts to impress his king had left him with little more than his weapons, his horse, and the clothes on his back. But the last gift, a talking sword seized from the hands of a dying werewolf, had earned him the right to undertake his tenth mission, his Dragonquest. *Now, if I can just find a way to get this gem into Shaharadesh's hands, he'll have to give me a Dragon!*

For a heartbeat Shashtah fancied that he heard his long-dead mother's voice carried on the fierce winds: "Dragons on the brain, I tell you! Don't you ever think about anything else?"

A harsh laugh tore from Shashtah's throat. Even his mother would have had to admit a Dragon might be handy at the moment. Blood flowed freely from a dozen cuts beneath rends in his sand-colored shirt and his leather trousers as he stared at the mouth of the canyon.

Mount Cinnamar wasn't much of a mountain. It looked a lot bigger than it was simply because there was nothing but barren wasteland around it for countless wingspans in all directions. Nothing had lived in Cinnamar for as long as the Dark One had ruled there. No grasses struggled to survive among the stones on the treacherous slope. No ants carved a home in the shade of the rocky shelf. Not even a fly stirred to bother Shashtah's wounds. Only ghosts and demons and devils and other things that had never lived, or that hadn't had the decency to die, populated the lifeless country. *How long can I survive out here, even if the Dark One's forces fail to find me after sunset?*

Shashtah mentally shrugged the question to the back of his mind. Daethian-style thinking had no place in the desert. Out here, faith was all that mattered. If he believed he would survive, somehow the Lord of Light would grant him the power to do so—even if his physical body died. Only the loss of his soul could change that, and he had no intention of losing his soul.

The panic Shashtah had felt in the clutches of the demons finally receded enough for his stomach to remind him he was starving. His last meal before he had left on his Dragonquest had consisted of unleavened bread, water and a single date. Some ancestral memory insisted that the hero's feast had been more elaborate in years gone by, when caravans had streamed across the barren wastes under the careful watch of the Dragonriders of Dumnonia. Now, almost all of the food the Dumnonians could scavenge went to their precious reptilian mounts, and Shashtah did not begrudge the fabulous creatures their sustenance one bit. Somehow the desert people's bodies had adjusted to the need, developing the power to subsist on a diet that would have killed a Daethian within a rotation— the twenty-day cycle that regulated the lives of the Dumnonian Dragonriders. The Daethian wisemen speculated that the powerful magics that warped the desert landscape had somehow mutated the desert dwellers as well. Shashtah preferred to think that the ability was a blessing granted to them by his god so that the Dragons might exist. Whatever the case, food was something that could wait until he reached safety.

His injuries, though, were another matter. If he wanted to be alive to eat when he did walk out of Cinnamar, he needed to do something to stop his bleeding.

Shashtah glanced around until he found his camel-colored turban lying on the sand. He picked it up and used his bejeweled jambiya to tear pieces from the cloth. He bound his injuries tightly enough to stop the flow of blood but not so firmly as to cut off his circulation. He worked with the speed of long practice. The last thing on Centuria he wanted was to give those living nightmares another chance at him. They would have just that far too soon if he failed to put enough distance between himself and the mountain before nightfall. Satisfied he was not going to bleed to death, he climbed up to the rocky shelf and raised his darkened amber eyes to scan the horizon.

Seif dunes stretched away from him, running for thousands of wingspans parallel to the north and south winds. Of all the realms on Centuria, only the countries of Rashtar, Daethia and Dumnonia remained free from the evil powers locked in the mountain beneath his feet.

Rashtar lay far to the northeast, beyond the Dragon's Back Mountains. The barbarians, who lived behind the formidable natural barrier, largely ignored the conflict with the Dark One except when a Cinnamarian or two actually managed to slip through Daethia's defenses or found a magical pool or other means to transport them into Rashtar. Then the Rashtarians made short work of their enemies.

Daethia and Dumnonia, however, shared borders with Cinnamar. Unwilling to abandon lush farmlands and magical forests for the open desert, Elves, Galantites and Krills had crowded within the Dragonslayers' tiny country of Daethia, about three days' ride to the east of Mount Cinnamar.

Shashtah could cut across the seif dunes and hope to reach the Elven or Daethian border patrols before the demons found him. To hide among so many until he could find a caravan to carry him to the King's Camp would be Hatchling's play. But navigating around the enormous dunes would be treacherous.

The vast expanse of Shashtah's homeland, Dumnonia, stretched several days' journey to the north. He could pick a gassi, a path sliced between the dunes by the vicious north wind, follow it part of the way, and then turn his horse loose. With luck, one of the patrols from a Dragonlord's basecamp would spot either him or his stallion if a sandstorm didn't bury them first. Or he might find a magical warp that would carry him far away from Mount Cinnamar. If he reached a basecamp, he could hire on with a caravan that was heading to the King's Camp. The mere prospect of trying to cross the expanse of Cinnamar toward the brutal deserts of Dumnonia instead of toward the farmlands and forests of Daethia seemed insane at best.

Then again, is not every warrior who dreams of skimming through the desert skies on dragonwings a bit sunstruck? Shashtah grinned as he drew a bit of horsehair from his second belt pouch. His slender fingers sketched the image of a horse in the air. Sparks glittered like diamonds as he prayed silently, *May I see the mount that Thou hast hidden for me.*

A black desert stallion and all of his tack shimmered into existence before him.

Shashtah crooned softly to the spirited animal as he removed the hobbles from the stallion's legs. Then he pulled a bit of multicolored ash out of the same pouch. As he scattered the ash on the wind he prayed, *May the hooves of my horse leave no mark upon the sand.* The second invocation was as unnecessary as the first had been, but, as a warrior several days' ride from any hope of help, he felt a prayer or two wouldn't hurt.

Shashtah vaulted onto the stallion's back. Water might be to the east, but Dumnonia and the Bronze Dragons waited for him to the north. The malevolent jewel safe in his pouch and dreams of his future Dragon in his heart, he dug his heels into his horse's ribs and rode for home.

For the better part of two candlescars Shashtah's stallion cantered north along the rocky gassi between two massive seif dunes. Only desert mounts had such stamina beneath the strength-sapping heat of the merciless sun. Any other horse would have dropped dead before running a hundred wingspans. But even the splendid stallion had his limits. Shashtah slipped to the sand and walked his mount, giving the horse small drinks from his nearly-empty waterskin. The sun was already sinking low in the sky by the time Shashtah judged that it was safe enough to ride again. Walking had helped to keep his wounds from stiffening, but the injuries burned, ever-present reminders of what would emerge from Mount Cinnamar when the sun finally set and Lord Criton's spells weakened enough for the demons to escape.

As Shashtah rode north into the growing darkness, he dreamed of the Dragon who would be his when he reached the King's Camp. Young or old, male or female, he didn't much care. All he wanted was to Bond with one of the magnificent creatures and to know that he would never be alone again. They would join a century and fly together over the glittering sands, carrying "Eternal Death to the Dark One!" with their fellow Dragons and Riders. They would soar effortlessly on the desert winds, crossing above harrats and kavirs and wadis, hunting their enemies, driving away lesser creatures with the Dragon's noxious breath and reducing powerful demons to ash with bolts of pure magic.

Shashtah felt his stallion stumble, jarring him back to his surroundings. The sun had set, and the shadows had grown too dark for most non-desert creatures to see. Shashtah slid to the sand and removed the stallion's tack. He gave his weary mount the last of his water. Then he held the sweat-drenched horse's head close to his own. "May the Light shine upon my tongue and my ears that the words of this noble creature shall be clear to me and that my words shall make sense to him," he whispered. Pure white light radiated from his fingertips.

"What more must you ask of me?" the stallion panted, his language suddenly comprehensible under the effects of the spell.

"Fetch help," Shashtah commanded.

The stallion nodded his willingness to obey, neighed his challenge at the desert winds, and cantered north.

May the Light protect my stallion and show him the way. The benediction whispered through Shashtah's heart.

The wind had shifted. A steady sirocco now blew out of the south. The silhouette of the Dark One's mountain had long been hidden by the great seif dunes, but Shashtah could imagine the shadows stirring on its slopes. The demons would soon be upon him.

Shashtah felt his soul quiver. He had best keep moving while he still could. He paused long enough to bury his horse's tack in the sand to hide his trail. Then he took a deep breath and trudged northward in his stallion's wake.

Not being a particularly bright lot, the demons took until well after moonrise to locate the weary Dumnonian.

Shashtah's heart originally leapt with joy at the sound of leather wings, envisioning a Dragonrider coming to his rescue. Then he remembered that the prevailing wind had shifted, and his heart sank. He scanned the sky with his sharp night vision.

Demons filled the air. Bat-winged they were for the most part, with more limbs and horns and eyes than any natural creature would have dared to boast. Patches of hide, fur, scales and decaying flesh in an appalling array of disgusting colors shimmered in the moonlight. Hell-flames ringed some of the monsters, while others seemed either too dull-witted or incompetent to understand that kind of torment. Atop one of the larger demons sat a being more jackal than man. Impressively tall in spite of a wicked curvature of his upper spine that betrayed a once-broken back, he—it was most definitely a "he"—strained with sturdy tendons and stringy muscles to maintain his perch on the demon's shoulders, just in front of its massive wings. The ribs of the creature's gaunt chest threatened to puncture his mangy yellow hide. A ridge of scraggly black hair rose along his spine from his tailless buttocks to the base of his canine skull, near equine ears that were flattened against the wind. Thirst-blackened lips pulled back in a sneer. Sadistic yet intelligent yellow eyes peered out from beneath the creature's heavy brow. He giggled obscenely as his glistening black nose scented his prey. The monstrosity wore no clothes except for a tattered black kilt he had stolen from a deceased member of the Kyondoca, Daethia's elite guards. The kilt did nothing to hide the fact that his organ was erect with the thrill of the hunt. He flourished a giant flail above his head. Three wicked, spiked balls flashed in the moonlight at the end of thick chains. Only one metal shone that brightly in any light: Galantite, for which the diminutive miners of Mount Paradin were named. Only one of the Dark One's henchman had ever amassed enough of the precious metal to have a magical weapon of torture forged in the hellfires of Mount Cinnamar: Yapada.

Shashtah shuddered involuntarily as he recognized the Demonlord and his deadly lash. *He's too powerful! How was he able to escape the mountain?* Fingers numb with fear, he reached into his belt pouch and extracted the pulsing black gem. "Let me go, or I'll destroy it!"

"What could you possibly do to the container of the Dark One's heart?" Yapada cackled.

Steal it. The words flitted through Shashtah's mind, but he had no time to dwell on the thought as he watched the demons perching along the crests of the dunes, blocking his escape in all directions.

Yapada vaulted to the sand and bowed toward the stone.

The black gem flared with dark light.

Yapada grinned, revealing hideously yellowed fangs. He tested the weight of his flail in his hand as his ears pricked forward, eagerly awaiting the sound of his victim's screams. "Prepare him."

Several demons rushed into the gassi.

Shashtah cringed as they grasped him with their claws and nails, but he resisted the temptation to struggle, knowing all too well that he would need every grain of his strength to survive what was to come.

The demons tore the cloak and shirt from their victim. Tentacles wrapped around Shashtah's wrists and ankles and held him spread-cagled, bare back to the Demonlord. They lifted him slightly off the ground so his feet could not take any of his weight.

The muscles on Shashtah's back stretched tight, which he knew would only increase his suffering. He took a deep breath and let it out slowly, trying to release the tension he could feel building within him. It did no good.

Yapada, a master of torture, held his blow for what seemed like an eternity, letting his helpless prey writhe in anticipation of the imminent pain.

The gem, still clutched tightly in Shashtah's left fist, pulsed wildly in time to his own frantic heartbeat.

The three spiked balls finally whistled through the chill night air and tore deep furrows across Shashtah's back. Instead of breaking bone, the magic in the weapon created the all-too-real illusion that the flail was also shredding his soul.

The evil gem glowed brighter and melded to Shashtah's hand, sucking at his torment.

When Shashtah's muscles stopped contracting uncontrollably with pain, the flail whirred toward him a second time.

Shashtah convulsed and arched his back in agony at the blow.

Yapada's giggle set the demons to gibbering with delight.

The stone blazed in Shashtah's hand as he contorted in pain beneath the merciless lash.

Yapada waited until Shashtah's muscles ceased twitching then landed a third blow.

A prayer that he might lose consciousness flittered through Shashtah's shattered thoughts.

He must have screamed the prayer aloud, for the Demonlord's laughter redoubled. "Why would I deprive my Lord of his feast?"

What was left of Shashtah's mind tried to recoil into unconsciousness, but the force within the stone kept him alert and fully aware of his lacerated flesh.

The Demonlord struck a fourth time.

The half-flayed Dumnonian realized that he must have screamed again, since his throat suddenly hurt worse than his back.

The gem in his hand became a beacon of darkness, splitting the air with its unholy light.

Yapada landed a fifth blow.

Shashtah's world twisted into a simoom of pain and terror as the evil within the stone suckled on the essence of his soul.

As the beating continued, Yapada held each blow, waiting for Shashtah's muscles to stop shivering with pain and for the expectation of the next lash to become almost unbearable.

Through it all Shashtah battled with the heart of the evil god. Long after he relinquished any hope of his physical body living through the night, he struggled to keep what he could of the divine spark within him intact. In some strange way the pain actually helped, clearly delineating what was flesh and what was not. He ceased praying to his god for aid, fearing that the effort would distract him from his internal war and doom him forever to such torments at the whim of the heart's owner.

At dawn the demons vanished, chased back into their prison by Lord Criton's spells.

Shashtah lay bleeding onto the sand where the demons dropped him. The grains felt cool against his feverish face. He concentrated on pulling air into his lungs and letting it out again even though his shredded muscles protested at every breath. For a few heartbeats he fancied he was dead, but he knew he had to be alive. *Being dead wouldn't hurt this much.* He had no idea how many lashes he had taken. He did know, though, that there was only one reason he had not been smashed to a paste candlescars ago. *Magic . . .* He had no way to fight such power. He could not pull his thoughts together enough to summon water to slake his thirst or manna to give him strength. *Even if I could think straight, I don't know a single spell that would be of any use against Yapada's power.* Depression wrapped around his heart. Strangely, the despair helped to calm him. His pulse slowed, and he opened his eyes.

The dark stone still shone in his left hand.

Shashtah's fingers remained cramped tightly around the gem. Either he could not drop it or it would not let itself be dropped.

Through the heat of the day Shashtah felt the evil presence in the stone keeping him alive, delighting in his thirst and hunger and anguish as he lay exposed in the midday sun. Fortunately, no native animals existed in Cinnamar, so there were no vultures nor anything else to feed on his torn flesh. The only wind was a zephyr from the north, too gentle to carry sand to settle on him. His injuries crusted over in the brutal heat, and his bleeding stopped. He pieced his thoughts together as best he could. *Maybe my horse will find help.* He clenched his teeth against the insane laugh that tried to follow the sunstruck notion. The nearest basecamps were far to the north, beyond the Border, hidden in secret locations among the dunes. Even if his stallion did stumble into a warp that brought him out near any of them, someone still had to spot the horse and figure out what message he was carrying. Then that person would have to retrace the stallion's path, travel through the warp—assuming that the warp even went two ways—and figure out which gassi to follow. Shashtah closed his eyes tightly. *It's impossible.*

The rays of the sun as it started to pass behind the peak of the dune touched the gem.

Shashtah saw the flash through his eyelids.

The light sliced through him, and he heard a voice: *Have faith.*

Why not? Shashtah seized the light and gathered it tightly in his heart. *I have nothing else.*

Night fell again, and, when the crescent-shaped moon rose in the star-filled sky, the demons and their commander returned.

At a signal from Yapada, tentacles hauled Shashtah's abused body into the air.

"Back for more?" Shashtah croaked through cracked lips.

The Demonlord grinned, his yellowed fangs flashing in the scant moonlight. "So willing! The Dark One will feed well tonight!"

Certain he could not endure another night under the vicious flail, Shashtah begged, "Just take the stone!" His harsh whisper hurt his ears almost as much as it hurt his throat.

Yapada giggled. "Prepare him!"

Why won't he take the stone? Shahstah's mind raced, searching for an answer as the demons spread-eagled him once more. His reason scattered as the first blow landed on his destroyed back. He was stunned that his body was still capable of feeling more pain.

The gem flashed in the darkness, pressing against his hand with a will of its own and feeding on his ever-increasing agony.

Slowly the truth began to take shape. *The demons can't touch the stone. But then why not carry me into the mountain with it? Unless they can't carry me into the mountain while I possess the stone. Or the stone possesses me.* Shashtah shuddered from the pain of another lash.

By the time dawn came again and the demons disappeared, Shashtah knew with dread certainty that the Dark One and his servants had no intention of letting him die. They planned to keep him alive until they completely destroyed his soul. He had used the last grain of his faith to maintain his true essence through the final blows from Yapada's cursed flail. He could not let the Demonlord flog him a third time. Slowly, in excruciating pain and trusting to the hungry god within the gem to keep him alive, Shashtah shifted his battered body to face the north and began to crawl.

Dragonrider Kashon

CHAPTER 2:

A Teacher's Folly

Keep, then, these laws, and forsake not my teaching. For the laws are as lamps in the Darkness, and the teaching is the fire to light them; and the penalties of discipline are the way of life, to preserve you from the treacheries of the Dark One.

—from *The Dumnonian Code,*
by Corin of Daethia

SHASHTAH WAS APPALLED to find that his arms and legs were almost as damaged from hanging from the demons' limbs as his back was flayed from the flogging. His muscles cramped, making it nearly impossible to move. The sunlight stopped his bleeding once more, and its warmth slowly eased the ache in his muscles. Still sheer agony accompanied every handspan he gained, and he feared he would black out every time he shifted his weight enough to creep forward once more.

Shashtah felt as if he had been crawling for leagues, but the part of his mind that was still coherent told him he could not have made it more than a few wingspans by the time a shadow fell across him. At first he thought that the darkening of the sky was caused by the setting of the sun. Blind with pain, he heard rather than saw the two immense forms that perched on the dunes on either side of him. Only the rapid exchange in a language that sounded more like a sword fight than an intelligible tongue, the unmistakable scent of Bronze Dragons, and the impact of something that felt like a suit of plate mail against his right side convinced him that the help he had sent for had arrived.

"Tphah!" cried an irate Dumnonian from somewhere off to Shashtah's left. "Don't smash him! He's in bad enough shape as it is." The Dragonrider leapt to the sand as a screech, which sounded like metal scraping against metal, caused Shashtah to groan and his Dumnonian rescuer to squawk in protest.

Tphah! The name sang through Shashtah's mind like a cool zephyr on a blistering day. *The Dragon from Dameth's court! She heard me praying and came to save me!* He gave a silent, insane laugh as he recognized his hysteria in the fantasy that Tphah could hear him think.

A friendly hand pressed gently against his head, brushing some of the sand out of his hair. "I am Kashon, Rider of Katrell. Can you hear me?"

Shashtah managed a groan.

Kashon stood up. "Katrell, hold him for me."

Shashtah felt huge, metal talons—not completely unlike those of the demons—slip under his breast and, careful to avoid the lacerations on his back, slowly raise him off the sand. He had no prayer of standing on his own, but he took note that the Dragon left his boots touching the ground so he did not have the sensation of dangling helplessly in the air.

Damp fingers rubbed against Shashtah's cracked lips. His mouth stung for a moment, then began to heal. The pressure of a vial replaced the fingers. "Drink. This will help."

Shashtah tried to follow the order, but he could not get his throat to work. The sweet liquid flowed over his tongue and out the corners of his mouth.

"Easy, friend," Kashon crooned. "Katrell, tip him backward a little."

Katrell complied.

Shashtah's head flopped back, and he felt Kashon pour the healing fluid directly into his throat.

A firm, calloused hand massaged the muscles of his neck, teaching them once more how to swallow instead of scream.

Shashtah melted into that touch, reveling in the human contact.

A concerned clicking came from somewhere off to Shashtah's right.

"Tphah, settle down!" Kashon commanded. "Sands, I can't wait until she learns to speak ClearTalk!" he groused to no one in particular.

Shashtah felt the warmth from the potion seeping through his body, starting to repair at least a little of the damage the Demonlord had done.

By the time Kashon had helped him drink a second vial, the pain receded enough for Shashtah to open his eyes. *That's it. I'm hallucinating.* The thought slipped unbidden through his mind as he stared at the stunningly handsome warrior who went with the comforting voice.

Kashon proved to be in his thirties. His blue-black hair, solid amber eyes and slightly pointed ears marked their common race. Yet somehow those features looked so much more impressive on the Dragonrider than they did on Shashtah. Kashon's deep-tanned, beardless face declared him to be a man of pride, honesty and sensitivity, someone who could be moved to anger or humor with a single word. He seemed to wear his soul on the outside, for everyone to see. Kashon sported a linen shirt, tough leather trousers and practical desert boots, but the clothes fit him better than Shashtah's clothes had ever fit him, conforming to his muscular frame instead of hanging haphazardly on a sack of bones. A white keffiyeh bound with a golden agal shielded Kashon's head from the merciless sun. A simple scarab fastened his sand-colored cloak at his thick neck. His mouth curled into a reassuring smile as he noticed Shashtah's scrutiny. "Think you might live?" He signaled for his Dragon to set their patient on the sand.

Katrell set Shashtah down more carefully than he thought possible.

"Y-yes," Shashtah stammered as he half-sat, half-lay in the gassi. He tore his gaze away from Kashon in an attempt to keep from staring—and gaped in awe at a completely different subject: the magnificent male Dragon.

A metal hide of pure bronze covered Katrell's wedge-shaped head, serpentine neck, powerful body, four muscular legs and whip-like tail. Tough, translucent leather wings sprouted from his sides. Wicked metal thorns protected his spine. The spiked ridge flattened out briefly where his neck hinged with his shoulders, providing the only place where a

Rider could sit. Glistening amber eyes sparkled on the sides of his armored head beneath transparent protective lids that were lowered against the desert glare. Katrell's pointed ears, not unlike those of a horse, swiveled forward with keen interest. The flaps of the two huge nostrils in his equine muzzle opened and closed and a forked tongue flicked out briefly from between his armored lips as he tasted Shashtah's scent.

Not wishing to appear rude, Shashtah tried to look in another direction. This time he spotted the smaller, female Dragon. His heart caught in his throat. *Tphah!*

Barely half the size of the adult male, Tphah studied Shashtah with glittering amber eyes. Her head was slightly more tapered than Katrell's, and her sleek muscles and sinuous curves suggested that her speed surpassed that of the powerful male. In the thirteen years since Shashtah had first seen Tphah at Dameth's court she had almost tripled her size, and, while still something of a gawky teenager as Dragons went, she was definitely showing the fine lines of the elegant adult she would become. *They must be from Dameth's century.*

Katrell distracted Shashtah by pointing with a talon at the stone still clutched in his left hand. "May I?" rumbled the Dragon.

Shashtah blinked at him, too stunned at being noticed, let alone spoken to in ClearTalk, by a Dragon to do anything but nod.

With talons dexterous enough to pluck a single gold coin from a pile in a hoard, Katrell pried the gem from Shashtah's grasp.

Shashtah marveled that his skin did not adhere to the stone, yet he wondered if the marks the gem left on his palm would ever go away.

A talon from Katrell's other forepaw pulled open Shashtah's pouch. He dropped the stone into the bag and tugged the drawstring closed. The great Dragon nestled into the side of the dune and extended his left wing over the two Dumnonians to shield them from the afternoon sun.

Tphah positioned herself nose to tail with the larger Dragon and imitated him with her smaller wing. She snaked her serpentine neck around so her armored head lay at Shashtah's feet. Her amber eyes glowed with light even in the shade beneath the wings. She made a series of clicking sounds.

Katrell glared at her and clattered something in response.

Tphah sighed unhappily but settled down.

"She has a crush on you!" Kashon guffawed. "She's even given you a nickname: Dragonheart."

Shashtah looked quizzically at Tphah. "Dragonheart?"

Kashon grinned, revealing straight white teeth, and handed Shashtah a third vial of the healing concoction. "Don't try to talk. Just drink. When your Dragonlord assigns you a Stripling to care for, you'll understand."

"My Dragonlord?" Shashtah echoed. He downed the contents of the third vial. The draught worked its magic in his veins. He felt his bleeding stop, and moisture returned to his mouth. "My name is simply Shashtah," he declared as the potion gave him back his voice. "I ride no Dragon. I am not worthy of a Dragonlord."

Kashon raised an eyebrow.

Shashtah felt the tips of his ears burn. *Oh, sands. He speaks Daethian. What on Centuria possessed my parents to name me "Precious Water?" At least he's called "The Giving One," Katrell is "The Extreme One," and Tphah's name doesn't translate in any language I've ever learned. He must think I'm some sort of pompous imbecile.*

"That was no ordinary bauble Katrell placed in your pouch," Kashon observed, deftly pulling Shashtah's thoughts in another direction. "I suspect I'll have orders—"

Katrell rumbled at him.

"Correction," Kashon's grin widened. "I have orders to take you straight to the King's Camp. I won't be at all surprised to see you with me in the skies before long, if that is what you wish."

Shashtah felt his heart skip a beat. "You mean I did it? I finished my Dragonquest?"

Kashon chuckled and held out a hand to help Shashtah rise. "And then some, I'd say by the looks of you." He pulled Shashtah to his feet. "Turn around."

Shashtah obediently presented his back to his rescuer for examination.

Kashon took an involuntary deep breath, held it for a heartbeat, and then observed in a reasonably steady voice, "Not to worry. There'll be someone in the King's Camp who can repair the rest of that. The Healers love a good challenge."

"That bad, eh?" Shashtah commented drily.

"I'd suggest that we stay here and let you rest for a few candlescars," Kashon said, "but I don't fancy getting caught in Cinnamar after nightfall."

"Neither do I," Shashtah agreed. He puzzled at the urge he felt to melt into Kashon's powerful, protective arms as he glanced at what he could see of the sky beyond the edge of the Dragons' wings.

Kashon removed his cloak and draped it gently across Shashtah's bare shoulders. "You'll need this."

Shashtah wondered why the cloth did not stick to his damaged skin, but Kashon's gentle touch as he fastened the cloak around Shashtah's neck diverted his thoughts once again. "Why?" He swayed slightly on his feet.

Kashon frowned. "You are well enough to ride, aren't you?"

"Ride?" Shashtah echoed. He glanced around for his horse.

Clicks and clangs rang through the air as Tphah hopped to her feet.

Katrell quickly stood up and raised his wing out of danger, a much put-upon look on his face.

Kashon planted his fists on his slender hips and scowled at Tphah. "What in the name of Corin makes you think that I'm going to allow someone who can barely stand to sit astride a Stripling who can't remember which way is up?"

Shashtah blanched. "Are you asking me if I'm well enough to ride a Dragon?"

Tphah bounced in place, showering the Dumnonians and Katrell with sand. "Yes! Yes! Yes! Ride me!"

Kashon and Shashtah coughed and spit the sand out of their mouths.

"Tphah!" Kashon raged in surprise. "How long have you known ClearTalk?"

If a Dragon could blush, Tphah did.

Kashon glanced at Katrell, then back at the Stripling. "That's what I thought," he growled. "You hold out on me about something like that for over three years, and you expect a reward? You are not worthy of the honor of bearing 'Dragonheart.'"

Shashtah and Kashon clapped their hands over their ears as the youngster screeched her distress.

"Tphah!" Kashon's plaintive cry was drowned out by Katrell's earsplitting roar.

Tphah cringed into the sand, amber eyes wide with awe as she blinked up at the mature Dragon.

"I think you'd better let me ride her," Shashtah ventured, "or we're both going to be deaf."

"What?" Kashon responded as he wriggled his finger in his ear. He glanced at Katrell, who nodded his massive head ever so slightly. "Katrell will have the honor of bearing 'Dragonheart,'" he sternly informed the cowering Stripling. "But, since you still need the practice, I shall endure the shame of riding you." He shot a look at Shashtah, mouthing the word, "Watch." His powerful fingers grabbed the training harness that Shashtah suddenly realized was strapped around Tphah. Kashon pulled himself up to the flat spot between the neck and backridges just in front of Tphah's wings. He lowered himself onto Tphah and wrapped his right leg around the spike in front of him so that he sat sidesaddle, not unlike the way a caravaneer would perch on a camel's back. He settled his legs into her harness, securing himself firmly in place.

Tphah skittered a bit.

Kashon grimaced as he was pinched between her neck and backridges, which were not quite wide enough apart yet to hold a Rider comfortably.

Faster than a cobra's strike, Katrell's head swiveled around until he was nostril to nostril with the young Dragon.

Tphah immediately froze into the statue-like pose of the perfect mount.

"Katrell just threatened Tphah with several unsavory fates if she so much as bruises me," Kashon translated, favoring his Dragon with an affectionate grin. "Go ahead. Mount him," he instructed as the large beast crouched as low as possible in the gassi.

Shashtah started to reach toward the great Dragon's harness, but stories of such splendid creatures slaying anyone other than their Rider who attempted to mount them stayed his hand.

Katrell saw his hesitation. "It's all right, Dragonheart. I permit it. Bearing you will indeed be my honor."

Reassured, Shashtah grabbed Katrell's fabulous carved and dyed leather harness and tried to haul himself up.

Katrell snaked his head around and gave Shashtah a gentle boost with the end of his armored snout.

Shashtah settled onto Katrell's back. He winced as he wrapped his leg around the metallic spike at the base of the Dragon's neckridge.

Kashon laughed. "Not as soft as a camel, eh?"

"You could say that. No offense, Katrell," Shashtah added hastily.

Katrell's eyes reflected Kashon's amusement. "None taken."

"You'll eventually acquire scars and callouses that will help," Kashon said, "but I'm afraid you'll be a bit sore today."

Shashtah dubiously fingered the thorn-like projection in front of him, then glanced south. He imagined the demons in the mountain, waiting impatiently for nightfall and another chance to come after him. "Not as sore as I would have been if you hadn't found me. Thank you."

Kashon brushed aside Shashtah's gratitude with a wave of his hand. "Thank Tphah. She's the one who spotted your horse and figured out what he was trying to tell us."

"Thank you, Tphah," Shashtah said in all seriousness, "for saving my life."

Tphah, afraid to move a muscle after Katrell's rebuff, accepted his gratitude by blinking her inner eyelids.

Kashon allowed himself a small grin, then stared at Katrell. He waited until Shashtah had secured his feet in the harness. Satisfied his patient would stay where he belonged, Kashon brought his right fist to his left breast in the Dumnonian salute and thrust his clenched hand skyward, toward the north.

Shashtah grabbed for the harness, slipping his fingers around the strap as Katrell craned his neck in the direction Kashon had indicated.

Katrell swung his head back around until one of his beautiful eyes could stare directly at Shashtah. "Do not be afraid, Dragonheart. I will not drop you." Then his head shot forward. He pushed off with his mighty legs and gave a swift downstroke with his wings.

Shashtah gasped as the great beast rose smoothly into the sky. From watching the flight of large desert birds Shashtah had imagined that the sensation of flying on a Dragon would be jerkier. But then the immense creatures looked as if they weighed too much to be able to fly at all. That was part of what made them so spectacular. He had always imagined that there was a dreamlike quality to dragonflight. Alone, astride Katrell, the sensation intensified, and soon, when they reached the King's Camp, Shashtah would share his joy in flight with a Bond Partner all his own. Thrilling anew at the wonders of the superb creations of Corin's magic, he glanced at Tphah, who had leapt in unison with the larger Dragon.

Kashon guided Tphah into position just off Katrell's right wingtip with a confidence born of years spent in the air.

As Shashtah watched the graceful pair, he suddenly realized that Katrell was right: He did not need to hold on. The force of the upward motion kept him firmly planted on the wondrous beast's neck with absolutely no chance of falling off.

The air began to cool as they rose high above the sand until the temperature seemed bone-chilling to the desert-adapted Dumnonian. Shashtah readjusted Kashon's cloak to free his left arm while pulling it tightly around him. He frowned as the pain he expected did not follow his action. *Why doesn't the cloth stick to me?* He immediately forgot the question as he poked gingerly at Katrell's scales. The scorching sun had heated the Dragon's hide to the point where the metal continued to shimmer with warmth, keeping the air around Shashtah at a comfortable temperature and easing the ache in his legs. *Riders must avoid mounting their Dragons at midday,* he speculated. *The sun probably turns these hides hotter than kettles over a campfire. I'd wager they could burn through even leather trousers in a heartbeat.*

Shashtah glanced at Kashon, longing to ask his rescuer the billions of questions that his mother and father and everyone else on his caravan had always refused to answer.

Kashon saw the curiosity dancing in Shashtah's eyes and shrugged.

Shashtah realized, with sudden disappointment, that there could be no verbal communication between them while they were in the air. Only through a Bond such as that which Kashon shared with Katrell could words be understood over the rush of the desert winds and the thunderous clap of dragonwings. Shashtah noted the preoccupied look in Kashon's eyes. He fancied that the Dragonrider was relaying messages to his inexperienced mount through the larger Dragon, who would then have to translate any replies back to Kashon.

Shashtah suddenly felt terribly alone, surrounded by nothing but wind and sun and dragonwings. *Did Corin guess at that loneliness when he helped a Dumnonian and a Dragon forge the First Bond? Is that why the Great Wizard made it possible for every Dragonrider to "talk" silently with his own mount the way all Dragons talked with each other?*

As they flew Shashtah felt his back, which had been only partially healed by Kashon's potions, stiffen with the effort of keeping his body upright. His right leg, wrapped around the metal neckridge, cramped as the night winds cooled Katrell's scales. Unable to suggest to either the Dragons or Kashon that they land and let him rest, he tried to distract himself from his present discomfort by daydreaming about what his own Bond Partner would be like. *Will Shaharadesh give me a newly trained Dragon, one scarcely older than Tphah? I could shape one like that to my own tastes. He or she would certainly rely heavily on me for guidance. Or will I share a Bond with an Ancient, set in his or her ways, who has served countless Riders before me and whose judgment I'll have to learn to trust? That won't be easy,* Shashtah admitted to himself. *Maybe my Bond Partner will be somewhere in the middle. That might be best.*

The ritual of Bonding between Dragons and Riders was the closest thing the Dumnonian culture had to the Daethian practice of marriage, but Shashtah knew that the effects of Bonding went far beyond the mere blessing of a relationship by a religious institution. Shashtah suspected that the Dumnonian aversion to such Daethian practices somehow stemmed from the responsibilities incurred by the formation of Bonds. *Still,* he mused, *it does seem rather like going into an arranged marriage without ever having met your bride and without knowing whether your intended is of the same or of the opposite sex.* He smiled at himself. Here he was, flying high above the sand on another man's Dragon, already having very unDumnonian wedding night jitters! He had no guarantee, beyond Kashon's reassurances, that Shaharadesh, King of Dumnonia, would agree to let him become a Rider of one of the magnificent creatures of his dreams. Somewhat sobered by the thought, Shashtah tried to ignore his growing discomfort and concentrate on the pleasures of what might be his one and only solo dragonride.

The Dragons and Dumnonians flew north at a leisurely pace that would not tire the incredible beasts. Unused to spotting landmarks from the air, Shashtah calculated that they crossed the southern Border of Dumnonia about a candlescar after nightfall. At least his eyes, dark as filterglass in the sun and sharp as a hawk's by night, began to register the presence of plants and animals on the ground where none had been before. Not anything spectacular. A lizard here. A tuft of half-dried grass there. But more life than he knew existed in Cinnamar.

A few wingbeats later, they approached a vast encampment, which was at least ten times bigger than Dameth's basecamp had been. The endless rows of tents could only be the King's Camp, but Shashtah knew that was impossible. Even on dragonback, the journey from the Border to the Valley of Ancients should have taken at least half a rotation and far longer than that by caravan. Shashtah glanced at Kashon, wishing for some explanation. That was when he realized that they were not alone in the air.

Kashon's grim face paled with fear in the moonlight.

Shashtah's heart sank into his boots as he fancied that he heard an all too familiar cackle above the roar of the wind. *Yapada!* The name screamed through his soul. *He's found me!* Panic momentarily shoved aside all thoughts of physical discomfort. *But how?* He became aware that Katrell was executing a banked turn that would bring him around to face the threat.

A quick glance showed him that Tphah, under Kashon's guidance, was performing a similar turn.

Shashtah's heart leapt from his boots into his throat. *Is Kashon sunstruck? I can barely hang on to Katrell's harness! What makes him think I can fly into battle on a Dragon I can't control?*

Then Katrell finished his turn, and Shashtah realized that, sunstruck or not, Kashon had absolutely no choice: Yapada and the demons would overtake them well before they reached the King's Camp.

Better to turn and face them, Shashtah admitted, *than to wait for the demons to attack from behind.*

Katrell bugled his war cry, which was echoed by Tphah. The two Dragons tore into the ranks of the demons, magical bolts of light blazing from their open mouths.

Shashtah gasped. He had never seen a Dragon breathe in battle before. He had only heard that such things were possible by listening to the ballads sung around the campfires of his father's caravan.

Katrell's bolt narrowly missed Yapada but slammed into a gibbering bear-thing that was riding a bat-winged monstrosity just beyond the Demonlord.

The bolt knocked the foul creature and its mount from the air.

The body of a second demon plunged toward the sand.

Shashtah guessed that Tphah's bolt had also found its mark.

Katrell shot upward at an angle just steep enough to keep Shashtah in his seat.

Sitting on Katrell as easily as he would on a racing camel, Shashtah forced himself to concentrate on the thrill of the massive beast's skill in combat rather than the all-too-real problem that he was about to die.

At the apex of his climb Katrell swiveled in midair, glided atop a thermal until he was certain his terrified passenger was hanging on as hard as he could, and then plunged, releasing a cloud of his scent as he skimmed above the heads of the demon horde.

With battle nerves banishing all thoughts of pain, Shashtah's eyes widened at the effect Katrell's odor had on him. While Shashtah had always loved the smell of Dragons, he was completely unprepared for his body's reaction to the concentrated scent: He could not decide whether he wanted to mate or fall asleep. *What is the matter with me? First, the Rider. Now, his Dragon. This is ridiculous. I've definitely been out in the sun too long.*

Most of the demons had a different opinion of the stench. They turned almost in unison and fled.

Katrell continued his swoop, razor-sharp talons extended in an effort to rake an unholy rider from the back of one of the few remaining demons.

Half a wingspan away, Yapada grinned and raised his deadly flail.

Too late Shashtah realized that he had lost track of Kashon and that he had no way to warn the great Dragon beneath him of the danger.

Katrell's dive carried him across Yapada's arc.

The spiked Galantite balls struck solidly against the armor plating of Katrell's right shoulder, actually denting the Dragon's metallic hide.

Katrell yelped in agony. With a crack of his whip-like tail, he swept Yapada from his mount and sent him plunging toward the ground.

A flurry of monstrosities returned to pluck the Demonlord from the air as Katrell spiraled downward, out of control.

Dozens of Dragons suddenly filled the sky, breathing bursts of magical light and clouds of their scent at the retreating demon horde.

Yapada gibbered his frustration at the desert winds as he directed his new mount to join the retreat.

The Dragonriders had chased off the last of the demons by the time Katrell plowed a deep furrow into a particularly large whaleback dune.

Horrified, Shashtah scrambled down from Katrell's neck and examined the injury.

Katrell's amber eyes glazed with pain. "I told you I wouldn't drop you."

The reply Shashtah tried to make stuck in his throat as a sob.

Tphah landed beside them, sending sand flying in all directions.

Kashon leapt from her back and rushed toward Katrell.

Shashtah watched in appalled silence as the Dragonrider caressed his damaged mount.

The sorrow in Kashon's eyes dulled their glow, causing them to look as if the light in them would flicker out.

Just as Shashtah thought his heart would break watching the Pair, another Rider carrying a Healer balanced on her right thigh ordered her Dragon to land near them.

The Healer dropped to the sand and pushed past Kashon as if he were beneath her notice. Her hands began to glow with healing light as she touched the injured Dragon.

Kashon stood to one side, too grief-stricken to move or make a sound, as the woman's magic repaired the damage to Katrell.

Finally the Healer stood back and studied her patient through narrowed eyes, checking to see if she had missed anything. "He'll be all right," she announced to the desert wind.

"As if that's what he cares about!" snapped a young girl's voice at Shashtah's elbow.

Shashtah looked around surprised to see the number of people who had gathered behind him. Only a few Dragons were still in sight, and those were all in the air. There was no sign of Tphah or any other Dragon on the dunes.

The girl beside him could have been no more than eighteen or nineteen. Her loose, long, black hair, which, after the fashion of the women at Dameth's court, declared her to be a virgin, was caught neatly beneath a veil of a Priestess of the Mother, yet the rest of her garb was that of a Dumnonian man.

"She healed the wound," Shashtah whispered, finally finding his voice. "Why isn't everything fine? I don't understand."

"Kashon allowed Katrell to be injured," the girl explained softly without taking her eyes off the grieving Pair. "He will be taken before the Council of Ancients for judgment."

"Judgment?" Shashtah echoed. "What will they do to him?"

The girl shrugged. "Whatever the Council wills. If the king speaks for him, they may let him go. If they punish him and Katrell becomes too upset, their Bond may break."

Shashtah drew a quick breath. "That can happen?"

The girl's head gave a terse nod.

Shashtah felt Kashon's grief wring at his own heart. "But it wasn't his fault!" he shouted, forgetting to keep his voice low. "I was the one riding Katrell!"

"That is his fault!" the girl hissed. She glared at Shashtah and then shook her head as if trying to make the scene around her go away. "He should have been carrying you on Katrell, not flying into battle on a nit of a Stripling."

"But," Shashtah protested, "he couldn't have flown into battle at all if he'd been carrying me!"

"It doesn't matter," the girl said. "Only the Council's judgment matters now."

Two powerful Dumnonians, dressed in white ceremonial abas and keffiyehs, stepped out of the crowd and took Kashon by the upper arms. "The Council summons you," the taller of the two informed the Dragonrider in a none-too-gentle voice.

Katrell roared his objection.

Everyone in the crowd backed away from the frantic Dragon, covering their ears.

"Katrell!" Kashon ordered, his voice sounding halfway between a plea and a sob. "Stop it! You know I have to go with them. Stay here until I return." He met the gaze of the guard who had spoken to him. "I am ready."

Katrell roared again.

"Be still!" Kashon begged. "Don't make this harder for me than it is."

Katrell hung his head beside his Bond Partner.

The silent guard relaxed his hold enough so Kashon could reach out to his Dragon.

Kashon touched the scales above Katrell's eye in a gesture that was so tender Shashtah felt embarrassed to watch. "Stay here. I will come back to you." Kashon drew himself to his full height and nodded his readiness at the guards.

The guards tightened their grip on him and led him away.

"Come on," the girl beside Shashtah said. "I'll show you to our tent." She glanced at the agitated Dragon, wiping tears from her eyes. She angrily licked the moisture from her hand, looking more as if she were drinking an enemy's blood than returning water to her body. "There's no point in trying to see a Healer just now."

Shashtah balked. "I can't go with you. They saved my life. I have to help them. I have to go before the Council and speak for Kashon."

The girl stared at Shashtah, strange wisdom shining in her solid amber eyes. "Kashon's fate is in the Council's talons, and the Council will not listen to any non-Dragon except the Dumnonian king. Come with me. I'd promise you sleep, but I doubt any of us will sleep tonight."

Shashtah, suddenly too tired to argue at the mention of sleep, let her lead him through the crowd and into the King's Camp.

The girl escorted him through rows of tents of varying sizes. Just when he thought he could walk no farther, she paused before a tent that was large enough to hold an entire family and held open the flap, motioning for him to step inside. "This is where we have been assigned."

Big enough to hold a Rider astride his Dragon, Shashtah mused as he entered the tent.

Two sets of poles, one on either side of the enormous enclosure, helped support the billowing canvas high above his head. Rich, jewel-toned rugs, woven with legends of great Bronze Dragons and their Riders and the images of djinn, phoenix, and other fanciful beings, covered the floor. Elaborate tapestries hung on roll-rods along the sides of the tent. Lowered for the night to help keep in the warmth, the hangings could be raised during the day to take advantage of whatever breeze happened to blow through the Camp. Some cooking utensils, dishes, goblets and a couple of wine skins were neatly arranged to the left of the entrance where a pot of qaffah simmered slowly on a brazier. A wooden couch, shaped vaguely like a throne and piled high with sapphire blue silk cushions, dominated the center of the tent. Shashtah knew from his visit to Dameth's court, which was held in a tent ten times larger than this one, that the area beyond the throne was considered the family's private space while everything between the tent flap and the throne was used to entertain guests.

The girl took one of the cushions from the throne and laid it on a rug on the left side of the tent in the public area. "Lie down," she ordered.

Aching in every part of his body, Shashtah unfastened the brooch at his neck and dropped Kashon's cloak to one side. He stretched out, stomach down, and lay his head on the pillow. He silently forgave the girl for failing to offer him the ritual greeting of a cup of qaffah. *I couldn't drink it anyway.*

"I'll be right back." The girl ducked outside.

Alone, Shashtah could not get the grief in Kashon's face out of his mind. It had never occurred to him that the relationship between Dragon and Rider could be broken by anything other than the death of one of the Partners nor that the Rider could be punished if something harmed the Dragon. Shashtah would have to face the Council of Ancients himself when he made his request to Shaharadesh to Bond him to one of the fabulous beasts. He had no idea what everyone thought the Council was going to do to Kashon, but the terror he sensed in Katrell and the grim looks on everyone else's face told him that whatever awaited his rescuer could not be pleasant.

The girl returned with fresh clothes and a new pair of boots. She set them on the carpet next to Kashon's cloak. She secured the brooch's pin so it would not stab anyone, then folded the garment and set it out of the way. She grasped Shashtah's upper arm. Her grip was powerful beyond all reason, though she took care not to injure him further. "Here. Let me help you." She drew him into a sitting position.

Shashtah let her pull off his boots.

The girl helped him rise, unbuckled his belt and slid it from around his waist. She dropped the leather strap beside his boots, then steadied him as he removed his trousers.

Shashtah stood still while she gently peeled away his makeshift bandages. The gashes beneath the fabric had closed thanks to Kashon's potions so the bindings came away much easier than Shashtah expected them to.

The maiden produced a damp cloth from somewhere and gently sponged as much blood and grime as she could from his skin. Then she handed him a new pair of trousers from the pile of clothes she had brought.

Shashtah slipped into the pants as she dropped the soiled rag beside the tent flap. He let her help him pull the new linen shirt over his head. The fabric didn't stick as badly as he feared it would, so the potions must have done more good than he thought they had. *Perhaps that's why the cloak didn't hurt me.* He tucked the shirt into the trousers.

The girl laced the pants closed for him and picked up his belt. She wrapped the strap around his waist and fastened it into place. "Sit down."

Shashtah hid a smile as he swayed uncertainly on his feet. *Good idea.* He complied. As the girl slid the new boots onto his feet, he marveled that she had guessed his size exactly.

The girl picked up the shredded clothing and damaged boots and dropped them by the tent flap with the cloth. Amending her earlier error, she asked, "Would you like some qaffah?" The tone in her voice indicated that she presumed he would refuse the gesture.

"No, thank you," Shashtah replied because it was expected of him.

"What about some broth?" the girl pressed, expecting him to accept this time. "You look as if you haven't eaten anything for days."

"I haven't," Shashtah grinned ruefully. "But I'm not fond of meat."

"Fruit juice, then?" She eyed him critically. "I don't think it would be wise for you to try anything solid just yet."

Shashtah found himself smiling again, enchanted by her concern. "Fruit juice would be wonderful."

The girl picked up one of the wineskins and poured some of the contents into a golden chalice. She knelt beside him and handed him the goblet. She watched closely as he drained the contents. Then she reclaimed the cup and brushed a strand of his blue-black hair away from his face. "That's better."

Shashtah suddenly felt himself sinking into a deep sleep. He was honestly surprised that he had not done so earlier. He stretched out on the carpet. His last conscious thought as he felt gentle hands turn him onto his stomach and arrange the cushion under his head was that the girl who tended to him had a Dragon reflected in her eyes.

Katrell and Shashtah

CHAPTER 3:

Another's Anguish

"Your actions have brought this upon you. This is your sentence, and it is bitter; it has reached your very heart. You shall suffer anguish. You shall writhe in pain. The walls of your heart shall be breached, and you will not be able to keep silent."

"How long, Lord of Light? Wilt thou shun me forever? How long must I bear this pain in my soul? Will I have sorrow in my heart all my days?"

—from *Patrek's Lament,*
by Valron Silvertongue

DARK SHADOWS TROUBLED SHASHTAH'S dreams. He sat on a vast, strangely-carved throne at the end of a large meeting hall. He could barely make out his surroundings. The palpable blackness that filled the room reminded him of the dungeons of Mount Cinnamar, and he shivered in his sleep.

A shimmering queen stood at his left elbow, just beyond his peripheral vision. A lone figure, who resembled Kashon, knelt in a small pool of light a few strides in front of the throne. A thick mist swirled around the edges of the hall. Eight stately figures, five males and three females dressed in white abas, grey streaking through their night-dark hair beneath their keffiyehs and veils, filed in from behind the throne and lined up on either side of the room, four to his left and four to his right. He could not make out their faces, but he sensed that he knew them.

The male at the far end of the right-hand line gazed down at the kneeling Rider. "You feel true grief," he observed, his voice filled with the compassion of the guard who had spoken to Kashon outside the King's Camp.

The woman opposite the speaker nodded. "You make no excuse."

The man next to her, who resembled the silent guard, nodded as well. "You seek no mercy."

"You admit your error," the woman across from him intoned.

"You understand what is needed," the man to her left confirmed. Something about the speaker reminded Shashtah vaguely of someone he had seen in Dameth's camp, but he could not find a name to put with the face.

The man who mirrored the familiar judge inclined his head. "You entrust yourself to us."

"It is decided." The man immediately to Shashtah's left gazed up at the throne.

Shashtah strained to make out the judge's features, certain that the smallest stray beam of light would reveal the speaker's identity. He had almost named him when the woman to the right of the throne stepped forward and, without saying a word, handed Shashtah a scroll. He stared, unable to take his eyes off her.

She was as ancient as the desert. Her face, worn with time and care, could have belonged to the great-great-grandmother he had never known. The bright, solid amber eyes that stared at him out of the ruin of her face were incredibly wise. She turned her gaze on the kneeling man. "Your punishment for allowing harm to come to your Dragon now begins." The woman shifted her stare back to Shashtah. Her wrinkled mouth curled into a small, sad smile as, with a wave of her age-gnarled hand, she commanded him to read the words on the parchment.

The queen at Shashtah's left looked over his shoulder as he unrolled the scroll and started to read.

The words vanished from the sheet as he pronounced them. His dream-self recognized the language even though he did not. His voice sounded strange in his ears, more as if he were listening to a battle than to his own speech. As he read he sensed the kneeling Rider grow very still. By the time two-thirds of the words had vanished from the parchment, the Rider was shuddering violently, as if he were being hit with wave after wave of pain. As the last of the words disappeared, the man collapsed on the floor, writhing in absolute agony.

The ancient woman reached out and took the empty sheet from Shashtah's trembling hands, drawing his attention away from the tortured man and back to her. Her mouth quivered briefly into an understanding smile. Her eyes silently promised him that everything would be all right. She banished the blank scroll with a wave of her hand, then once more took her place and turned to watch as the helpless man lay screaming on the floor.

Shashtah sat bolt upright, echoing the shrieks of terror and pain from his dream.

Outside the darkened tent, earsplitting, inhuman cries shattered the night, drowning out Shashtah's screams. Murmurs of fear and occasional sobs filtered through the tapestry-covered walls. Sounds of people running in all directions and oaths as bodies collided unexpectedly only added to the cacophony.

The girl sat cross-legged on the rug beside Shashtah. Her head was bent forward so her veil hid her face, but he could tell that she was weeping. "I—I'm sorry. I sh-shouldn't have p-put that s-spell on y-you, b-but you needed s-sleep so b-badly."

"Spell?" Shashtah winced at the blood-curdling chaos around him. "What are you talking about? What is going on?"

"Katrell . . . cries for . . . Kashon," she answered.

"Kashon?" Shashtah grew very still. "Is he dead?"

The maiden shook her head, no.

Horror crept into Shashtah's heart. "Did their Bond break?"

"No." The girl took a deep breath and controlled herself. She pushed aside her veil far enough that he could see the sad smile, not unlike the old woman's, on her tear-streaked face. "Kashon is in so much agony, though, that Katrell fears his Rider will be driven mad." She wiped the tears from her cheeks. "If he is, then their Bond will break, whether or not anyone wills it so." She licked the moisture from her delicate hand, eyeing Shashtah expectantly.

Shashtah took the news like a blow to his heart. He lay back down and buried his face in the pillow. *What on Centuria does she want me to do?* The images from his dream still haunted him. He tried to remember what was written on the scroll. Only the last two words came to mind. "*'Tlact tah,*" he whispered.

"What?" the young girl prompted.

"*'Tlact tah.*' I dreamed . . . " Shashtah sat up and grabbed the girl by her shoulders. "Do you understand *'Tlact tah?*' Do you know what it means?"

The maiden almost cringed, but blind trust suddenly replaced her fear. She pressed her lips tightly together for a heartbeat before she spoke. "'Until dawn,'" she translated. "It means 'until dawn' in the ancient language of the Bronze Dragons." She touched his beardless cheek. "Help them, Dragonheart. You know what to do." She let her hand drop to his chest and pressed against the place where his heart beat behind his ribs. "Please, help them."

Shashtah swayed to his feet, not knowing where he found the strength to remain upright. *From her?* he wondered. *How could she do anything to help me? She's little more than a child.* The depth of the belief he saw in the girl's eyes unnerved him. His sensitive ears picked out a sound that was half moan, half keen above the havoc. His fear drove away all thoughts of his own pain. He stumbled to the tent flap, pushed it aside, and plunged blindly into the chaos of the King's Camp.

Dragonriders chased after non-Riders as Katrell's heart-wrenching cries tore through the night. Children of all ages ran haphazardly through the Camp, screaming for parents who were nowhere to be found. One little boy, no more than four years old, slammed into Shashtah's leg.

Instinctively Shashtah scooped the child into his arms. "Here, now," he murmured. "I have you. What's wrong?"

"Don't let their Bond break!" the boy sniffled.

Shashtah hugged the child tightly to his breast. "Hush." He closed his eyes as he whispered to the youngster. "I'll make everything all right. I promise." He thought he had lied, but then he felt his skin tingle for a moment and every hair on his head seemed to stand on end.

The boy in his arms grew suddenly calm.

Shashtah opened his eyes to see the child gazing at him with awe and trust, the same look he had received from the girl. Shashtah hastily set the boy down. "Wait here. Your parents will come for you."

The child stared at him in wonder. "Dragonheart!"

Shashtah groaned and staggered off into the night, fighting the urge to clap his hands over his abused ears. He would have to have a talk with Tphah about that nickname the next time he saw her. But first he needed to help Katrell—and Kashon.

Shashtah found Katrell where Kashon had left him. The miserable creature sat atop the whaleback dune where he had crashed, head craned skyward on his serpentine neck, howling, not completely unlike a wolf, at the scimitar-shaped light of the moon.

Shashtah's heart quaked at the cry. He stumbled to within a wingspan of the hysterical Dragon, put his hands on his hips and shouted in what he hoped was his most authoritative voice, "Katrell!"

The Dragon, seeming not to hear him, screamed at the stars again.

Shashtah sighed, strode forward, and tugged on the Dragon's harness. "Katrell!"

The great Dragon leapt into the air with an infuriated roar.

Shashtah, in spite of his certainty that he was about to be reduced to a pile of ash, stood his ground. He spread his hands slightly, signaling for Katrell to calm down. "You have to help Kashon!"

Stunned, Katrell settled back onto the dune. "How?" he boomed, a world of sorrow in his voice.

"I saw the scroll in a dream," Shashtah explained hastily, knowing he was arguing for his life. "The Council's punishment will only last until dawn. Do you hear me? Kashon heard. Somewhere deep within him he knows. You have to remind him: The pain will vanish at dawn. Your despair is sapping his courage, making him forget. That's what will break your Bond. You have to stop thinking about your own sorrow and lend him your strength. You have to tell him that you are proud, not ashamed, of him. You have to tell him how you do not hold him responsible for what happened. You have to let him know that you are still with him in his head and that you will be with him again physically at dawn. Do you understand? You have to remind him that the pain is only temporary, that you love him, and that he is not alone!"

Katrell hesitated a heartbeat, then closed his glistening eyes and stretched out on the sand.

Shashtah watched as the great Dragon began to shudder and whimper with a pain that was not his own. He shuddered himself at the sight. He closed his eyes briefly against the scene and said a silent, wordless prayer. Then he turned and staggered back toward the Camp, amazed that he was still alive.

With the cessation of the grieving Dragon's cries, the steadier Riders began to get everyone else in the Camp under control. Having no better idea where to go, Shashtah trudged back to his hostess's tent. Exhausted and only dimly aware of his surroundings, he fancied that he saw a Hatchling curled up where he had left the little boy. He smiled to himself as he thought of his mother's words once more, "You have Dragons on the brain!" *Yes,* he admitted to himself, *I suppose I do.*

Shashtah lurched through the opening of the tent and collapsed on the pillow beside the girl. His right leg ached abominably from where he had wrapped it around the spike on Katrell's neck, and the muscles in his back protested with each breath. All he wanted to do was sleep for a rotation, but something in the maiden's amber eyes made him reach out and lay his hand on her knee, inviting her to speak.

She stared at him for a moment, then hugged herself. "I am sorry I was rude earlier. I was frightened."

A small sound escaped from Shashtah's throat, and he pulled the trembling girl down into his arms. "So was I." She had to be at least ten years his junior, but suddenly that mattered little. Simply holding her seemed to numb the burning of his back. "I didn't want their Bond to break. How did you know I could stop it?"

"*You* didn't want their Bond to break?" she laughed nervously.

Shashtah noticed that she failed to answer his question, but he kept silent.

She pressed herself close to the reassuring presence of his body. "No one wanted it to break. Bonds are not severed lightly for a reason." She placed her ear against his chest so she could listen to his heart beat.

An image of Katrell baying at the sky came unbidden to Shashtah's mind. "It upsets the Dragons," he commented drily.

The girl twisted slightly in his arms and gave him an inquisitive look. "How did you know?"

Shashtah relaxed his hold on her, let his head fall against his arm, and closed his eyes. He kept his left arm draped across her. If she was not going to answer his questions, he saw no reason that he should answer hers. Besides, he didn't know the answer anyway.

The girl accepted his silence. She reached down to where Kashon's cloak lay folded at their feet. She drew the wrap over them, then she touched her fingers to his temple. "Sleep," she whispered. "I'll wake you at dawn."

Sleep overtook Shashtah almost instantly, and this time the only shadow that disturbed him was the face of an incredibly old woman with an Ancient Dragon in her eyes.

The maiden, true to her word, woke Shashtah at sunrise. "Dragonheart."

A heartbeat later, the two guards from the previous night pushed aside the tent flap. They carried Kashon's limp body inside and laid it amidst the pillows on the throne-like couch. A tall, haggard warrior in his early thirties followed at their heels. Both guards clapped the stranger sympathetically on the upper arm as they left. The warrior did not seem to notice them as he sank to his knees beside Kashon.

The young girl sat frozen as Shashtah got to his feet.

This is his tent? Shashtah touched the girl's arm reassuringly as he bent and picked up Kashon's cloak. *Then who is she? He's too young to be her father. Perhaps his mate?* He straightened and folded the garment, unable to take his eyes off Kashon and the strange man.

There was something heart-wrenchingly tender about the way the exhausted Dumnonian took Kashon's hand in his and pressed his lips to the calloused palm.

Shashtah hesitated for a moment, feeling like an intruder. Then he strode over to them and held out Kashon's cloak to the warrior. "Here. He may want this."

"Thank you, Dragonheart," whispered the stranger in a voice that was almost too soft to hear as he lay the cloak over the unmoving Dragonrider.

Shashtah grimaced. "Is there no one in the entire Camp who does not know that name?"

The stranger smiled up at him, and Shashtah fancied for a moment that he saw a Dragon in the man's solid amber eyes. "I doubt it after last night." He looked down at Kashon's drawn face and gently stroked the line of his cheek. "Thank you for showing me how to save him. I can't believe you found the courage to give him back to me after I almost killed you."

"Katrell?" Shashtah asked in spite of himself.

The warrior favored him with a knowing look. "I told you I wouldn't drop you."

Shashtah's lips curled into a bitter smile as he gazed at the still form on the throne. "Perhaps it would have been better if you had."

Katrell suddenly glanced over at the girl, who was literally cowering on the rug. Then he cocked his head and stared at Shashtah, curiosity flickering in his amber eyes. "Is it true, Dragonheart? You do not know that Dragons can take humanform?

Shashtah blushed a deep, molten bronze. "I grew up in a dragonless camp. I guess there's a lot about Dragons I don't know." His gaze went involuntarily to Kashon's slack face, still lined with remembered pain. Instinctively Shashtah reached toward Kashon. He hesitated and glanced at Katrell. "May I?"

Katrell tightened his grip on Kashon's hand. "Someone who has been punished by the Council may not be healed by magic, Dragonheart."

"I have no healing talents, Katrell," Shashtah assured him. "His touch meant a great deal to me after an inhuman experience. I only want to offer that same comfort to him now."

Katrell gazed at Shashtah for a moment, judging his words, then nodded. He held Kashon's hand firmly as Shashtah settled onto the far edge of the couch.

Shashtah cupped his left hand along the curve of Kashon's jaw. "Poor payment, I'm afraid, for saving my life." He suddenly fancied that he saw the dark hall and the eight intimidating judges. One by one, the stately figures inclined their heads. The ancient woman paused the longest. She seemed to stare directly at Shashtah and then inclined her head as well. He felt his skin prickle again.

Both Katrell and the girl gave a startled squawk.

Shashtah snapped his eyes open. For a moment he imagined that he saw a shimmering light surrounding Kashon and Katrell.

The light vanished as suddenly as it had appeared.

Kashon stirred. "Katrell?" he whispered.

Shashtah saw something that frightened him in Katrell's eyes. He hastily stood and backed away.

Kashon patted Katrell's forearm reassuringly. "Easy," he whispered in an exhausted voice. "The Council let him wake me so I could be with you."

Shashtah flushed at the pain that he saw on Kashon's face. "It should have been me, not you. It was my fault."

"No," Kashon murmured, closing his eyes. "My fault, my guilt, my pain."

"You're both wrong," the girl declared. "Don't you see the wisdom of the Council? They've punished all four of us by hurting Kashon."

The images of Shashtah's dream came unbidden to his mind. He frowned. "Did I do this to you? Did I read the scroll?"

Kashon opened his eyes and squinted at Shashtah. "How did you know there was a scroll?"

"I dreamed . . . " Shashtah's voice trailed off. He lowered his eyes and focused on the toes of his boots. He noted absently that he stood atop an image of the long-dead king Bahakesh, Rider of the Dragonprophet Tchang.

Kashon settled deeper into the cushions. "Shaharadesh read the scroll," he said softly. His voice held a bitterness Shashtah had not heard there before.

Shashtah studied Kashon warily.

"Don't mind me." The tone in Kashon's voice did nothing to reassure Shashtah. "Even if you had stood there and read the words yourself, I could not be less grateful to you than I am now." He twisted so he could stare passionately into Katrell's eyes. "I would have been barely conscious for half a rotation. This way I can talk with Katrell and at least make some sense."

Shashtah averted his gaze, disturbed by the power of the Bond between them. *Could Dragons take their Riders as mates? But if they are mates, then who is the girl?*

Katrell pressed his lips to Kashon's forehead. "Tphah is correct. None of us is likely to risk this happening again."

Shashtah narrowed his eyes, suddenly remembering what the girl had said. "'Four of us?'" he echoed her words. He turned and stared at her as if he were seeing her for the first time. "Tphah?"

The dragongirl quivered beneath her veil, as Katrell glared at her.

"Yes," hissed Katrell.

"Stop it," Kashon groaned. "Both of you. I'm too exhausted for you two not to get along."

Tphah bared her throat to Kashon as Katrell gave his Rider's hand an apologetic squeeze.

Shashtah rubbed his forehead. "Demons, dreams, Dragons, Bonds, shapeshifting . . . I'm not thinking straight."

"Perhaps you are not meant to, Dragonheart," Tphah volunteered.

"Will you stop babbling, child?" croaked Katrell. "It's not time. He doesn't even have a Dragon yet."

Tphah flared at the words. She swayed to her feet in a single, elegant movement that made Shashtah's heart catch in his throat and a strange warmth flood through his loins. "Yes, he does."

"Who?" Katrell demanded.

"Me!" Tphah's chin jutted out as she met the older Dragon's disbelieving stare.

"What are you two blithering about?" Kashon demanded, half rising from his throne. He collapsed back onto the pillows, unable to stay upright.

"A Prophecy. Nothing more." Katrell stared pointedly at his Rider.

"Words, not thoughts," Kashon grunted, pressing his hands to his temples. "It's rude to think at me in the presence of others who cannot hear you. Plus my head hurts. What are you trying to hide from him?"

Katrell sighed. "He's a Dragonheart, but he doesn't understand. There's some reason the Council doesn't want him to know."

Kashon studied Shashtah's tense face. "Why would the Council not want him to—?"

"Please," Katrell begged.

Kashon pinched the bridge of his nose with his right thumb and forefinger. "I doubt the Council would be sending him dreams and having him wake me if they didn't want you to make him understand. They are practically hitting you over the head with a scimitar, you nit." Kashon's voice quavered with weariness.

Shashtah closed the distance between them, lay his hands over Kashon's calloused fingers and pulled them gently away from his face. "Rest," he commanded. "I don't need to understand."

"I think you do!" Kashon objected, trying to sit up again. He shook violently. Sweat from weakness trickled down his face and neck, dampening his linen shirt.

Concern flooded Katrell's face. "Please, lie—"

"I will not lie back until you tell him what a Dragonheart is!" Kashon threatened.

Katrell paled visibly but bared his throat in submission to Kashon. He locked stares with Shashtah. "Bonded Dragons and Riders generally dislike mating among themselves because of the way breeding with someone else's Partner can...complicate relationships. A few Bonded Pairs make arrangements with each other, but usually UnBonded Dumnonians mate among themselves or with Riders to produce Dumnonians and UnBonded Dragons mate among themselves or with Bonded Dragons to produce Dragons. Things don't always go as planned, though, so the blood of our two races has mixed. That's why the Dumnonians have Dragon eyes and why the Dragons can take humanform. Corin's magic gave us that."

"Get to the point," Kashon growled as he barred his teeth with his effort to stay partially upright.

Katrell bared his throat again. "Dragonhearts are said to be born when an UnBonded Dumnonian mates with an UnBonded Dragon in humanform and the dragonblood runs exceptionally strong."

Shashtah belatedly recognized the strange look in Katrell's eyes as awe.

"A Dragonheart is neither Dragon nor Dumnonian but somehow both. All of our greatest heroes and heroines have been Dragonhearts," Katrell finished decisively, as if that simple statement explained everything.

Shashtah worried at his lower lip for a heartbeat. "And you think I'm one of these Dragonheart things."

Katrell nodded slowly, purposefully. "I am certain of it."

Shashtah guffawed. "I hate to disappoint you, but I am the son of a merchant's daughter and a dragonless trader, both of whom had an inordinate aversion to Dragons. My parents always insisted I avoid Dragons whenever we ran into Riders on leave and even when our caravan was trading in Dumnonia. Until five years ago, when I came to tell Shaharadesh I had completed my first mission in his name, the nearest I'd ever been to a Dragon was when my father traveled to Dameth's basecamp to congratulate him upon receiving Tphah as a Fledgling. Yesterday was the only time I've ridden a Dragon, and it has been made unforgettably clear to me that I should not have done that. There is simply no way that I could be a Dragonheart."

Katrell glared at him, irritated. "Yet I swear to you that you are. One of your parents was an UnBonded Dragon trapped in humanform."

"Perhaps you should ask them," ventured Kashon as he finally gave into his exhaustion and lay back down.

Shashtah clenched his teeth. "That would be difficult." Images of blood and slaughter rose before his eyes, obscuring his vision. "My parents were killed by Cinnamarians while I was on my first mission for our king." Shashtah bristled at the memory. No one had spoken his father's name, Garesh, since, after sixty-seven successful missions into Cinnamar, the trader had fallen in battle against the Vampire King, Eschlend. Garesh's followers and Shashtah's mother had also been slain. The injustice continued to rankle, and Shashtah was deeply offended by the notion that his father had either been mated to a Dragon or had been a Dragon himself.

"For an UnBonded Dragon to be trapped in humanform long enough to create you, oversee your birth, and raise you would be a tremendous sacrifice," Katrell persisted. "That is part of why Dragonhearts are so rare. Once you had flown from the nest, the Dragon may have left as well. With the Dragon gone, nothing would have stood between the rest of your caravan and the Cinnamarians."

Shashtah stared at Katrell, appalled. "The Council would never allow such a massacre!"

Katrell lowered his eyes. "Oh, yes, they would." He gently brushed Kashon's hair back from his sweat-dampened face. "Look at what they have done to my Rider even though he is Bonded to me. Do you think they would place greater value on the lives of UnBonded beings?"

Shashtah gaped, completely aghast. "You can't be serious!"

"That is why I dread telling you now," Katrell said in a too quiet voice. "I fear that I risk causing my Rider more pain if the Council still does not want you to know what you are."

Shashtah surged to his feet. "I am not a Dragonheart!" he thundered. "I am not responsible for the murder of everyone on my caravan! And I absolutely refuse to be the cause of any more suffering or pain!" He strode toward the tent flap.

"Where are you going?" called Kashon.

"To the Council!" Shashtah boomed. "To put Katrell's fears to rest and to settle this 'Dragonheart' business forever!" He charged out of the Camp, his fury driving away all thoughts of his own weariness and pain. But as his feet carried him over the dunes toward the Valley of Ancients he could not dispel the growing suspicion that he might indeed have more than his share of dragonblood. At the very least, he most definitely had inherited a Dragon's roar.

Council Leader Tkai

CHAPTER 4:

Harsh Judges

Behold! The Judges stand at the doors to my Tomb in the Valley of Ancients. With them stands the king. If you have triumphed over Darkness and a Dragon will accept you, he will grant you to be Bonded as he himself triumphed, was accepted and was Bonded. But ask not lightly, for those whom the Judges love, they will reprove and chasten.

—from *Charge to the Dumnonians,*
by Corin of Daethia

SHASHTAH STOOD IN THE CENTER of the desolate box canyon, surrounded by ashes and the magic-charred bones of his fellow Dumnonians and the Dragons they had loved. His fury at the Council of Ancients vanished at the uneasy thought that he might be treading on the remains of his honored ancestors, Dragon and Dumnonian alike, of the near and distant Past. Sheer stone walls rose on either side of him. The cliff faces displayed centuries' worth of erosion. The deep crevices, gouged in the surface of the solid rock by wind-driven sand and torrential rain, cast eerie shadows even in the morning sunlight. *Climbable? Probably,* Shashtah decided. *But nothing I'd want to try.*

The gorge's rim was smoothed at even intervals, four on each side and one at the box end, as if impressive waterfalls had once tumbled over the edge, plunging at least three dragonlengths to the floor of the ravine. Massive whaleback dunes piled around the mouth of the canyon, creating a natural ramp. Although Shashtah remembered passing some desert plants on the long trek to the greatest *kanīsa* of the Dumnonian people, absolutely nothing grew in the Valley of Ancients itself. *Almost as if a bit of Cinnamar found its way into Dumnonia,* he mused.

Shashtah immediately prostrated himself and silently asked forgiveness for the sacrilegious thought. He knew quite well that the holy place felt nothing like Cinnamar. Something powerful and protective resided here. Something that valued and created life. The char-marks from magical fire that streaked the cliff faces more than explained the lack of plants in the ravine. *Plants would probably grow quite well if the whole place wasn't turned into a pyre every time a Dragon or Rider died.* Shashtah rocked into a kneeling position and brushed the ashy sand from his face.

At the far end of the box canyon stone steps led to a shelf at the base of the highest cliff. The massive, gilt-bronze doors of Corin's Tomb glittered too brightly in the shadows. *Magic,* Shashtah's mind whispered. *Lots of it.* He shivered. *What did I expect?* Legend had it that the Great Wizard Corin had forged the First Bond in the depths of the caves behind those doors and that, when he died, the Bronze Dragons of Dumnonia brought his body back to the Valley of Ancients and laid it in the sepulcher. Shashtah had hiked here from the King's Camp because the Council of Ancients was said to guard the site of Corin's Tomb and the bones of the champions that littered its doorstep. *Maybe I would have been wiser to approach them through the king,* he thought belatedly. *After all, I did earn the right to request an audience with him by completing my Dragonquest.*

Shashtah rose shakily, marveling at the extent of his sin in coming here. He started to turn and retrace his steps off the holy ground.

A Dragon's roar stopped him. "Stay, Dragonheart. The Council comes!"

Shashtah's heart skipped a beat as Makara, Dragonqueen of Dumnonia, bearing the Dumnonian king, Shaharadesh, perched on the cliff of the sacred valley above the doors to Corin's Tomb.

A flame-shaped brooch fastened Shaharadesh's cloak around his shoulders. Other than that and the Dragon-shaped ring on his right hand, he was completely indistinguishable from any other Dragonrider, except perhaps for the weariness that lurked behind his amber eyes.

One by one, eight enormous Ancient Dragons, half again larger than Katrell, settled onto the smooth stretches along the canyon's rim.

Shashtah felt his knees buckle under him as he recognized one of the males as Dameth's Dragon, Tlee. Kneeling, Shashtah bowed his head before the Council, wondering how Kashon had found the nerve to face their displeasure alone.

"Speak!" Makara commanded.

Shashtah stared up at the Dragonqueen.

Makara was smaller than the Ancients, being only about one fourth of their age and roughly the same size as Katrell. The memories of all the previous kings' and queens' Dragons glistened in her stunning eyes.

Shashtah opened his mouth, but no words came forth.

"He grew up in a dragonless camp." Shaharadesh's voice echoed against the canyon walls. "You're scaring the poor man into the Afterlife."

"We can't frighten a Dragonheart," an Ancient Female to Shashtah's right protested.

"Only if he knows he's one," an even older male, who stood at the king's left, observed softly.

Shashtah's gaze shifted abruptly to the sympathetic Dragon. Something about the beast's voice sounded vaguely familiar.

"How can you say he doesn't know after that nit Katrell told him everything?" sniffed another female, who was younger only by comparison to the female Dragon at the king's right.

The compassionate male gestured toward Shashtah with a sword-sharp talon. "Look at him! He's understanding every word we're saying, and he doesn't even realize that we're not using ClearTalk. His powers are awakening, all out of control, because of last night. If he listened to anything Katrell said, he did not believe. But how long is he going to be able to ignore the fact that he is glowing like Galantite in the desert sun? He's a dreamer with sand for brains, I'll grant you that, but he's not blind."

Shashtah's puzzlement at the Dragon's use of his father's favorite oath vanished like the desert wind as he realized that his skin was once more prickling as sparkling light swirled around him.

The Ancient Female to Shaharadesh's right roared with laughter. "You do have a point."

"Perhaps if you all tried treating him like a Dumnonian instead of like a Dragon," Shaharadesh suggested, "he might be able to get his power under control?"

The Ancient Female stared down at Shashtah for several heartbeats. She nodded slowly. "We include the king in our meetings to remind us of the Dumnonian point of view. We should take his advice." She melted into the shape of the frail, old woman from Shashtah's dream.

Shashtah gasped and his magic flared as the other Dragons, including Makara, followed her example. His eyes widened as he recognized two of the males as the guards who had arrested Kashon.

The understanding male beside the king was the last to shift, and as he changed, Shashtah heard an unearthly sound ricochet through the canyon, a sound that he belatedly recognized as his own scream. "Garesh!" He surged to his feet.

Garesh pondered the look in his son's shocked eyes. "You called me 'Father' once." The dragonman wore a keffiyeh with the same elaborate, bejeweled agal that Shashtah remembered from his childhood. Muscles on Garesh's powerful arms, legs and chest rippled beneath his embroidered vest and billowing pantaloons. No one who had ever sat across a bargaining table from that hawk-like face would ever forget those chiseled, impassive features. Now, though, sorrow beyond measure, instead of the sharp wit and impish humor that had once captivated Shashtah, dulled the trader's solid amber gaze.

"But you were killed by Eschlend the night Mother was slain!" Shashtah protested, refusing to believe what his senses and heart were telling him.

Garesh cocked his head slightly, and his lips curled into a sad smile. "Have you heard any stories about my undead body walking around?"

"No," Shashtah admitted. "But that doesn't mean—"

"Shashtah," Garesh argued in his most reasonable voice, "would you stop dreaming for one heartbeat and think? Eschlend is a Vampire King. If he had killed me wouldn't someone have noticed a too well-known trader in the Dark One's ranks by now?"

Shashtah swallowed hard. "But if Eschlend didn't kill you, then you killed—" He choked on the Truth and staggered to his feet, his magic churning around him like a ten-winter storm.

"Would you rather have your undead mother and the rest of our caravan coming against you out of Cinnamar?" Garesh snapped.

Shashtah jerked his head as if he had been punched in the jaw.

"Do not judge him, Dragonheart," thundered the elderly woman in her dragonvoice, "until you understand what he has done!"

"What is that," Shashtah demanded, "besides murder my mother and all of his followers?"

The woman stared at Garesh, great respect and boundless compassion shining in her ancient eyes. "He spent a quarter of a century trapped in another being's form, had a child with a member of that creature's race, grew to love his child and his mate, and defended them, a task that would have been so easy in his true form but that was ever so difficult in theirs. He experienced the love of another even after he reverted to his dragonform and then found it within himself to slay all of those he loved to save them from a worse fate at the Dark One's hands. When you have done as much, only then can you judge Garesh."

"'Judge Garesh'?" Shashtah repeated. "Only the Dragons judge. I am simply a Dumnonian."

"You are a Dragonheart," the Ancient Female corrected him.

"What difference does that make?" Shashtah's voice reverberated with confusion.

Garesh placed his fists on his hips and bent his head. He could have been mortified or furious. His face revealed nothing.

"You are neither Dragon nor Dumnonian, but somehow both," the woman half-chanted as if she were reciting an ancient text. "You would not be speaking with me here if you were simply a Dumnonian."

Actually, Shashtah admitted, I am sunstruck enough to do precisely that.

Where on Centuria was I when the Lord of Light passed out brains? "Why are you all so sure I am a Dragonheart?"

"All Dragons can see you for what you are," the old woman said indulgently, "even without you glowing like the midday sun. Tphah is too young to know when she should hold her tongue. There is no excuse for Katrell, though. He should have called for help the heartbeat he found you and realized how injured you were. We will have to speak with—"

"You will not hurt him!" Shashtah roared, sending his magic soaring almost as high as the clifftops. "I forbid it!"

The Ancient Female raised her eyebrow. "You what?"

"I—" *What am I doing? I can't talk to her like that!* Shashtah prostrated himself in the sand and ashes faster than he thought possible. The invisible force surrounding him discharged into the ground, taking the shimmering light with it. "I'm sorry! I—!

"Well," Garesh's voice rumbled, "I suppose that's as safe a place for that much magic as any. Corin will have some idea what to do with it. If that had happened in the King's Camp . . . " He sighed. "Shashtah, stand up."

A lifetime of obeying that voice jerked Shashtah to his feet. He stood at attention, awaiting his father's orders.

Garesh smiled slyly. "You look like a sandhog in a dust storm. Wipe your face."

Shashtah quickly used his sleeve to rub away as much of the sand and ash as he could.

"Better," Garesh said in a tone that suggested there had not been that much of an improvement. His features hardened into those of a caravaneer with decades of experience in command. "You bear the heart of the Lord of Cinnamar in your pouch. You have held that heart in your hand. You have felt it feed on your fear and pain. If you had known you were a Dragonheart, do you think you could have hidden the fact that it was your power and not the Dark One's that kept you alive?"

Shashtah suddenly felt like a child again beneath his father's stare. His back stung at the memory of Yapada's flail. He clenched his left fist where he had clutched the pulsing black stone, feeling the imprint the vile gem had left there. "How could I do anything like that? I barely have the brains necessary to cast the simplest of spells."

"Not all magic is of the head. Some is of the heart." Makara, now a stunningly beautiful Dumnonian woman at Shaharadesh's side, tossed her shiny black hair beneath her shimmering white veil. A nation's ransom in jewelry sparkled at her throat, waist, wrists and ankles, and Shashtah fancied that he could hear her jingle as she moved.

A dazzling middle-aged dragonwoman who stood on the canyon rim closer to Shashtah laughed. "Yapada could not be certain you were anything other than the common thief that you appeared to be. The Dark One would not have been pleased to be presented with something else than what he truly prized: a captive Bronze. The Demonlord could not force you to take the shape of a Dragon, though, because your natural form is that of a Dumnonian. He did not realize that something far more valuable than a Bronze had fallen into his paws. The fool will pay for his mistake."

"But I'm not a common thief!" Shashtah protested, completely failing to hear anything else the Councilor said.

One of the guards guffawed. "Of course, you're not! That's what the Cinnamarians didn't see. Nits, all of them. Just because they are evil, that doesn't make them smart. They all thought the Dark One was keeping you alive. It never occurred to them that you did not need his help."

"As if a common thief could have gotten anywhere near the Dark One's heart!" Tlee crowed. "Someone with even half a brain would have chosen a Krill for that job. Or at least sent someone who knew something about magic to collect that prize. I doubt anyone in Cinnamar suspects the Council has created another Dragonheart."

The second guard joined in the laughter. "It took him ten tries to come out of that mountain with what we wanted. I almost gave up hope!"

Shashtah found himself nodding at the Council's wisdom even though he was fairly certain that they were all out of their ever-loving draconic minds. "Ten tries," he echoed. "My Dragonquest." He looked up at Shaharadesh and decided that engaging in a ritual conversation with his monarch seemed much less nerve-racking than saying another word to the Ancient Dragons. "Sire, I have completed ten quests in your name. I bring the Heart of the Dark One as proof that I fulfilled my Dragonquest. I formally ask that you allow me to Bond with a Dumnonian Bronze." His soul trembled as his roar resonated off the canyon walls.

Shaharadesh blinked with surprise at being addressed with the words from the timeless tradition. Uncertain what to do, he turned to the most Ancient Female.

The Council Leader nodded her consent. "It is permitted. He has earned the right."

The king regarded Shashtah uncertainly. "He's a Dragonheart. Once he is Bonded, the Dark One cannot touch him without all of the Dragons of Dumnonia coming to his aid. You know that as well as I. Why would you want to take such a risk?"

The elderly woman beamed benignly. "Because it is Prophecy."

The king and the Councilors bared their throats to her.

The Ancient Female accepted their submission with a regal nod.

Shaharadesh signaled to Makara, who shifted to her dragonform.

The Council melted back into their true shapes and called their summons to the sky as Shaharadesh climbed to his perch on Makara's neck.

Bronze Dragons of every size, all old enough to bear a Rider, all currently Riderless, appeared in the morning sky above the Valley and settled onto the canyon rim.

Shashtah gazed up at them in awe. *I could never choose from so many!* He said a silent prayer of thanks to the Lord of Light that his king would select his Bond Partner for him.

When all the Dragons had found a perch, Shaharadesh raised his hands for silence. "A Rider presents himself! A very worthy one. In his pouch he bears the Dark One's Heart. Upon his back he bears the scars of a Demonlord's flail. In his veins runs the blood of a Dragon. I give to you Shashtah Dragonheart! Is there one among you who will consent to Bond with him?"

Shashtah gaped as Shaharadesh grabbed his head and fell from Makara's back.

Makara hastily shifted to humanform and gathered her Rider into her arms.

The Council Leader bellowed, "WILL ALL OF YOU NITS SHUT UP?"

Shaharadesh shook his head and let Makara help him to his feet. "I guess I didn't need to ask." He kissed the Dragonqueen on her forehead. "I'm all right." He motioned for her to resume dragonform.

Makara hesitated a moment, then took her true shape and glared at the Dragons on the rim.

Shaharadesh remounted Makara and carefully braced his legs in her harness. He held up his hands again. "Since so many are agreeable, who is the most worthy?"

The Dragons looked at each other, and Shashtah could sense a heated, if silent, argument among them that he could do nothing to stop.

Shaharadesh's brow furrowed as if he had a terrible headache. He swayed in the harness and seemed about to collapse again.

Suddenly Tphah in dragonform appeared out of nowhere and landed beside Shashtah. Her abrupt arrival shocked the Dragons into a real silence. "He's mine!" Tphah bugled at the would-be Bond Partners.

"You are too young!" one of the unBonded Dragons called back.

"I saw him first!" Tphah insisted.

"I'd say Garesh saw him first," a female Councilor observed with a chuckle.

"Let it be Garesh, then," a male Councilor agreed.

"No!" Tphah wailed. "I'm his Dragon! I know I am! I see him flying with me—"

"Hush, child," the Council Leader ordered.

Shashtah threw the elderly Dragon a grateful look as the ear-splitting argument ceased.

The end of Tphah's whip-like tail curling possessively around Shashtah's left leg.

"First Dragon Bond with Dragonheart," the Council Leader chanted, "Five too-short years, then they must part."

All the Dragons seemed to hold their breath.

Even Tphah slightly loosened her hold on Shashtah's leg.

Garesh suddenly swooped to the canyon floor. "Let it be me, then."

An image of Katrell caressing Kashon's face came unbidden to Shashtah's mind, and he recoiled from his father.

Sensing Shashtah's distress, Garesh took his humanform. "Fear not, my son. Bond Partners do not have to be lovers. They can be parent and child or simply friends. Perhaps I kept you too sheltered. You do not understand. But you could not find out what you were until your powers began to manifest themselves. It was too dangerous. For you. For me. For Dumnonia."

Shashtah shook his head. "I can't. I just learned you slew everyone I loved. It will be some time before I can understand that let alone figure out if I can forgive you."

Suddenly, the extremely ancient woman was standing beside Garesh. Shashtah had not seen her glide to the canyon floor or shift into humanform, but she must have done so. She smiled at him, more than a millennium of wisdom in her amber eyes. "Take me then."

"No, Tkai!" Garesh protested. "You cannot fly in the face of your own Prophecy!"

A bemused smile shifted the wrinkles on Tkai's face not unlike the way the winds caused dunes to creep across the desert. "At my age I have earned the right to do anything I please. You are still young by my standards. The Council will need your wisdom and your understanding when I am gone."

"No!" Tphah keened.

Tkai reached out and chucked the Stripling under her chin. "Hush. I don't think there's a Dragon alive today who's not related to me in some manner. When you can't remember how many mates you've watched Hatch and die, it's well past time for you to join them."

"But he's mine!" Tphah whined. "I'm afraid, but I know. I saw!"

Tkai tapped Tphah's snout between her nostrils, causing the Stripling to go nearly cross-eyed. "You saw, but you saw far into the future. You haven't learned to control your Prophecy yet. Stay with Kashon: He knows more than he thinks he does. You might even learn a thing or two from that nit Katrell."

Tphah shook her head, freeing herself from the trance Tkai had nearly lulled her into. "Katrell is not a nit!"

"Hush!" Tkai hissed. "He wants us all to think he is, and because he wishes this, it is so."

Tphah bared her throat to Tkai, then hung her head.

Tkai turned to Shashtah. "I'm not as fast as I used to be, but I still have much to offer. I've borne two Dragonhearts in my lifetime. Will you deign to make it three?"

Shashtah felt his heart quivering in his breast. *The Leader of the Council of Ancients wants to Bond with me?* "I thought you said that after five years the Dragon or the Dragonheart will die."

"I said they must 'part,'" Tkai said. "That could mean anything. Perhaps their Bond breaks. Perhaps something makes it physically impossible for them to be together. But as it happens, in this case you are correct. One of us will die."

"You've borne two Dragonhearts, and they both died at the end of five years?" Shashtah asked worriedly, suddenly not liking his odds.

"Ah, Garesh, you are right. This one leads with his heart, not with his head!" Tkai laughed. "Think, Dragonheart! Think!"

"You're expecting a lot of him," Garesh sighed.

Shashtah's brow furrowed at the challenge from his father. He turned possibility after possibility over in his mind until he found the only one that made any sense. "You were the UnBonded Dragon in humanform. You weren't their Bond Partner; you gave birth to them."

The old woman beamed. "Such a clever boy, Garesh! Perhaps you underestimate him."

Shashtah suspected that Tkai was being sarcastic. He blushed and looked away from her. His gaze fell on Tphah. "How can I become Tphah's Rider if I die?" He turned back to Tkai, defiance in his eyes.

Tkai grew somber. She waited for him to see the answer.

Horror spread across Shashtah's face. "Oh, no. No, no, no, no, no. I will not be Bonded to the Leader of the Council of Ancients when she dies!"

Garesh put his hands on his hips and stared at the sand, clearly trying to control his temper. "Shashtah, we're Dragons, not immortals. We die. So do our Riders." He raised his eyes and glared at his son. "Or has that never occurred to you in all the years you've spent dreaming about becoming a Dragonrider?"

Shashtah clenched his teeth to keep himself from admitting to his father that the terrifying thought had indeed not occurred to him.

Tkai lay her hand on Garesh's arm, silencing him. "Your son will add glory to my final years, and perhaps one day, because of him, the bards will sing a line or two about Tkai." She released Garesh and pulled herself erect. "What is your answer, Shashtah Dragonheart? Will you walk through the doors of Corin's Tomb with me?"

Shashtah glanced quickly at Tphah, then looked up at Shaharadesh. "It is not my choice to make. You are supposed to choose."

Shaharadesh stared pointedly at each of the eldest Dragons, apparently taking a silent vote. "I choose Tkai, Leader of the Council of Ancients and Prophetess of the Bronze Dragons, as the Bond Partner for Shashtah Dragonheart."

Shashtah had not thought it possible to be thrilled and horrified at the same time. He covered his conflicting emotions by holding out his arm to the Ancient Prophetess.

Tkai rested her hand lightly in the crook of his elbow as if for support and let him lead her on the long walk toward the great bronze doors.

Shashtah suspected her apparent feebleness was a show intended to calm his nerves. The pressure her fingers exerted on his arm felt more like the grasp of one of his father's centaurs than like that of the elderly woman Tkai appeared to be, and it did nothing to reassure him. He also had the definite impression that she was shoving him toward the Tomb even though he appeared to be escorting her.

Tphah raised her head and keened softly, unable to take her eyes off them, as if she were watching the marriage of another woman to the man she loved.

Garesh took his dragonform and moved closer to the Stripling. He stretched his left wing over her protectively.

Makara glided to the canyon floor with Shaharadesh.

The king dismounted and climbed the stone steps just as Shashtah and Tkai reached the entrance to Corin's Tomb.

Bronze Dragon and would-be Rider bent in deep salaams before their king.

Shaharadesh waited until they straightened themselves, then he gazed into Shashtah's solid amber eyes. "Shashtah Dragonheart, having completed ten missions in my name, you come before me to claim your reward. I remind you that it is your right to ask for an entire band of warriors to command. You will never be given another chance to make this request. Will you give up that command to be joined instead with the Honored Ancient Tkai, Bonded soul-to-soul, heart-to-heart, until Death or Judgment severs that Bond?"

Shashtah thought carefully about his answer. It was a blind trade. He knew everything about the life of a dragonless warrior. He knew nothing about Dragons nor Riders nor the lives they led. His father had seen to that. Garesh. The Master Trader. The Dragon who had made a blind trade to give Shashtah his life. *There's no logic to it. It's a matter of faith.* He took a deep breath. *Please let me be right, Lord of Light!* "Yes, I will give up that command."

Shashtah's hesitation brought approving smiles to the faces of both his king and Tkai.

"Will you," Shaharadesh continued, "care for her needs before your own in both her dragon- and her humanform?"

"I will," Shashtah swore in a much steadier voice. *As if I would do anything else.*

"Will you submit without protest to the Judgment of the Council if, for any reason, be it your fault or no, she comes to harm?"

The memory of Kashon's pain-filled face and Katrell's heart-wrenching cry came unbidden to Shashtah's mind. *In five years she's going to die. What if it's my fault? What if it's not my fault? Tphah said the Council would only listen to Shaharadesh. Will he speak for me? Did he speak for Kashon?* Shashtah tried to read his king's impassive face and failed. He could almost hear his father's disapproving snort inside his head as he took too long to answer. "I will," he said at last.

Shaharadesh acknowledged the oath with a nod. He turned to the Ancient Councilor. "Will you, Tkai, give up your freedom and do the bidding of this warrior, serving him to the best of your ability with body, mind and soul?"

Tkai remained silent for a heartbeat. "I will, sire. This Dumnonian pleases me. It will be my honor to Bond with him."

"Will you give up all wealth to him that he might purchase what he needs to care for you?" Shaharadesh asked, watching the Ancient Dragon with a critical eye.

Tkai sighed. "I will. I understand the need."

Shaharadesh looked deep into Tkai's eyes. "Will you guard yourself against harm so that your Rider will never have to face the Council on account of you?"

Tkai turned and caressed Shashtah's cheek like a grandmother touching a treasured grandson. "I will try. With all my heart, I will try. But one day I will fail." She took Shashtah by the shoulders and turned him toward her. "Dragonheart, do you understand my Prophecy? In five years our Bond will break. At that time, I know that I will die and you shall live. I give my last five years to you, and I will serve you in that time as best I can, if this is truly what you wish. But do you comprehend what you will face the day I die? The breaking of a Bond is not an easy thing to endure. Having let one Dragon die, there is no guarantee another will agree to Bond with you. Are you truly willing to pay that price for what little I can give you in those five years?"

Kashon's dream image, writhing on the floor of that great, dark hall, came into sharp focus in Shashtah's mind. With a broken Bond, he'd have no Dragon to help him endure such pain. There was a very real chance that even if he survived he would be insane. He could ask for a band of warriors instead, comrades in arms who would never force him to face the prospect of a broken Bond. He could run a caravan with them as his father had, helping to supply the front line centuries and the King's Camp with the goods they so desperately needed. If, however, he survived Tkai's death, Tphah might still want him. If not, after a lifetime of wanting a Dragon, he would have lost the only one he would ever have. Shashtah stared steadily at Tkai's eyes. *She knows so much. Is it worth the trade?* "Your Prophecy says I will survive?"

Tkai smiled her approval once again. "Yes, Dragonheart. You will survive. You may not wish to, but you will survive."

Shashtah nodded his acceptance of that truth. "Then I am willing." He turned to face Shaharadesh. "We are agreed. Create the Bond."

Tkai lowered her hand to her side.

Shaharadesh reached out and drew Shashtah into an embrace.

Shashtah closed his eyes and wrapped his arms around Shaharadesh. He gasped at the speed with which the true essence of his soul was laid bare before his king's probing mind.

Shaharadesh released him and turned to embrace Tkai.

Shashtah shivered, feeling naked and exposed. A disconcerting loneliness flooded through him at the absence of his king's touch. He watched a haunted look that must have mirrored his own spread across Tkai's face as Shaharadesh released her.

"Do not touch," Shaharadesh charged them, "until the magic of Corin instructs you to do so." He turned and muttered a spell that opened the doors to the Tomb. "If you will be Bonded, enter herein. Seek the Wizard's Heart that you might be whole."

Shashtah fought the overwhelming urge to grab Tkai and crush her into his arms as he stood before the doors. "What's in there?" he whispered.

"Our test," Tkai's voice shrugged. "I know no more than that. The Challenge of Corin's Tomb is different every time, designed to form a Bond between a specific Pair."

"Tkai," warned Shaharadesh.

Tkai hastily bared her throat to him. "Forgive me, sire. My instinct to protect him has already stirred." She focused on Shashtah, waiting for him to enter before her.

Shashtah took a deep breath and studied the ancient dragonwoman carefully. Then he exhaled slowly and stepped through the doors of Corin's Tomb.

The Shade of Corin

CHAPTER 5:

A Rock in a Hard Place

And His Tomb will become a sanctuary, and a stone of offense, and a rock to stumble over for both Dragons and Riders, a trap and a pit to the inhabitants of Dumnonia.

—from *The Prophecies of Tchang*
by Bahakesh, Dragonlord of Dumnonia

SHASHTAH SENSED TKAI STANDING at his side, just beyond his touch, as the doors slammed shut, locking them inside Corin's Tomb. His desert-adapted eyes strained at the darkness, unable to make out ceiling, floors, walls or even Tkai. "What do we do now?" he tried to ask, but no sound formed. He could not hear himself breathe. Quickly it occurred to him that he did not want to: The dungeon reeked. He started to panic but recognized the magic pulsing in the air. *An illusion*, he decided. "*Seek the Wizard's Heart.*" Shaharadesh's words echoed in his breast. *Without touching Tkai. Right.*

Although Dragonriders were the closest thing the desolate country had in the way of a military force, Dumnonians were not well known for obeying orders. And Shashtah had grown up about as far away from Dragonriders as a Dumnonian could get. Having served as a lone operative on every one of his missions for the king, he did not have the first idea how to go about working with a partner. He did know, however, that he had absolutely no intention of taking the king's injunction not to touch Tkai too literally. He felt the Bond magic making him ache for her the way he suspected she was aching for him. Find the Wizard's Heart he would, but he was not about to leave her standing alone in the dark while he did it. He was going to take her with him.

With deft fingers he rapidly unfastened his belt buckle and slid off the pouch that contained the unholy gem. He dropped the pouch down his shirt, feeling the heavy stone come to a rest where the loose-fitting garment was tucked tightly inside his trousers' waistband. He made a slip knot out of the belt and drew it snugly about his right wrist. It was not his strongest arm, but he had a feeling he was going to need his good hand free. Knowing Tkai was somewhere to his right, he gently flicked the free end of the belt in that direction.

The leather touched something that flinched away from the contact.

Shashtah stifled an exasperated sigh and tried again, a little harder this time. He felt the leather pass close to something that he hoped was Tkai. Shashtah took a step to his right and swung the leather out a third time.

Someone caught the other end.

Shashtah imagined Tkai's gnarled fingers gripping the leather strap. He felt a hesitant tug. He tugged back, careful not to tear the leather from her grasp. Then he reached out with his left hand and felt for the tunnel wall.

He had to coax Tkai into following him by using a few small tugs on the strap. After two steps his fingertips brushed the glass-smooth surface of volcanic stone. *Lava tube*, he identified the tunnel to himself. *Only one way to go.*

Or maybe two.

Shashtah leaned back as soon as he felt his right foot come down on nothing but air. If he had not been following the wall, he would have fallen all the way into the pit, pulling Tkai in after him. As it was, his left forearm slammed flat against the ledge that ran along the wall and his right arm slapped down hard on the obsidian floor at the edge of the pit. The glass-sharp rim cut into his right underarm and through his shirt, reopening some of the wounds Kashon had tried so hard to heal. The soles of Shashtah's desert boots scrabbled helplessly against the polished sides of the pit wall. His throat felt as if he had screamed, but still no sound reached his straining ears.

A gentle tug came on the leather strap from somewhere near the level of the tunnel floor.

Shashtah allowed himself a sigh of relief. He had gone down so fast, there had been no chance of warning Tkai. He had been half afraid that she would continue forward and step blindly into the pit just as he had. But then again, she did have a few centuries' experience on him at this sort of thing. *In spite of her age, maybe I should let her lead. If I can ever get out of this cursed pit!*

Shashtah let himself hang for a moment. The sword-like edge of the pit bit deeper into his back, driving him to move as quickly as possible. He would have to be careful how he climbed out or he would be sliced to shreds.

Shashtah was about to push himself up when the ledge under his left hand began to move. The side of the pit pressed inward, toward the center of the tunnel, threatening to scrape him from his precarious perch. His experiences inside Mount Cinnamar told him that the side near the other wall was probably pressing inward as well.

Panic pushing aside all thoughts of caution, Shashtah heaved himself up and rolled onto the moving ledge.

As the moving surface carried him toward the center of the tunnel, the belt attached to his wrist pulled taut and began to swing out over the moving surface.

Shashtah scrambled to his feet and stumbled after Tkai as she led him across the ledge and deeper into the tunnel. Walking at an angle to avoid the gap in the center of the pit, he had just gotten the hang of keeping his balance when he felt the ledge click to a stop and then reverse its motion.

The belt tugged urgently at his wrist.

Shashtah did not need the warning. He gave Tkai the slack she needed and started to move after her as fast as he dared, wondering exactly how quickly the elderly dragonwoman could run.

There was scarcely enough of the ledge for him to place one foot after the other by the time the sole of his right boot came down on solid ground. The shock almost sent him toppling back into the pit.

The belt around his wrist tightened and yanked him forward into the tunnel.

Shashtah sprawled face first onto the tunnel floor. The black gem beneath his shirt dug into his belly, and he felt himself groan. He lay there for a heartbeat, trying to catch his breath, grateful that Tkai could not see him.

He used the strap to haul himself to his feet in response to her worried tugs. He pulled on the belt again to let Tkai know he was ready to move on, then stumbled after her into the dark silence that lay beyond.

They had not gone more than a dozen paces when Shashtah felt every ounce of energy left in his battered body receding in the absence of an immediate threat. The strain of the last three days had taken a dreadful toll on him, and he wondered absently if he honestly had the strength to go on. He contemplated lying down on the tunnel floor and sleeping for a few candlescars, hoping he would awake refreshed.

Shashtah had slowed almost to a stop and was about to sink to his knees when Tkai tugged sharply on the strap, almost yanking him off his feet.

The effort it took for Shashtah to recover his balance on the slippery floor cleared his head. With some surprise he recognized the telltale wave of dizziness that accompanied the breaking of a magical suggestion. But unable to see or hear he could not grasp how the spell had gotten a hold on him. He sent a tug of thanks along the belt to Tkai, then followed her lead once more.

They seemed to walk forever, down one heat-polished corridor after another. Shashtah wondered for a while if Tkai had any idea where she was going or if she was just wandering through the maze waiting for something to happen. He hoped the blood, which he could feel dribbling down his back once more, would congeal before he lost too much and collapsed.

Shashtah was never sure exactly when he noticed that his feet were getting uncomfortably warm through his desert boots. *How hot does something have to be before something like that happens?* He cut a corner too close and startled backward into the opposite wall. He screamed as the blistering stone cauterized the wounds on his back. He felt almost as if his flesh were turning to scales. Several notions about what could be causing the heat abruptly followed, none of which pleased him in the slightest. He stopped dead in his tracks.

Tkai gave a curious tug on the strap.

Shashtah frowned, doing his best to think in spite of the terror that threatened to paralyze his mind. *Can she feel the heat through her Dragon-tough skin?* Her pace had never varied. *Has the increase in temperature really been so gradual that neither of us noticed? Can she feel what's bothering me now?* Shashtah pulled the strap toward the wall until he felt the hand on the other end jerk back suddenly. His stomach cramped uncomfortably at the belated thought that he might have hurt Tkai, but he desperately needed her wisdom. He knew he had no other way to alert her to the danger. *Does she know where the heat is coming from? Is it simply because we're going deeper into the crypt? Then again,* Shashtah shivered as the horrible thought that had refused to take shape before suddenly formed all-to-clearly in his mind, *this* is *a lava tube.* He led Tkai back along their tracks for a few steps.

Shashtah had never personally walked into a blacksmith's forge, but the blast of heat that hit him as he tried to retrace their path gave him an excellent idea of what the experience would be like. He started to yank on the strap and was nearly hauled off his feet as Tkai, finally catching his panic, did her best to sprint down the corridor in the way she had originally been heading.

The now-sweating Dumnonian ran after her, wrenching away from the corridor walls in agony every time he missed a corner and slammed into the searing rock. The stench of his blistering flesh caused his stomach to twist, but stopping to throw up was not an option.

A small voice in his head kept repeating the words :*Don't panic. Don't panic.*:

Shashtah knew he was losing his nerve badly, but going back was impossible and an infinitely more terrifying prospect than going on. He ran blindly through the panic and pain that had become his world.

The strap on his wrist abruptly went slack.

Frantically, Shashtah grabbed at the belt with his good hand and followed the leather to the conclusion that his heart already knew: Tkai was no longer on the other end. Sheer horror shot through him, giving him the courage to ignore the king's injunction not to touch her. He used both hands to sweep the darkness in front of him.

His fingers brushed against something larger and furrier and tougher than anything Shashtah had ever seen in all the years he had been raiding in Cinnamar. Muscles like bone ridges stretched beneath the creature's skin, and Shashtah had the distinct impression that he had only found the beast's lower abdomen. He recoiled both physically and mentally from the certainty that the monster blocking his path had Tkai's humanform in its clutches and was probably well on its way to slaying her. His scimitar long since lost to the demons of Cinnamar and not even a jambiya to cut food with in his borrowed clothes, Shashtah ran back down the hall as far as the heat would let him. He turned, took a deep breath, sprinted into the darkness before him and threw himself into the air, feet first, at where he hoped the creature was.

Shashtah felt the ridges beneath the creature's hide snap and the skin of the beast enfold him. His leap carried him through the monster's insides. Shashtah had absolutely no time to wonder why he had been able to jump through the beast. He landed on his abused back and continued to slide at an alarming speed into the darkness, away from the monster and Tkai. He flailed, trying to stop. Slowly it occurred to him that he could no longer find the walls. He felt his throat screaming, but his brain could not form a rational thought. Then he was in midair, with the unpleasant sensation that he was shooting upward, feet first.

The stone and pouch inside his shirt flew out and slammed against his chin.

Instinctively, Shashtah caught the pouch in his left hand. In spite of Garesh's assurances to the contrary, he still believed that the evil in the rock, rather than his own power, had sustained him beyond all reason when he should have died in the desert under the torture of Yapada's blows. He felt the heart inside the stone calling to him now, suggesting that he take the throbbing black gem out of the pouch and hold it in his hand once more.

Shashtah, his soul appalled at the notion, threw a desperate cry at the darkness that rushed past him. ":*Tkai!*:"

Silence answered him as the horrible gem inside the pouch continued to pulse.

Almost as if it really were a heart, Shashtah thought in abject horror.

:*Like a Wizard's heart*,: commented a crystal-clear voice, an amplified version of the one in his head that had been telling him not to panic.

Something snapped inside Shashtah's skull. :*Do you mean to tell me the king asked me to find what I had all along?*:

:*You don't need to shout*,: laughed the voice. :*I can hear you just fine.*:

That's it, Shashtah thought as he suddenly realized that the voices in his head were now talking to each other. *I've lost it. I'm insane.*

Laughter filtered through his mind, setting up a strange, tingling sensation in his brain. :*No, Dragonheart. You're not insane. It's the Bond.*:

Shashtah's vision suddenly cleared. He sensed the dim outlines of an absolutely enormous cavern surrounding him. He stopped shooting upward and began to fall. The thunderous clap of dragonwings nearly deafened his suddenly-hearing ears. He saw the gleaming form of the Ancient Bronze Dragon rise beneath him, and he felt himself settle between the wide, metal ridges on her neck and back as if he had always been there. He hugged the thorn-like spike in front of him and held his breath while Tkai drifted gently down to the cavern floor.

Tkai landed with scarcely a jar and nestled into the sandy ground.

Shashtah slid from her back and sat, panting, his right shoulder against her armored side.

Tkai craned her neck around and contemplated him with one of her twinkling amber eyes. :*That was fun!*:

Shashtah gaped at her, still a little shocked at the sound of her voice in his head. :*Fun? You call that fun? I never want to find out what you think a life-threatening situation is, if you think that was fun!*:

Tkai's eyes sparkled with laughter as her dragonjaws opened and she roared her amusement.

Shashtah clapped his hands over his ears, only to be painfully reminded that he still held the pouch with the stone in his hand. He stared at the bag for a heartbeat, then realized that he was sitting in a circle of blue-white light. He looked up and saw the Wizard who was the source of the magical glow.

A strikingly handsome Daethian in his late thirties gazed down at the startled Dumnonian. Physically powerful beyond all reason, the man, Shashtah suspected, could have wrestled Garesh's giant to the ground. At least seven feet tall, the Wizard boasted a mane of bronze hair, combed straight back and streaked with the scar-white strands that come only from the habitual use of major magic. He wore a sleeveless tunic, Daethian trousers and boots, and no weapon. The last detail made Shashtah's heart quiver. Corin studied the newest Dragonrider with magnificent silver-grey, Daethian eyes that belonged to a man millennia older than his apparent age. "Think, Dragonheart," the Wizard scolded in the bemused voice of a patient teacher talking to a particularly dim pupil. "If the object is to create a Bond between a Rider and a Dragon, what would be the point in killing one or both of them?"

Somewhere in the course of the Wizard's brief speech, it dawned on Shashtah that he was in the presence of the shade of Corin and that he should probably be prostrating himself. He scrambled to his knees but was unable to take his eyes off the radiant figure long enough to stretch himself fully on the ground.

The Wizard laughed, a thunderous sound. "Oh, this is indeed a bright one! You have every right to be proud, Tkai."

Shashtah felt the tips of his ears burn as he suspected the spirit was mocking him.

Tkai ruffled her scales. "You know brains never get the Dumnonians anywhere. They need to follow someone with a heart."

Tkai's final word reminded Shashtah that he indeed had a heart that he desperately wanted out of his possession. He extended his hand with the pouch that contained the pulsing black stone. "The Dark One's Heart," he whispered in a hoarse voice. "I think I'm supposed to give this to you."

"Keep it safe," Tkai requested, "just as we guard you, until we can destroy the foul creature to whom it belongs."

Corin started to reach for the pouch but stopped when his fingertips were almost brushing the leather bag. "Not that long," the shade whispered. He glanced at Tkai. "Do you see the Prophecy?"

Tkai's great head swayed. ":*Dragonheart and Elven King,*:" she chanted aloud in the ancient language of the Bronze Dragons, translating silently for her Rider, ":*o'er the Dark Heart with Criton sing. Two-edged the spell, two-edged the pain, for Magic's sake some time to gain.*:"

Shashtah blinked at Corin, hearing Tkai's Prophecy echo uncomfortably inside his skull. "What does that mean?"

"It means," Corin said sadly, "that you will join with the Lord of Daethia and the Elven King to cast a spell against the Dark One, not unlike the spell used for punishment by the Council of Ancients. One of those who casts the spell will share that pain with the Dark One for all eternity, and I tell you now that when you cast that spell Tkai will be dead and your Bond with her will have been broken. You will face the uncertainty of that torment alone, a few days more than five years from when I touch the Wizard's Heart."

Shashtah felt his own heart grow cold. He looked at the Ancient Prophetess, tears glistening in his eyes. His Bond with her was so new, he could not bear the thought of losing her or imagine how he had ever been able to contemplate forging another Bond with a different Dragon after her death. Perhaps he would never Bond again. Maybe that is why Corin and Tkai saw him alone. *But Tphah sees me with her . . .*

:*You are a Dragonheart,*: Shashtah heard Tkai whisper softly in his mind. :*Dragons find the courage to form more than one Bond. You will, too, when it is time.*:

Shashtah looked back at Corin. "Take the stone."

The shade's fingers closed on the pouch and lifted the evil gem from Shashtah's grasp.

Shashtah felt as if somehow the Wizard had taken his own heart with the stone.

"It is done," Corin stated in a barely audible voice. "Now, go. Seek the White Wolf; tell him I said it is time to come home."

"Go?" Shashtah asked in spite of himself, suddenly having trouble facing the prospect of fighting his way back through the scorching hot, death-dark corridors with Tkai.

Corin's shade abruptly shifted into the shape of the Demonlord Yapada, the throbbing stone clutched in one hand and the deadly flail in the other, poised to bring the punishing weapon down on both Shashtah and Tkai. Saliva dripped from the yellowed fangs of his dog-like head. "What does it take to make you think?"

Shashtah grabbed Tkai's foreleg, closed his eyes and screamed and screamed and screamed.

After an eternity it occurred to him to wonder why he had not yet felt the blow of the flail.

:*Dragonheart*,: Tkai's stunned voice whispered through his mind. :*Open your eyes.*:

Shashtah obeyed. He was standing beside Kashon's throne-like couch, but there was no sign of his friend. In fact, all he could see was a wall of bronze scales, which he belatedly recognized as his Dragon.

Tkai's dragonform, which had instinctively curled around her Rider inside the straining cloth of the tent, melted into the shape of a Dumnonian woman. "Don't scare me like that!"

"Corin scared me!" Shashtah protested. He looked at her face recognizing it only after several heartbeats as a younger version of the face of the ancient woman he had seen in his dream and with whom he had Bonded.

Tkai embraced him like a mother trying to comfort a frightened child. Her voice smiled in his head, echoing the physical voice that sounded in his ears. "*:I only took my older shape before because I thought it was less likely to frighten you. I can appear as any age you like. I can even shape myself to the form of a man or another race, if that would please you more.:*"

Shashtah held her at arm's length and stared at her, a million questions once again piling up behind his solid-amber eyes. The words tangled in his mouth and faded into silence as he became aware of the three people blinking at them from just inside the tent flap. Slowly he recognized Katrell and Tphah supporting Kashon. Shashtah hastily released Tkai.

Kashon licked his lips, which were dry with shock. "That was a little close, Honored Ancient," he observed in the language of the Bronze Dragons.

"Do you think I'm sunstruck enough to transport into a tent even with the aid of my Rider?" Tkai snapped, switching to the Dumnonian tongue, which was easier on human throats. "I'm as amazed as you are that we don't all have bits of each other coming out of us and cooking pots for insides!"

Kashon quickly checked to make sure his brazier, pots and utensils were still in place, then shifted his gaze to Katrell who shook his head in denial.

Kashon and Katrell turned to look accusingly at Tphah, who shrugged her innocence.

All three of them turned and stared in disbelief at Shashtah.

"Oh, no!" Shashtah tried to reassure himself as much as them. "I didn't do it. Riders don't transport Dragons. It's the other way around."

Tkai sniffed and sat cross-legged on the carpet-covered floor beside the throne. "Well, Corin apparently believed you could do it enough to make you try."

"I'd say he succeeded," Kashon said.

"M-may I suggest," stammered Katrell, "that you try something a little easier next time? Like open sky?"

"Oh, Tkai!" Tphah wailed. "You don't know half of what he can do! None of you do! I'm the only one who knows! The only one who sees! He was supposed to be mine, I tell you! He was supposed to be mine!" She thrust Kashon into Katrell's arms and fled from the tent.

Shashtah saw a glazed look flash over Kashon's face at a rapid mental exchange with Katrell.

"It's rude not to use physical speech when you are in the presence of someone who cannot hear you," Tkai snapped, apparently irritated by something the two had said.

Fear returned to Kashon's features. He bared his throat as he pressed deeper into Katrell's protective embrace. "I ask your pardon, Honored Ancient."

"I'm not the one whose pardon you should ask," Tkai snapped.

Shashtah saw Kashon's eyes shift to his own face and the words of an apology start to form on his new friend's lips. "Don't." Shashtah lost all patience with his Dragon and completely forgot he was speaking to the Council Leader. :*Leave the poor man alone!*: he thought directly at Tkai in blatant and unrepentant violation of her rebuke of Kashon. :*Haven't you hurt him enough for one day?*:

Tkai blinked at Shashtah in utter surprise. :*What?*: she responded silently, breaking her own rule.

In for a copper, in for a gold. Shashtah stood his ground. :*I am half of this Partnership, and you swore to our king that you would do my bidding! Leave him alone! He has done nothing wrong!*: A trifle surprised he was still in one piece, Shashtah felt Tkai's tumble of thoughts sort itself out in his mind.

"You are right." Tkai rose gracefully to her feet and turned to smile gently at Kashon. "I am sorry. I should not be lecturing so brave and honorable a Rider who has already been taken to task."

Fear fled before confusion as Kashon's eyes met Shashtah's gaze. Awe, wonder, gratitude and finally blind trust flashed across Kashon's face while Katrell's features registered nothing but a deep, heart-wrenching concern for his Rider. "The king sent Tphah back to me so she wouldn't see you come out of the Tomb with Tkai. He thought she might react like this. Tphah is so upset I fear she might come to harm. Would you be generous enough to go after her—alone? Seeing Tkai with you will probably only set her off again. I am not strong enough yet, or I would go, and Katrell will not leave me. "

Shashtah favored Kashon with a lopsided grin. "On one condition."

"What?" Katrell asked before Kashon could blindly accept the Shashtah's terms.

Shashtah's grin widened. "That you call me 'Shashtah.' That Dragon nickname is starting to make my skin crawl."

"'Shashtah,'" Kashon echoed with a relieved smile. "Now, please, go. We'll still be here when you return."

Shashtah started to leave as Katrell helped Kashon toward some cushions in the private area, behind the wooden throne.

As they passed, Kashon reached out and clasped Shashtah's left forearm.

Startled, Shashtah returned the grasp.

Magical light flashed softly around their grip.

Shashtah sensed a Bond form between them almost as deep as the one a Rider and Dragon shared. Embarrassed and touched, he released Kashon and ducked out of the tent in search of Tphah.

Dragonrider Shashtah
and the Prophetess Tphah

CHAPTER 6:

Suntouched

And the Lord of Light said, "I was starving, and you fed me. I was parched, and you found me water. I was an outsider, and you brought me into your tent. I was naked, and you stretched your wing over me. I was injured, and you healed me. I went into the Dark One's prison, and you joined me."

And the Bronzes shall say, "Lord, when did we do these things?"

And He shall answer them, "Truly, I say to you, even as you did this for the least of my warriors, you did it for me."

—from *The Book of Light*

THE WHITE-GOLD LIGHT of the sun beat down on the King's Camp from its perch in the sapphire sky. The sunlight flashed off crystals of sand with an intensity that would have blinded anything but Dumnonian and Dragon eyes. The stillness of exhausted sleep settled over Dragons and Riders alike after the chaos of the previous night. Battle-weary Dumnonians took shelter from the midday heat inside the billowing tents and beneath the wings of sleeping Dragons.

Tphah's tracks were painfully easy to spot in the sand. To Shashtah's surprise, he was even able to tell when she had shifted to dragonform and taken flight at the edge of Camp. Hands on his hips he stared at the horizon in the direction he knew she had gone.

The leather strap that still dangled from his wrist slapped gently against his leg.

Shashtah stared at the belt for a heartbeat, then slipped it off his arm and wrapped it once more around the waist of his borrowed pants. As he did so, it occurred to him that the belt was the only thing left in all of Centuria that belonged to him.

Shashtah raised his farseeing eyes to the horizon once more.

A bronze glitter glided in the air above the Valley of Ancients.

Practiced ears separated the distress cry of a Bronze Dragon from the lonely howl of the desert wind, and Shashtah sighed. With measured steps he struck out across the desert, wondering what on Centuria he was going to say to Tphah when he finally reached the Valley.

As Shashtah trudged across the dunes, every muscle in his body reminded him exactly how long it had been since he had had any true rest. His stomach finally gave up complaining about his need for food. Thirst burned in his throat, which was still raw from screaming. Cuts, burns and bruises covered him from head to foot, and he smiled grimly at the thought that, with his clothes shredded once more, he must look like a walking corpse. *Hope no one mistakes me for a Cinnamarian.* The muscles in his back had settled into a grating throb that made him feel as if he were standing shirtless in a sandstorm. The ministrations of a Healer, a skin of water, a feast fit for a king, and a tent where he could sleep in peace for the next three days were all he wanted, in no particular order. He had stopped being fussy about how he received the comforts of life sometime during the first night under the Demonlord's flail. A part of him knew that he would honestly rather be pursuing such mundane pleasures instead of walking several leagues over the blazing sand to talk some sense into an adolescent Dragon. But he had promised Kashon, so he walked on.

Shashtah was sweating profusely and more than a little dizzy by the time he reached the sacred valley. He decided to sit down atop the box end of the canyon before he fell down. He squinted at the sky, waiting for Tphah to notice him.

The Stripling saw Shashtah on her second pass but circled a third time before she alighted on the rocky ground half a wingspan away from him. Tphah stared at him with her grief-dulled eyes. She finally shifted to her humanform. "What do you want?"

Shashtah sighed. "I want you to go back to Camp and start acting like an adult before Kashon frets himself into the Afterlife with worry about you."

Tphah turned and stared out over the ravine.

Shashtah followed her gaze. They were positioned almost exactly where Makara and Shaharadesh had been, and he fancied that he could see the Dragons of the Council perched along the canyon rim.

"Can you see them?" whispered Tphah.

Shashtah squinted against the glare of the sun. The images of hundreds of Dragons and their Riders flickered across the deep blue sky. Candidates beyond number seemed to kneel on the gorge's floor. Every Dumnonian on Centuria appeared to stand behind them, covering the sand. A chill ran along Shashtah's spine as he thought he heard his name carried on the desert wind.

"Can you hear them? The greatest fighting force Centuria has ever known: They call for you." Tphah rounded on him. "And I am there beside you. Here. In the place reserved for you, for our king. I am your Dragonqueen. Me! Not Tkai!"

Shashtah closed his eyes against the power of the vision and the sight of the petulant girl before him. "Of course you are," he said at last. "But before your Prophecy can come to pass, Tkai must die." He opened his eyes and looked at her. "And before that there is so much I must learn that only she can teach me. I don't know how to wage a war on dragonwings. I don't understand why I'm a Dragonheart or what that means. I don't know what powers I have or how to control them. I don't know either the Lord of Daethia or the Elven King or why their lives will intertwine with mine. I can't begin to understand what it is that Corin's shade wants from me. Yet I sense that in five short years Tkai can teach me all of that. Please, do not begrudge me her wisdom and those five years."

Tphah made a strangled sound and ran toward him. She collapsed to her knees at his side. "And what am I supposed to do in the meantime?

Watch you with her night and day? Flying with her? Sleeping with her? Doing the Mother's Dance with her?"

Shashtah laughed at the image Tphah's words conjured in his mind. He reached out and cupped his hand along her jaw. "Tkai may be the greatest shapeshifter I've ever seen, but the idea of Dancing with her is like me thinking about mating with my own great-great-grandmother. I'm a Hatchling she has taken under her wing. The Bond is different between us than it will be between you and me one day. In the meantime we both have a lot of growing up to do. You stay here and learn everything you can from Kashon and Katrell—"

"Stay here?" Tphah squawked in alarm.

:*Careful, Hatchling,*: Tkai's voice shimmered affectionately in Shashtah's mind. :*She's going to transport away from you.*:

:*Are you planning to eavesdrop on me for all of the next five years?*: Shashtah groused as he quickly reached out and embraced the skittish dragongirl.

:*Maybe,*: came the jovial reply.

Shashtah forced himself to concentrate on the distraught Stripling he held in his arms. "I'll come back to you, Tphah. You know I will. But tomorrow Tkai and I have to leave on a mission for Corin. That mission will take me five years to complete. Please, be ready for me when I return. I'll need a strong Dragon who is fully trained, not a silly girl who falls to pieces when she doesn't get her way."

Tphah pulled away from him in protest.

Shashtah grabbed her shoulders, again surprised at the steely muscle he felt beneath her skin. "In five years my Bond with Tkai will break, and last night I got a sense of what that will be like. When that happens, you will have to fight like all the demons in Cinnamar to keep me sane enough to Bond with you. Do you want me enough to stay here and train to be ready to do that?"

Tphah grabbed him and pulled him into her arms with a strength that belied her humanform. "Yes," she whispered in his ear.

Shashtah felt a strange warmth pass over his back as one of her hands closed on his neck and the other wrapped around his waist. His pain dulled, though it did not vanish entirely.

"You know," Shaharadesh's voice boomed from somewhere above Shashtah and to his left, "most new Bond Partners transport out of Corin's Tomb above the Valley so the Council can congratulate them on their success."

Shashtah and Tphah disentangled themselves and staggered to their feet, dropping simultaneously into deep salaams as Makara landed on the ledge with the Dumnonian king astride her.

Shaharadesh slid to the sand and motioned for Shashtah and Tphah to rise.

Shashtah felt his king stare deep into his suddenly exposed soul.

Shaharadesh grunted. "I did Bond you to Tkai, didn't I? Is there some reason that you're out here on a cliff, carrying on with a Stripling who has been told to stay away from you instead of getting to know your new Bond Partner?"

Shashtah lowered his eyes. "Family squabble," he muttered, the words sounding stupid even to his own ears.

Unexpectedly, Shaharadesh laughed. "Has there ever been anything but family squabbles in the House of Tchang?"

Shashtah looked up to see Tphah blushing. He felt the heat of her shame somehow reflected on his own cheeks, and he suspected that Tkai was eavesdropping again. "I'm sorry, sire, but Tphah got upset when I returned with Tkai, and Kashon wasn't well enough to go after her. I didn't want him—her," Shashtah corrected himself, "to come to harm because of me."

Shaharadesh's face hardened into an unreadable expression. "Kashon is a very responsible Rider," he observed in a tone that left Shashtah wondering what exactly his king meant by "responsible." "I'm surprised he asked you to undertake his duty."

"I can stand without help," Shashtah practically snarled. "He can't. Not enough dragonblood in him, I suppose." He tried to control his temper. And failed. *What on Centuria has gotten into me? I know better than to address my king like this!* "I didn't have to go after Tphah; I chose to. Someone had to do it. Kashon couldn't. Katrell wouldn't. Tkai—" He took a deep breath and bared his throat to his monarch. "Forgive me, sire. I am acting like—"

"A newly Bonded, overprotective Dragon who outranks the king,"

Tphah said softly. "Can't anyone else see it? He was already a mess, and now you've scrambled his brains with Tkai's instead of melding them to mine!" She stamped her foot and roared her frustration at the canyon walls.

Shashtah reached out and lay a quieting hand on Tphah's shoulder.

Tphah spun into his arms and sobbed against his chest.

Shashtah met his king's gaze over Tphah's head. *Maybe she's right. Maybe she was supposed to be my Bond Partner. She certainly seems to have a better idea about what's going on around here than anyone else does. But she's so young . . .*

Shaharadesh glanced at Makara then focused on Tphah. "Tkai has prophesied that she will die in five years but the Dragonheart will live. When that happens, you will become our last living Prophetess. I swear to you now that, if you wish it and if he agrees and if you are fully Trained, I will Bond you to him even though you will still be too young. In the meantime, you will go back to Kashon and Katrell. They will keep you safe until the Dragonheart returns."

Tphah stopped crying.

Shashtah wiped her tears from her face and let her lick the moisture from his hand.

"Yes, sire," Tphah murmured. She stepped away from Shashtah and shifted into her true form. She sprang quickly into the air, taking care not to spray any of them with sand.

As soon as she was out of sight Tkai's dragonform appeared above the gulch, gliding smoothly toward the rim. She landed gently beside Shashtah and spread her left wing protectively over him.

Shaharadesh looked up at the Ancient Dragon critically. "Not so swift in deciding for punishment where your own Rider is concerned, eh, Tkai?"

Shashtah heard Tkai's scales bristle.

"He has done nothing wrong," Tkai's voice boomed.

Shaharadesh's face suddenly relaxed. "No. Unusual, yes. But wrong? Not yet."

Amusement danced in Makara's eyes. "I, for one, would have liked to have seen you crammed inside Kashon's tent, Honored Ancient!"

:*Sorry*: Shashtah hastily apologized to Tkai as he felt her mortification spreading through his mind. "I didn't mean to transport us into the tent. I just got scared," he confessed aloud, "and it was the only safe place I could think of."

Shaharadesh's laugh echoed off the ravine's walls. "If that's scared, remind me not to be around if you are ever truly terrified."

"A good point," Tkai observed, recovering her composure. "I know it is customary for you to assign a new Rider and his Dragon to a Dragonlord for the Training. In this case, however, I ask that you allow me to take my Rider somewhere a little safer for our people while he tries to get his new powers under control."

"When the Dark One rules so much of the world," Shaharadesh mused, "just where do you think is safer than under the watchful eye of a Dragonlord?"

"The Northern Wastes," Tkai answered promptly.

Shashtah glanced at his Dragon, wondering just what was going through that antiquated brain of hers but not wanting to interrupt.

Shaharadesh coughed his own surprise. "That's your definition of 'safer'?"

"For a Dumnonian," Tkai replied.

"Let them go." Makara's voice shimmered with mirth. "There will be time enough to Train them when they return. It will be entertaining to see a Rider, used to his freedom, try to break himself and his Dragon, especially the Leader of the Council, to a Dragonlord's command."

Shaharadesh squinted at the Dragonqueen, clearly wondering whether he had heard her correctly.

"Fear not," Tkai assured Shaharadesh. "This is a debt that will be paid in full."

Shaharadesh narrowed his eyes even more as he studied the Ancient Prophetess. "And what is Dumnonia supposed to do while the Leader of the Council is off flitting around Centuria on perpetual leave? We cannot keep summoning you back to this Valley every time the Council needs to meet."

"Garesh will take over in my absence," Tkai said promptly. "He has been prepared to replace me, and he will likely do a better job of leading the Council than I have. He has more recent experience in what it is like to think in Dumnonian terms than I do."

Shashtah felt distinctly as if everyone had forgotten he was there, but he stayed silent. *My father is right. I don't have sand for brains. I'm about to make a murderer the temporary leader of the Council of Ancients, and Tkai's death will make that position permanent. Wonderful. What other damage can I do to our people while I'm at it?*

Shaharadesh apparently made up his mind. "So be it. After the Feast, you have my leave to go."

"Feast?" Shashtah's ears pricked up at the promise of some long-overdue food.

Tkai craned her head around to look at him, affection gleaming in her amber eyes. "To celebrate our Bonding. New Pairs are always given a Feast."

"Besides," Shaharadesh added grimly, "I think we all need one after last night."

Makara nodded her agreement. "Yes." The word sounded strangely like a hiss.

Tkai shot a disapproving look at the Dragonqueen but said nothing.

"Get your Rider cleaned up, and have a Healer tend to him," Shaharadesh commanded. "He looks as if you just dragged him off the battlefield."

Tphah did. Shashtah bit his lower lip to keep from saying the thought aloud.

Tkai bent her head to Shaharadesh in what Shashtah suspected was the draconic version of a salaam.

"I'll see you both at nightfall." Shaharadesh waved his dismissal and agilely climbed onto Makara's back.

At some unseen signal the Dragonqueen rose swiftly into the air, then flew through a warp.

Shashtah let his knees buckle, and he collapsed against Tkai's unyielding foreleg. :*Thanks,*: he whispered mentally, his throat suddenly too dry to work.

:*For what?*: Tkai's voice washed softly between Shashtah's brain and his skull. :*You can't be expected to deal well with Shaharadesh until you* understand him any more than Tphah can be expected to deal well with a Rider until she understands what it means to be a Dumnonian.:

:*I don't think Tphah has her heart set on just any Rider,*: Shashtah confessed.

:*All the more reason she needs to understand what it's like to be a Dumnonian.*: Tkai's practical answer echoed inside Shashtah's head. :*Now, climb up so I can get you to a Healer before Shaharadesh has a fit.*:

:*I think he's already having a fit.*: Shashtah reached for her harness, then leaned against her, suddenly all too aware of every aching muscle in his body. He sighed. :*I don't think I have the strength to climb.*:

:*Fine. You don't care about your dignity,*: Tkai rumbled, :*then neither do I.*: Her great head reached around behind him. Her fangs closed on the back of his torn shirt, and she lifted him into the air rather like a mother cat picking up a kitten.

Shashtah panicked briefly, then realized that there was something oddly flattering about the care with which she treated him.

The Ancient Dragon set him gently behind the great spike at the base of her neckridge. :*Hang on,*: Tkai warned as she reared on her haunches and rose into the air with a great clap of her enormous wings.

Shashtah did not need the warning. Suddenly possessed of the strength he thought he lacked, he gripped her harness so hard that his knuckles turned white.

:*Silly man,*: Tkai's chuckle resonated in his brain. :*If that nit Katrell didn't drop you in a battle, do you think I would in so brief a flight?*:

Shashtah swiftly realized that he was actually soaring through the sky above his beloved homeland on his very own Dragon. He felt an unexpected closeness with Tkai. Just hearing her voice in his head drove away the terrible loneliness he had felt during the flight with Katrell. The comfort of their Bond far surpassed anything he had ever experienced with every woman he had known. *Better than doing the Mother's Dance.*

:*I'm like your great-great grandmother, remember?*: Tkai teased.

:*You're still eavesdropping,*: Shashtah chided as he felt his cheeks burn from something other than the sun.

Tkai rose abruptly in the air then glided easily toward the camp. :*I'd forgotten how wonderful it feels to fly with a Rider on one's back!*:

A brief image of Kashon's pain-racked face flashed unbidden through Shashtah's mind. :*Maybe that is why you need me,*: he ventured. :*To remind you how Dumnonians feel.*: He sensed Tkai's mind balk at the notion and then settle into submission.

:*I am not the only one with something to teach, Dragonheart.*: Tkai landed just beyond the edge of the King's Camp, etiquette forbidding her to enter in other than her humanform.

Shashtah slid from her back, a puzzled expression on his face as he wondered how he suddenly knew things such as why all the Dragons in the King's Camp were always in humanform.

:*It's the Bond. As needed, things I know will pass through it to you,*: Tkai explained patiently. :*The Council is not as random and inflexible in its decisions as you suppose. We follow our ancient Traditions, whether we understand them or not. Those Traditions are there for a reason. The Bond will make it clear to you what is and what is not wrong. Corin's magic gave us that.*: She was silent for a heartbeat, then shifted into humanform, taking the shape of the old woman he had seen in his dream. "All of the Councilors had a Rider once, you know." She reached out and gently touched his arm. "It grieves us to hurt another's Rider as if our own Bond Partner had been hurt. Please, understand."

"I'll try," Shashtah promised. "I'm afraid I can do no better than that for now."

Tkai smiled affectionately at him. "We can ask no more." She turned to lead him toward the portion of the Camp where the Healers' Tents were pitched. As she did so she readjusted her shape to that of a woman in her middle years. Guessing that her appearance disturbed him, she flashed him a grin. "You're the patient, not me," she explained. "I want no mistake when we get to the Healers."

Shashtah returned her smile. He was so covered in blood and grime that he knew the Healers could never make such an error. He sensed that her older form bothered her, though, so he kept silent and let her lead him onward as she had through Corin's Tomb.

The Healer Tkai chose for Shashtah was a male, he noted with amusement. *Not that it matters. All the Healers in the King's Camp are wonderful, and not a one of them thinks of me as anything more than a piece of ground camel meat to patch up and send back out to fight once more.* He slipped off what remained of his torn shirt to give the man a clearer view of his damaged back.

The Healer took a sharp breath, then asked politely, "Would you mind telling me what you are doing still walking around?"

"Hoping you can fix me," Shashtah replied with a quick look at Tkai. :*Not a word out of you,*: he ordered. Somehow he felt that it would not be a good idea to let every Dumnonian in existence know about the extent of his wakening powers.

Tkai blinked her innocence at him.

"You worship the Sun?" the Healer asked, dragging Shashtah's eternally wandering attention back to him.

Shashtah spread his hands apart in deep reverence. "Above all others," he swore, knowing that healing spells worked much better if they were attuned to the patient's god.

The Healer nodded. "Lie down." He gestured to some cushions on the floor.

Shashtah obediently stretched out, face down, on the pillows as Tkai watched.

The Healer rolled up the sleeves of his white caftan, then knelt and laid his hands on Shashtah's neck and tailbone.

Shashtah closed his eyes, feeling the healing warmth spread through his damaged muscles, knit his skin, and drive away his pain. He was almost asleep when the magic touched his soul and the Healer flew backward as if he had been hit by skyfire.

Shashtah's eyes snapped open in time to see the sun's aura flickering along his skin.

:*HEAL!*:

The single word snapped through Shashtah's mind. It sounded more like a command than a suggestion.

The bright magical flame around him collapsed into a tiny flicker deep within his heart as abruptly as it had appeared.

Shashtah slowly looked at Tkai, all too aware that the physical evidence of his injuries, except for a few completely healed scars on his back and the marks the stone had left on his palm, had vanished. Never having been healed of such serious injuries before, he ventured, "I suppose that happens all the time."

Tkai wordlessly shook her head in denial of what she had seen.

The Healer simply sat where he had been thrown and stared at his still-glowing hands.

Shashtah pulled himself to his knees. "I think we had better leave at dawn before I accidentally blow the whole Camp to ashes."

Tkai nodded her assent. Then she remembered to close her mouth.

Shashtah rose hesitantly to his feet. He offered the Healer his hand.

The man shook his head and rose without touching Shashtah. "W-what are you?" he stammered, finally finding his voice.

"A Dragonheart," Tkai replied. :*And then some,*: she added silently to her Rider.

Shashtah grinned at her, trying to take the edge off the awkwardness that had descended on the tent. "It's not polite to think at me when we're in the presence of others who cannot hear."

Tkai blushed. "I am terribly sorry," she hastily bared her throat in apology to the Healer, who completely missed the gesture because he was too busy examining his hands. "Being old is no excuse for being rude."

Shashtah checked for a belt pouch before he remembered that he was completely out of everything, including money. "I'm afraid I can't pay you for your services."

The Healer finally shifted his awe-filled gaze to his patient. "I think you already have."

"Nonsense," Shashtah assured him. "When I can, I will pay in full." With that, he turned on his boot heel and, still shirtless, walked out of the tent.

Tkai hurried after him. "We have to get you out of here," she muttered in a voice pitched so low that only he could hear.

"The only thing we have to do right now is get me some decent clothes," Shashtah countered. "I'm not about to appear in rags at a feast Shaharadesh is throwing in our honor."

Tkai protested, "But—"

"But nothing. I haven't eaten anything solid in three days." Shashtah growled. "Help me find some clothes that are in one piece and someone who can clean me up. I'm tired of looking like a poor excuse for a wraith."

Tkai laughed in spite of herself. "You are looking a bit wraith-like. Guess I don't get first pick at the Feast."

Shashtah threw her a sidelong glance. "Do you honestly think I would give you anything else?"

Tkai snaked her arm around his waist possessively. "No, Dragonheart, no. You are as traditional as Dumnonians come. If you were starving to death and I had just gorged myself, I truly believe you would offer your only morsel to me."

"Just don't test me on that, okay?" Shashtah grinned as they turned into the Tailor's lane.

Dragonqueen Makara

CHAPTER 7:

Rising Sun

There shall be a time of trouble, such as never has been since the First Bond. Then a Prophet shall arise among you, a dreamer of dreams. He shall shine like the brightness of the Land of Light, and those who follow him shall glitter like the stars forever and ever. And the signs of the Prophet shall be these: The starving man shall feed you, and the injured man shall make you whole.

—from *The Prophecies of Tchang*
by Bahakesh, Dragonlord of Dumnonia

SHASHTAH SAT AT SHAHARADESH'S left, bedecked in a simple white aba and headdress that a simpering tailor had loaned him under the threat of Tkai's vicious glare. He felt absolutely ridiculous in the billowing garment, but at least he had won the battle with his Dragon to let him wear trousers and a linen shirt underneath. He was hotter than Galantite in the desert at midday, but he could shed the outer garment in a heartbeat if he needed to fight. Tkai had rolled her eyes at the very suggestion that anyone might attack him at their Bonding Feast. A lifetime spent on caravans, though, had taught Shashtah to see demons in every shadow and potential enemies even among friends.

Makara lounged in her humanform to Shaharadesh's right. She wore a chador of white samite that glittered with golden filigree, and she was bedecked in so much treasure that Shashtah marveled she could remain upright—until he remembered that she was a Dragon and still had a Dragon's strength hidden beneath her willowy appearance. The brazen display of wealth turned Shashtah's stomach, though Shaharadesh seemed positively bewitched by his Bond Partner.

Tkai had been offered a seat at the Dragonqueen's side, but she had flatly, and more than a little rudely, refused. The newly Bonded Ancient had taken Shashtah so firmly by the left hand as she led him to his place that he was still trying to work the feeling back into his fingers.

Shashtah let his eyes wander over the scene before him as he tried to ignore the silent war that raged between Tkai and Makara who were separated only by him and his king. The enormous Festival Tent was crowded with people: Dumnonians, Dragons in humanform, clerics, crafters, supply personnel and caravaneers. Shashtah suspected that at least some of the Dragonlords were in the throng. Since there was nothing to distinguish them from other Riders, though, except a ring shaped like a Bronze Dragon on their left hand, he could not figure out who they were. *It doesn't matter. The only one I have to care about is the one Tkai and I are assigned to for the Training when we return,* he thought. *If we return,* he amended.

The "feast" itself consisted of four not particularly large piles of unleavened bread, a few urns of qaffah, two vats of water, half a dozen skins of fermented mares' milk, two rounds of pungent white cheese, two serving bowls of dates, and a single roasted calf, which Shashtah suspected had been Dragon-supplied by a raid on some poor Daethian farmer's herd. *Surely there are a few skympsam or addax left somewhere in the desert, or have the Dragons eaten them all? Why antagonize our allies when the one thing they hate almost as much as the Dark One is us?* Shashtah took mental stock of the number of individuals at the feast, then gazed disconcertedly at the paltry offerings that were spread on the table that ran along the center of the tent to make it look as if there was more food than there really was. *Hardly enough to give each Rider a single taste let alone feed their Dragons and all the others who are here.* No clearer evidence could have been presented of how truly desperate the Dumnonian situation had become.

Tkai rose and started to help Shashtah to his feet.

"Where are you taking him?" Shaharadesh demanded.

Tkai frowned at her monarch. "To eat. He's starving."

Shaharadesh shook his head. "This is a ritual feast, Tkai. You and the other Dragons must eat your fill before any Dumnonian can touch the food. And," he looked meaningfully at Shashtah, "your Rider should have the grace to set the example for all Dumnonians by eating last."

Shashtah placed a quieting hand on Tkai's thigh. "Our king is right," he insisted before the outburst he sensed gathering in her exploded. "Dragons eat first." He released her and watched as she took her plate and made her way to the food. *I'm actually more likely to fall asleep than to die of starvation.*

Makara used the disturbance to sneak away from the head table and beat Tkai to the front of the line. The Dragonqueen proceeded to heap her dish to overflowing from the meager piles.

Tkai watched in stunned disbelief.

Shashtah sat frozen beside his king. He had never seen anyone so important look as furious as Tkai did. Rider or no Rider, he knew he had no hope of containing the Councilor's fury if she chose to unleash it.

Tkai took the place behind Makara and pursed her lips. She snatched an entire haunch from the roasted calf, took one small bite, and strode to the head table. She deposited the remainder of her prize on Shashtah's plate. "I am sated," she said pointedly. "It is a sin to eat too much when so many are starving." She glared at Makara.

Shashtah looked warily at Shaharadesh for his reaction, but the king was too busy scowling at Katrell, who was slipping through the crowd toward them, to pay any attention whatsoever to Tkai. Shashtah stared at the haunch. His stomach twisted. *I forgot to tell her I don't eat much meat.* Certain that Tkai expected him to consume every last morsel, Shashtah covered his revulsion by shifting his attention back to Katrell.

Katrell stood before the high table, a single date in his hand. Shashtah felt his stomach lurch again as the dragonman nibbled a bit off the end, approached the head table and deposited the uneaten portion next to the calf's haunch. "I am also sated. The Dragonheart is more than welcome to the portion I cannot finish."

Shashtah glanced hastily around, fervently praying that the next Dragon to come forward would not be Tphah. He eventually spotted the Stripling at the rear of the tent, supporting Kashon, but he soon lost sight of his friends as Dragon after Dragon, not having the nerve to imitate Tkai's brazen action, followed Katrell's example, placing one barely-touched titbit after another on Shashtah's plate.

This time when Shashtah glanced at his king, Shaharadesh was peering at his newest Rider with suspicious eyes. Shashtah gave his ruler a beleaguered look, then turned to Tkai. "You are not helping me."

Tkai favored him with a smug smile. "You think not?" She gestured at the table where the feast had been laid.

Kashon, aided by Tphah, was standing near one of the demolished piles of bread. He picked up a piece, bit off a corner, and let Tphah half-carry him to the head table.

Shashtah met his friend's blazing eyes. "Kashon . . . "

Kashon deposited the remainder of his piece of bread atop the Dragons' gifts. "Accept it, Drag—" He grinned a quick apology and corrected himself. "Shashtah. I have nothing else to give." He made an elaborate salaam, then motioned for Tphah to help him back to his place.

Immediately every other Dragonrider in the room crowded around what was left of the food in an attempt to imitate their Dragons and Kashon. Several of them had pained expressions on their faces as if they were being mercilessly hounded into action by their Bond Partners even though they feared retribution from their king. By the time they and the civilians who joined them finished, the rest of the feast had been heaped onto Shashtah's plate. From there the offerings spilled off the table and onto the carpeted floor. *At least they didn't bury me,* Shashtah thought a trifle hysterically.

When all motion in the tent had ceased, a blushing Makara rose and added the barely-touched contents of her own plate to the pile.

All eyes turned to Shaharadesh.

Shaharadesh stared at Shashtah for several heartbeats. "Well?"

Shashtah glanced from face to face. Dragons, Riders, Dumnonians, non-Dragons, . . . *What in the name of the All Holy Sun do they expect me to do?* There was absolutely no way he could eat all that food. He had been raised on a starvation-level diet, and a single piece of bread, a slice of cheese, and a couple of dates were all he generally managed to consume in a single day. His body just didn't need, and wasn't able to handle, more. A childhood prayer suddenly flitted through his mind. Not having a better idea, he rose to his feet, spread his hands over the gifts, closed his eyes and intoned, "Lord of Light, we thank you for your bounteous gifts. May they nourish us in the same way Thy Orb fills us with warmth." As Shashtah finished his prayer he heard everyone gasp. He opened his eyes slowly, dreading what he would see.

A ball of pure sunlight was sparkling less than half a wingspan from him about the level of his hands. The beams danced, twining around themselves and almost blinding him in spite of his desert adapted eyes. The image of a stunningly handsome young man, whose eyes shone with pure white light, appeared in the center of the miniature sun. :*Because they have nourished you for me, I will nourish them for you.*: Rays of light shot out of the glowing ball, touching the empty plates. Food in marvelous abundance appeared in front of everyone. The vats along the edges of the tent filled almost to overflowing with the finest of wines. Even when the magic subsided the food and drink seemed to glow with an otherworldly light. :*I give you the power to ease their pain. This is all I can do. I cannot stop my Dark Son from causing more. But perhaps my brother has found a way. Seek the Elven King, and tell him that the Lord of Light has sent you.*: With that the shining sun vanished, and the tent settled back into the relative gloom of the festival lamps.

Although everyone else was still blinking from the after images of the light, Shashtah quickly decided that only he had seen his god and heard his voice. Instinctively he knew that he had better say something before the situation got even more chaotic. He opened his mouth, whispering a silent prayer for wisdom as he began to speak. "The Bonding Feast is not one of the body but of the heart. We should not celebrate a joining by a tearing asunder. Our king provided us with everything he had, although his heart wished to give you the bounty that is before you now. My god has chosen to grant our king's wish. Do our king the honor he deserves by enjoying this food and drink and by reminding yourselves that, in spite of the harshness the Dark One has brought into our world, we are still alive!"

A general cheer arose, and the revelers promptly began to gorge themselves on the marvelous food.

Shashtah sank back into his seat with a wary glance at Tkai. He felt Shaharadesh's hand close on his right arm. He looked at his king.

Shaharadesh's lips were curled into a grateful smile. "Thank you," he murmured. "My crown appears to be yours for the taking whenever you are willing to stretch out your hand."

Shashtah took his king's right hand and kissed the Bronze Dragon-shaped ring of office in the traditional gesture of fealty. "The Dumnonian king has no crown to take. The Dragons choose our monarch. Besides, I am a nomad. I don't know how to sit in one place. I have no desire to be king. That burden you may gladly carry until the day you die." He released Shaharadesh's hand and turned to Tkai. "I'll thank you to do no more grandstanding with Makara until we figure out what my powers are and how I can control them."

Tkai bared her throat to him in submission.

"Eat," Shaharadesh's voice commanded. "I think your needing food is what started this commotion."

Shashtah accepted the command with a slight bow of his head. He applied himself to the pile of food before him. He made something that resembled a dent in it before he became certain that he would be ill if he ate another bite. He declared himself sated and leaned back on his cushions.

Gaiety and a truly festive atmosphere flooded through the tent. Musicians played tunes to ancient stories Shashtah remembered from his childhood. Several of the revelers began to dance.

Tkai rose and helped Shashtah to his feet. As the guests of honor, passed through the crowd, exchanging a private word with everyone who wished to speak with them. A few Dragonlords proved to be in the throng. Kassandra, Dumnonia's most vicious Dragonlord, appraised

Shashtah with a look that made him feel as if she had stripped him down to his soul. His heart trembled at the possibility that he and Tkai might be assigned to her after they completed their task. Dragonlord Corban, whose main job seemed to be preventing Kassandra from terrifying everyone else, caught Shashtah's attention as someone he might enjoy serving under. Shashtah congratulated himself that Dragonlord Dameth did not stare completely through him the way he had stared through Garesh so long ago. Shashtah wondered briefly how much Dameth knew about what Garesh truly was and what that meant about his son, but the Feast was neither the time nor the place to ask. Even Katrell and Makara seemed to make up. Shashtah spotted the Dragonqueen offering her subject something to drink and Kashon's upset Bond Partner making every effort to accept the draught with passable grace.

As the revelers swirled about the tent, Shashtah found himself having trouble staying with Tkai. She appeared to forget he was there and let a dragonman coax her into a dance. Having absolutely no idea what the dance was or how to do it, Shashtah let her go and concentrated on enjoying the people around him. He had been alone for so long that he was starved for contact with his fellow Dumnonians, and they were thrilled to give it to him. In the press of bodies, slaps of congratulations and exchanges of drinks, he almost failed to notice Tphah's urgent tug on his sleeve.

"Kashon needs you," Tphah whispered when she finally gained his attention.

Shashtah immediately glanced toward the back of the tent where he expected to see Katrell standing guard over Kashon.

Instead, the exhausted Dragonrider sat alone, a circle of emptiness around him in the otherwise packed tent. Kashon had thrown aside whatever food had been in front of him, and he stared unseeingly at the crowd. His hands clasped the edges of his empty plate so hard that Shashtah marveled that he had not yet bent the gold.

"Did he have an argument with Katrell?" Shashtah asked.

Tphah shook her head "no," but apparently would not or could not say more.

Shashtah took her answer for what it was, patted her arm in thanks, and shoved his way through the celebrants to sit beside Kashon. "If you need to go back to your tent and lie down, I understand."

Kashon shook his head violently, more as if he were trying to banish an unwanted thought than in reply to his friend. "I'd just see them more clearly if I were alone."

Puzzlement spread over Shashtah's concerned face. "See whom?"

"Makara is with Katrell," Shaharadesh's voice said from Kashon's other side. "They are mating." He picked up one of Kashon's grapes and ate it absently.

Shashtah frowned his bewilderment. "But I thought Katrell and you were—"

"We are." Kashon looked at Shashtah, a deep sorrow in his eyes.

"But if he doesn't want to be with her, then why does he agree?" Shashtah suddenly remembered the draught Makara had handed Katrell. "She makes him drink love potions."

Kashon nodded.

"But why?" Shashtah persisted.

"Because she needs to be carrying fertilized eggs in order to lie safely with me," Shaharadesh answered, claiming a piece of unleavened bread from Kashon's rejected meal.

Shashtah stared blankly at his king.

"If I do the Mother's Dance with her while she's in humanform and she's not already carrying fertilized eggs, she could conceive my child," Shaharadesh explained with infinite patience. "We cannot afford to have a Dragonqueen trapped in humanform for a quarter of a century."

Shashtah closed his eyes briefly and rubbed the bridge of his nose with his left hand. *So much I don't know. So much I don't understand.* He opened his eyes and focused on Kashon, who was still trying to bend his plate in two. *There are, however, some things I do understand.* He gripped Kashon's trembling hands and gently pried his fingers from the plate. "There must be several hundred other males around here tonight. She didn't have to choose Katrell."

Shaharadesh nodded. "I admit, my Makara doesn't have a very good understanding of the way Dumnonians see things. Most Dragons don't."

A flush spread over his face as he spoke, as if he had unexpectedly walked in on a pair of lovers.

The revelers continued to swirl incongruously around the trio.

Kashon sat, shaking violently, the same flush on his own face that was evident on his king's.

Shashtah suddenly felt the flame, which had been glowing in his heart since the Healer's touch, flare within his breast. He draped his arm across Kashon's trembling shoulders and pulled him close. "Listen to me," he whispered. "Don't think of the two of them. Think of the two of you. Katrell is struggling, and you are tearing at his heart just as surely as he was tearing at yours last night. Make him forget about the present, and promise that you will be eagerly waiting for him when he returns."

Kashon shook his head yet again. "I can't. That's a promise I won't be strong enough to keep for at least a rotation."

"Nonsense!" Shashtah snapped, drawing his friend into a full embrace and praying that he had truly understood the words of the Lord of Light. The magical flame spread like skyfire through his veins. He felt the healing light burst out of him and into Kashon, seeking out the broken places in the Dragonrider's soul. He seared away the distraught man's fears and despair. He cauterized the unseen wounds that had been inflicted by the Council's spirit-racking pain. He found the flagging courage in Kashon's breast and fed it with his own heartfire. Finally, he located the places where the Bond between Dragon and Rider was dangerously frayed and wove them together, making them even stronger than they had been before.

When he released Kashon, Shashtah felt utterly drained, but the look of wholeness in his friend's eyes reassured him that the effort had been worth anything it might have cost him.

"Impossible," Shaharadesh whispered. "No one can heal someone who's been punished by the Council! Only time. The wounds aren't physical; they're of the heart."

"So is a Dragonheart's magic," snapped Tkai, who had finally pushed her way over to join them. "How many times do I have to tell you that?"

"You repaired our Bond!" Kashon marveled. "But I thought only a Dumnonian king—"

"I'm not dead yet," Shaharadesh growled. "But I'll lay you odds I know who will rule Dumnonia when I'm gone."

"Not if I don't get him out of here long enough to teach him to stop working miracles right and left," Tkai barked. "If the Dark One realizes that we have created another Dragonheart before my Rider's powers mature, the Cinnamarians will try to eat us alive with him as the first course. They would rather leave their entire flank exposed to the elves and the Daethians than risk having another king who is a Dragonheart coming at them out of the north. If they found out he was an immature Prophet as well—" Her voice trailed off, leaving Shashtah wondering exactly how many deities he had offended in a former life to deserve all the horrors that were stacking up against him in this one.

The effects of Katrell's mating still ruled Kashon, but he was no longer completely consumed. "You are the Council Leader!" he protested as he desperately tried to think through the haze with which his Dragon's passions wrapped his mind. "You can't just leave Dumnonia and wander around Centuria with an unTrained Rider who will attract the Goddess only knows what danger!" Thoughts flickered frantically behind his amber eyes. "Katrell and I are the most expendable Pair who have the most skills. We should go with you to protect you."

Shashtah shook his head. "No. I need you to stay here and train Tphah. Tkai can call for help if we need it."

"My life is yours to command," Kashon swore.

The left corner of Shashtah's mouth jerked slightly as he tried not to grin. "Your life belongs to Shaharadesh. Only when he is done with it will it be yours to give again."

"Well, you aren't a power hungry asp, I'll give you that," Shaharadesh observed. "In that at least my luck shines like Galantite. If—" He bit off the rest of his thought as draconic appetites momentarily blinded him to the people in his company.

Kashon closed his eyes and looked equally preoccupied, apparently promising Katrell sun, moon, stars and everything in between.

After a few heartbeats, Shaharadesh and Kashon relaxed, settling into themselves again.

"Corin's magic leaves a lot to be desired some days," Shaharadesh griped.

"It doesn't seem to leave much at all to be desired is more the problem," Shashtah commented drily. He rose stiffly to his feet. "If I were you, Kashon, I'd get myself back to my tent as fast as I could."

Kashon rose, but then paused. "Where will you spend the night?"

Shashtah threw Tkai a troubled look, trying unsuccessfully to see himself sleeping with the old woman he knew she was.

Tkai laughed. "First, he's going to go find some compassionate young woman to help him work off the frustration you and your Dragons have just finished filling him with. Then he's going to find my dragonform somewhere outside Camp and sleep under the stars with me the way a proper Rider should."

Shashtah bristled slightly at what he knew was her thinly veiled disapproval of Kashon's taste for Katrell's humanform.

Kashon good-naturedly shrugged the comment aside and left.

"And I," Shaharadesh declared to no one in particular, "am going to have a long talk with Makara about toying with other people's feelings to fulfill her own needs." He heaved himself to his feet and jerked his head to the side, cracking his neck. "Not that she'll listen to me."

Shaharadesh and Shashtah slipped out of the tent while Tkai slid through the throng and swirled back into the dance. Monarch and Dragonrider rushed in separate directions, each seeking his own desires in the desert night.

Shashtah quickly turned his steps toward the edge of the encampment where the Mother's Tent was pitched. He probably could have gotten any of a number of the female revelers to share her carpet with him, but he had had quite enough of romantic entanglements with the Riders and their Dragons for one day. Tkai was right. After four days of pain, suffering and misery he was in sore need of a refresher course on the simpler joys of life.

Shashtah was yanked out of his reverie at the sight of Katrell's humanform slithering through the shadows. Even in the darkness he could see the humiliation burning in the dragonman's amber eyes. Shashtah swiftly changed his course to intercept him. "Here, now," he crooned as he planted himself in Katrell's path, forcing him to stop. "Kashon's looking forward to seeing you far too much for you to show him a face like that."

"Don't." Katrell averted his eyes. "You can't know what it's like."

"Perhaps I do," Shashtah mused. He looked up at the star-filled sky and into the past. "There was a temple of the Mother that was little more than a few caftans stretched between a stunted tree and a sandblasted rock." His voice shifted into the sing-song rhythm of a storyteller, instantly captivating Katrell. "Garesh had discovered the place while deflecting a raid on another caravan, and the grateful trader had offered his savior the services of their Tent. Garesh declined for himself but chose to accept the offer on behalf of his son, who had recently turned fifteen. The boy was initially curious and thrilled at the prospect of losing his virginity to a genuine Priestess. But then came the discomfort of being poked and prodded by a Healer to make sure he was clean. That, followed by what seemed like several candlescars of lectures about what behavior was and was not acceptable in a temple, left him far more interested in a nap than in any kind of physical activity with a woman. As it turned out the merchant had been a little too grateful and had selected the rare gift of a girl who had just attained her womanhood and had chosen the life of a Priestess over a life as someone's mate. If possible, the girl knew even less about the art of doing the Mother's Dance than did the boy. The two children laughed and cried at their clumsy attempts to please the adults who had thrown them together, and, as was bound to happen, they wound up hurting each other far too much. The merchant was furious and threatened to flog the boy within a handspan of his life, but Garesh and two of his fastest horses arrived on the scene with a preferable alternative. As the boy fled into the desert with his father, the teenager glanced back once at the girl, blushing at her last words to him: 'At least neither of us will have a lover who is worse.'"

"I have," Katrell whispered.

"No." Shashtah reached out and touched Katrell's burning face. He could almost feel his inner flame leaping from his fingertips, searing away the Dragon's shame. "You have given Makara a great gift: the ability to lie with Shaharadesh as easily as you can lie with Kashon. In return you have earned your Rider the much needed favor of his king. That doesn't make what Makara did right, but it doesn't make what happened to you any worse than a young girl and me hurting each other just to please our elders when neither of us gave two figs about anyone or anything. Few people understand how special it is to truly care about your partner when you are doing the Mother's Dance. For Kashon to have been blessed with a Bond Partner like you who honestly knows what that means, I count him as one extremely lucky Dumnonian."

Katrell grabbed Shashtah's hand in his own and pressed it to his lips. "Thank you for healing him, for giving him back to me. I can never repay you."

Shashtah's laugh sounded harsh even to his own ears. "Train Tphah as you've never trained anyone before, and keep your Rider and yourself alive for the next five years. I'm going to need you, all of you, and I will owe each of you a debt I will never be able to repay."

"Prophecy?" Katrell ventured.

"I certainly hope not!" Shashtah winced. "I have quite enough complicating my life without that! Now, go. Kashon is waiting for you."

Katrell flashed him a sympathetic smile and slipped away into the darkness.

Shashtah watched until Katrell was out of sight. Then he remembered his interrupted plans and turned his steps once more toward the Mother's Tent.

The Tent of the Mother was deserted when Shashtah arrived. That did not particularly surprise him since he was fairly confident that nearly everyone in the King's Camp was at the Feast. He shed his borrowed agal, keffiyeh, aba and shirt. He folded them neatly into a pile just inside the tent flap. His hands paused on his belt buckle. He let his fingers trace over the carved stories of Dumnonia's greatest heroes. The tales that flowed beneath his fingertips seemed unreal, almost as unreal as his life had become. *Dragonhearts*. He simply could not believe that he was also one. He had grown up listening to bards recite those tales, and his paltry life sounded nothing like them. He slipped the piece of leather from its place and added it to the pile.

Shashtah sat beside the ever-burning lamp to remove his desert boots. The subtle scents of the Mother's incense rose from the lamp, channeling his passions into his body, away from his mind. He had always liked the smell of the incense used by the Priests and Priestesses of the Goddess of Fertility. Most other religions relied on the heavier odors of the desert's meager gifts: jasmine, cinnamon, and sandalwood. But the Mother's worshipers favored the almost pure scent of the desert wind, that vast, unpredictable force that swept over the endless sands, mingling faint traces of life and death into something ethereal that always set Shashtah's pulse to pounding. The smell of heat, the child of the sunlight, that mercilessly hammered the sands by day and rose again to warm the weary desert dwellers by night mingled with the scent as well. That heat was the gift from Shashtah's own deity to the otherwise cold and bitter world, and he found himself drawn to the Mother's clerics because they treasured that scent as dearly as did the clergy of his own religion.

Shashtah finished undressing and sat, cross-legged, in the middle of the tent, awaiting the Healer he knew would come. Even though he had seen a Healer just candlescars before and knew his body was clean, the Mother was notoriously careful of the health of her Children. No one could worship her without seeing a Healer first. Then would follow the inevitable interview with one of the cult elders to determine his likes and dislikes so that he would enjoy the service as much as the other worshiper would. Finally the lamp would be shielded and a woman would be sent to him, probably young, most likely beautiful, and, if he were truly lucky, a virgin. Shashtah smiled at the irony of how much his own taste in women had been shaped by his encounter with that poor girl in the merchant's makeshift tent. Sometimes he felt as if he were apologizing by making sure that the first service of other virgins in the Mother's name was nowhere near as unpleasant for them as it had been for that unfortunate Priestess in his childhood. Other times he thought he was extracting a punishment from himself as real as any flogging would have been by forgoing a more mature woman's love and forever repeating his first mistake.

In any event, he was absurdly pleased when he heard Tkai's voice drift through his mind. : *The Healer has vouched to an elder for your health, and I have sworn that I know precisely where you have been and what you have been doing ever since. I have selected an appropriate partner for you so you won't have to go through the interview. She's on her way.:*

Shashtah shielded the lamp and stretched out comfortably on the elaborately woven carpets that covered the floor of the tent. After a few heartbeats his eyes stopped straining against the darkness, and he relaxed.

A slender hand drew the tent flap aside, and against the starry sky his sharp eyes made out the silhouette of a young woman wearing a simple veil over the unbound hair of a virgin.

:Is she afraid?: Shashtah found himself asking Tkai before he had really considered the thought himself.

:Hardly,: the old woman's voice chuckled in his head. *:Enjoy!:*

Shashtah sensed his Dragon's presence withdraw to a discrete corner of his mind, and he found himself feeling more like a simple man than he had in days.

The virgin let the flap fall behind her. She laced it shut.

He heard the rustle of her clothing as she crossed the rugs and knelt at his side, bending her head so he could remove her veil.

Following an odd custom he had developed over the years, he waited for her to tire of his inaction, reach up and remove the veil herself. Only then did he stir, rising to help her out of her white silk robes. He ran his fingers through her long, soft hair. He traced the outlines of her arms, breasts, waist, hips, and legs. He stood patiently while she repeated the motions, seamlessly joining him in the Mother's Dance.

As the beginning of the ritual drew to a close, Shashtah thought he felt a Dragon's tail wrap around his left leg. Then the sensation went away, and he concentrated on the feel of the virgin's hands on his feet.

Instead of straightening herself and embracing him, she worked her way slowly up his legs and thighs, a gentle warmth emanating from her hands and driving the tension from his muscles.

An apprentice Healer, Shashtah guessed. *I hope I don't blow her across the tent.*

She took his left palm in her gentle grasp and licked at the depressions made by the evil gem until they disappeared. She slid her arms around him, placing one hand at his neck and the other at his waist.

Shashtah felt her magic spread across his skin, restoring sensitivity and flexibility where he never thought to have such things again. *Not a Healer. Her power is different.* He placed his hands upon her hips and kissed her. His eyes widened as her tell-tale power surged into him. *Tkai found me a virgin Priestess of the Mother?* He felt a sense of smug pride flash through his mind then withdraw again. He was too preoccupied to care about Tkai's eavesdropping. He closed his eyes and let the warmth of the incense fill his lungs. Gently he lowered the Priestess to the carpet. He returned her kiss, breathing her breath, tasting her pleasure, flinching away from any hint of her discomfort or pain.

In delighted shock at his gentleness, her passion danced in time with his. She embraced him with sure arms that spoke more of a fighter's training than of a Priestess's, and if, in her abandon, she accidentally clawed at his freshly healed back, he took no notice as he thrilled at her response to him.

The Mother's Blessing washed over them, outshining all but the glittering of the Bond Shashtah could feel with Tkai. As he broke their kiss and relaxed, panting, into the girl's arms, he wondered absently what kind of blush he had just sent over Tkai's face, or whether the venerable dragonwoman, knowing what was in store, had fled the Feast, nestled safely atop a dune in her dragonform, and trusted that his passion would only color her dreams.

The worshipers lay quietly for a long time, wrapped in each other's arms, until their pulses steadied.

Shashtah had almost drifted off to sleep when the girl rose, dressed, tucked her veil under her arm, and slipped out of the tent. Finally feeling like a human being again, he sent a mental note of thanks to Tkai for her choice, then dressed himself and went in search of his Dragon.

Shashtah found Tkai sleeping peacefully just beyond the edge of Camp. A thousand stars glittered in the black velvet sky, and the desert wind caressed him like a lover's touch. He stared for a moment at the slip crescent moon, then lay down contentedly next to his Dragon, rested his head on his folded arms, and quickly drifted off to sleep.

Elven King Farador

CHAPTER 8:

Illusions

Beware of Him who rebels against the Light! The murderer rises in the Darkness, and He comes as a nightmare in the shadows. An adulterer who disguises His face, He feeds on barren women. Darkness is as Light to Him, and He befriends the terrors of the night. Yet the Lord of Light shall sustain the life of the valiant by His power, and they shall rise up against the Darkness even when they despair of life.

—from *Dumnonian Visions,*
by Shane of Corin

SHASHTAH AND TKAI TOOK their leave of Shaharadesh as the King's Camp began to settle for its midday rest. Shashtah had slept late and felt as if he could still use another half rotation in bed. Yet his god had called, and he knew he had to answer. Part of him dreaded traveling beyond the Border of Dumnonia with Tkai while knowing so little about Dragons. Another part knew it was deeply wrong for them to leave without undergoing the Training, but his mission would not wait. He glanced at Tkai. If he stalled their departure much longer, her hide would become too hot for him to mount.

Tkai looked resplendent in the new harness Shaharadesh had supplied for her. Legends of her ancestor, Tchang, danced along its surface in a rainbow of colors. The king himself had shown Shashtah how to put it on the Ancient Dragon before giving his newest Rider the traditional farewell salute.

Shashtah felt at least somewhat better now that he had returned the borrowed aba. He had kept the keffiyeh since the draping cloth seemed more practical than a turban on dragonback. A simple leather thong, which Tphah had presented to him, had replaced the agal and would hold his keffiyeh firmly in place against the winds of dragonflight. Katrell had spent the morning locating a not-completely rusty scimitar from somewhere. Shashtah silently admitted that he felt far more comfortable with a weapon once more strapped securely to his hips. Kashon's own cloak draped across his shoulders. "I'll have another one made," Kashon had insisted in response to Shashtah's protest. "You'll need the cover while traveling far more than I'll ever need it in Cinnamar."

Shashtah climbed to his perch and wrapped his right leg tightly around the spike at the base of Tkai's neck. He settled his feet into their proper places on her harness. His scimitar dangled loosely against the scales on her right side. He would rather have had the scabbard tied to his leg, but there was no way he could do that and ride sidesaddle. *Apparently Dragonriders aren't supposed to be left-handed.* He marveled at how something he had no power to change could still rankle him. *As if I haven't been dealing with everything being reversed my entire life!* He brought his right fist to his left breast in the Dumnonian salute and thrust his clenched fist into the air, giving the Ancient Prophetess the command to rise. As Tkai took to the air, Shashtah said a brief prayer of thanks for the inspiration that had made him stop by a Healer's Tent to have a salve applied to the fresh scratches on his back. He felt his recently-healed muscles straining at the new activity and tried not to remember that he would be injured again soon enough. He looked down at where Kashon sat, mounted firmly on Katrell, just beyond the edge of Camp. The head of Tphah's dragonform lay in the older Dragon's forearms. She dozed, apparently worn out from her adventures at the Feast. Shashtah waved and flashed a grin at Kashon.

Kashon saluted him in return.

Shashtah concentrated on staying erect as Tkai's great wings carried him ever higher into the sky.

The blinding sun beat down mercilessly on Dragon and Rider as Tkai's wingstrokes sent them hurtling into the unknown. Although Shashtah found it a lot easier on his right leg to ride the Ancient Dragon than it had been to ride Katrell, Tkai's ridges gave him room to slip that Katrell's had not. Still, he was in the air on a Dragon, and she was all his.

Shashtah had crossed the vast desert of his homeland many times, and the journey never seemed the same. On the ground, magic left over from countless battles against the forces of the Dark One warped the landscape, sometimes making long distances mercifully short and other times separating short distances by virtually impassable mazes of illusions and traps. Before the War, the Dumnonian traders had taken two to three rotations to lead their caravans from their homeland to the border of Daethia. Or so the stories said. Shashtah wondered idly if his horse, perhaps guided by a divine hand, had stumbled into one of the desert warps, which brought the stallion close enough to Dameth's Camp for Tphah to spot him, or whether Kashon had actually been patrolling with his Dragons deep in the barren wastes of Cinnamar.

:*Where do you think it would be a good idea to train a Stripling in the use of magic and breath weapons?*: Tkai's voice thundered inside his head. :*Where she could accidentally wipe out half a century of Dragonriders, or where she couldn't destroy anything if she tried?*:

:*Then how did Katrell make it back to the King's Camp in the space of a single night?*: Shashtah wondered, not expecting a reply, as he rearranged Kashon's cloak to shield himself from at least a little of the heat that shimmered along his Dragon's hide. He frowned absently, realizing that the Ancient Female's bronze scales were becoming uncomfortably warm even through his leather pants.

Tkai craned her great head around to look at him, her total surprise reflected in her amber eyes. :*You don't know?*:

Shashtah failed to answer as the rest of her body twisted to follow the lead of her head. Ignoring everything he had learned from decades of riding horses and camels, he grabbed her harness, praying that the suddenly feeble-seeming leather would not break. He screamed both silently and aloud.

Tkai somersaulted in protest, causing him to scream again.

:*DON'T DO THAT!*: Shashtah shrieked.

:*Then don't scream!*: came the disgruntled reply as the great Dragon leveled off.

Relieved to find himself at least upright, Shashtah swallowed his heart back into his chest. :*Are you trying to kill me?*: he inquired in what he hoped was his most quiet, deadly and disapproving voice.

:*I'll think about it if you scream again,*: Tkai warned. :*That hurt!*:

:*You scared me!*: Shashtah echoed her accusatory tone.

:*You surprised me!*: Tkai countered without missing a wingstroke.

:*What? How?*: Shashtah demanded, too preoccupied with maintaining his grip on her harness to remember what had started the argument.

:*Exactly how many nits do you think sit on the Council of Ancients?*: Tkai asked. :*Kashon found you a good two rotations' journey by caravan outside of Dameth's camp. That's about half a rotation of straight hard flying with rests in the midday heat for the Rider and Dragon. Instead of summoning help once he realized you were too injured for him to carry on Katrell, he decided to have you ride Katrell even though you could not talk silently with him. To make the trip from Cinnamar in one night Kashon had to order Katrell to create a warp and take you through it to within easy flying distance of the King's Camp, which is even farther north than the Dragonlords' basecamps. That provided a way for the Dark One's forces to fly closer to the heart of everything we hold dear than they usually do. Allowing Katrell to be injured in battle because he lost track of him was not Kashon's only mistake.*:

Shashtah shuddered, suddenly feeling cold in spite of the growing heat. *How could a Dragon carry me through a warp without me knowing it?*

Tkai's voice smiled in spite of herself. :*You daydream on dragonback, Dragonheart.*:

Shashtah made a mental note to take up the issue of her eavesdropping on him later. He glanced down and reassured himself that he could still see the dark blotch of the King's Camp on the horizon.

The Ancient Dragon sniffed. :*Do you really think I would have the audacity to carry you through a warp without telling you when I have so recently rebuked another for doing so?*:

Shashtah's cheeks burned from more than the growing heat. :*No.*:

:*All right then,*: Tkai responded in a more amiable tone. :*Let's get somewhere cooler before I have to set you down. Warping. Lesson One. Traveling to an Unpopulated Region. I've been in the general area of where we want to be three times. How about you?*:

Shashtah almost laughed. :*More times than I can count.*:

:*You've really gotten around for a dragonless warrior,*: Tkai commented, genuinely impressed. :*Fine, then. Call up your memories, focusing on a specific location you desire. I'll call up my general memories and overlay them on yours. When the memories join, the warp will be created, and we will be where we are going.*:

:*Sounds simple,*: Shashtah replied as he recalled a particular journey with Garesh to barter captured gems and stolen goods for elven spices and Galantite-forged armor and swords. His images of woods, mountains, rivers and streams blurred together unexpectedly with an aerial image of glaciers, crevasses, and lifeless snow.

With sudden terror Shashtah felt himself freezing from an abrupt change in air temperature. Panic set in as he realized he could not breathe. Only then did it occur to him that Tkai was in a steep dive, barely skimming the rocky, snow-covered surface of an enormous mountain. :*Where in the name of Cinnamar are we?*:

Tkai's wings finally caught enough air to pull them out of the dive. She landed heavily on a half-frozen cliff and greedily filled her lungs with icy air. She scanned the vast expanse of forest at the base of the mountain, then gazed north at gently rolling plains. Far off to the west, beyond the edge of the Great Woods, a lone peak rose ominously from desert sands. The setting sun turned the sky blood red. :*Offhand I'd say we're perched on a cliff in the Dragon's Back Mountains somewhere above the Great Woods of Daethia,*: she replied in a too-quiet voice. :*Is there something you want to tell me, Dragonheart?*:

Lightheaded from the thin air and the sudden fright, Shashtah swayed precariously in his seat and tried to tighten his already vicelike grasp on

Tkai's harness. The lighting was all wrong. Used to crossing distances by caravan, the drastic change from the King's Camp to his present location befuddled him. He slowly recalled his geography as his mind struggled to make sense out of what his eyes were telling him. The Dragon's Back Mountains formed the eastern border of Daethia. The giant peaks rose too high for anything to live near their summits. Only one pass through the massive range had ever been found, and that was guarded by the Daethian capitol, Tor, far to the north. According to legend Corin had caused his own death by transporting himself to the top of one of those impressive peaks. The general queasy feeling that had been sweeping through Shashtah abruptly settled into his stomach. :*I think I'm going to be sick.*:

:*Serves you right!*: snapped Tkai, finally recovering enough to be angry. :*Don't you ever lie to me again when it comes to warping! We could have been killed!*:

"I didn't lie!" Shashtah's screech echoed off the peaks just as he hoped his frustration was ringing inside the Ancient Prophetess's head. Irrational fury replaced his terror. He reverted to silent communication alone as the thin air caused his lungs to ache. :*It never snows in the Great Woods! The Elven King's magic won't let it!*:

"The Great Woods?" Tkai spat in her sword-sharp voice. Apparently the altitude bothered her as well, since she also slipped back into sending her thoughts through their Bond. :*Since when are the Northern Wastes in the Great Woods?*:

Shashtah winced at her telepathic roar. He pointed at the setting sun. :*My god told me to take a message to his brother. His brother is the Elven King, isn't he?*: he asked silently. :*And the elves still live in the Great Woods, don't they? Or did I miss something important while I was on my Dragonquest?*:

Tkai frowned. :*What are you talking about? Corin told us to find the White Wolf. The White Wolf is somewhere in the Northern Wastes.*: She glanced again at their surroundings. :*Which we most definitely are not.*:

":*Are you telling me,*:" Shashtah growled, once more adding his exasperated voice to his thoughts, ":*that you eavesdrop on my lovemaking but you don't know anything about the vision I had last night? I thought you were a Prophetess!*:"

"*:Apparently,:*" Tkai's speech grated in the crystal-cold air, echoing her silent reply, "*:the Sun God's message was a private communication to you that he did not see fit to share with me. You failed to share it with me as well. We are going to be useless as partners if you won't open your mind to me:*"

:Admit it!: Shashtah challenged. :*You just made a mistake that was potentially as dangerous as the one Kash*—:

The rest of his accusation was cut off by a bloodcurdling scream from somewhere in the forest below.

:*DIVE!*: Shashtah ordered.

Tkai flinched at the power of his mental roar but obediently sprang into the air and sent them plunging toward the tree tops with a sharp crack from her great wings.

Shashtah's farseeing eyes searched the woods as the scream echoed off the mountains again.

Flashes of white pursued by a dark hunter showed through branches of aspen, pine, oak, willow, and all the other trees that grew in the Great Woods without regard to climate or season.

Shashtah was never quite sure what he had expected to see in the clearing beneath them, but a young Daethian woman, half dead from a difficult birth and clutching a newborn, was not at the top of his list.

Tkai, as startled as her Rider, pulled out of her dive and landed in the woman's path.

The woman screamed again, this time at the sudden appearance of a Bronze Dragon and her Rider. She whirled around to face the Daethian warrior who came crashing into the clearing after her. "No! Davit!"

The enraged fighter wore the black kilt and golden armbands that were the uniform of the Kyondoca, Lord Criton's elite guards. He efficiently drew back the string of his impressively-carved bow and sent a deadly arrow through the woman's throat, instantly killing her.

Tkai roared in rage.

Shashtah sensed his own throat echoing the sound as the Daethian nocked another arrow.

Instead of targeting Tkai, though, Davit took aim at the child in the dead mother's arms. "May the Light save us from the Dark One's spawn!"

Tkai opened her great jaws and sent a bolt of magical light crackling through the air toward the archer.

Davit interrupted his shot and easily deflected the bolt by raising his right armband.

A tree at the edge of the clearing burst into flames as the surge of power hit.

"Call off your Dragon, Dumnonian!" Davit shouted as he took aim at the child again. "I'll slay you both if you interfere again!"

:*Tkai!*: Shashtah shrieked telepathically. He had seen Kyondoca warriors in battle, clashing their armbands together to create magical bolts that could destroy powerful demons in a single blast. He would never survive such an attack and neither, he feared, would Tkai. :*Do what the nice man says, and back off.*:

:*He's not a nice man!*: Tkai protested, breaking her own taboo about talking telepathically in the presence of others.

:*He's a member of the Kyondoca,*: Shashtah tried to reason. :*He has to be a "nice" man. He'd be a pile of dust on the ground if he weren't. You know as well as I do that those armbands can't be worn by anyone who's not "nice."*:

:*Since when do nice people go around slaying unarmed Daethian mothers?*: Tkai asked.

:*They used to go around slaying Dumnonian Bronzes, remember?*: Shashtah countered.

The warrior apparently took what he heard as an extended silence as assent to his command. "May the Light save us from the Dark One and His son!" Davit bellowed. He released his bowstring.

An enormous winged devil, at least twice Shashtah's height, suddenly materialized between Davit and the baby and smashed the arrow from the air with a wave of its clawed hand.

:*A devil?*: Shashtah gawked. :*It won't be nighttime for candlescars yet!*:

:*In Cinnamar,*: Tkai reminded him. :*Look at the sky. Night is already falling here. The Binding loosens on the exits to the Great Woods first.*:

Abruptly, the significance of the setting sun hit Shashtah. Garesh had always made certain their caravan never traveled the Great Woods at night for a very, very good reason.

Two more devils materialized behind Davit as darkness descended on the clearing. They grabbed the Daethian's arms, forcing him to drop his bow.

With one clawed hand the first devil tore Davit's beating heart from his chest.

Sheer panic washed over Shashtah, followed by utter horror as Davit did not die.

Terror and despair filled Davit's eyes. His fading gaze fell on Shashtah. "Kill me!" he begged, loathing the undead thing he was starting to become.

Shashtah slid to the ground. Leaves crackled beneath his feet. He awkwardly drew his scimitar.

The two devils holding Davit suddenly lost their balance and fell backward as the warrior's armbands flared and plummeted to the ground, severing Davit's hands from his undead arms.

The devil with the still-beating heart in his claws laughed and flapped into the air.

Tkai rose into the sky after the monster as Shashtah, ignoring the other devils, darted across the clearing and swung with all his strength at the undead warrior's throat.

Otherworldly light sizzled along the edge of his blade. The scimitar sliced through Davit's neck as easily as a jambiya cutting through soft cheese.

Shashtah sensed the sickness he had felt on the cliff returning as Davit's head reattached. Shashtah's scream echoed the Daethian's as he saw madness spreading across Davit's face. Shashtah lunged forward and, driven by some instinctive reaction to the large whites and pinpoint pupils in Davit's eyes, wrestled the gutted body to the ground. He felt the abomination's teeth sink into his throat and his blood flow into the unholy creature's mouth. He held Davit tighter and prayed. Suddenly Shashtah felt the warmth of his god rushing through him. He sensed his power surging into Davit, seeking the dying magic of the Daethian's soul. Power touched power, and magical bonds snapped.

Davit's body shimmered into flames, and his corpse crumpled into a pile of ash beside his now-charred bow.

Shashtah scrambled backward.

Overhead the flying devil shrieked as the heart flared, turned to ash and scorched him.

Tkai sent a magic bolt crackling toward the flying horror.

The devil vanished abruptly through a warp.

The warp was apparently one of the temporary kind created by a spell, since Tkai's burst of power flashed through the spot where the monstrous form had been and struck a second tree.

Tkai roared in frustration as her bolt kindled another fire.

The two devils still in the clearing picked themselves up and stared, dumbfounded, at Shashtah.

Tkai swooped back toward the clearing, the woods echoing with her scream of rage.

The devils screeched and dove through the warp at the clearing's edge.

Shashtah blinked at the rust-encrusted scimitar, which by some miracle he still held tightly in his left hand. "What in the name of—?" His frozen brain could not complete the thought.

Tkai landed at the far end of the clearing and shifted to humanform. :*You didn't think Katrell would give you a completely useless scimitar, did you?*: Tkai asked reasonably as she crossed the clearing and pried the newborn infant from its dead mother's arms. :*He really isn't the nit everyone thinks he is.*:

"That's not what I—" Shashtah's comment was cut off as the newborn took one look at Tkai and decided it was safe enough to squall. A relieved grin crossed Shashtah's face as he was finally presented with a problem he could handle. He quickly wiped his scimitar on the moss at his feet and sheathed it. "Here. Let me." He carefully picked his way over the ash and charred remains of the bow, holding out his arms.

Tkai handed him the shrieking infant. "I'd forgotten how much I hate children."

Shashtah gathered the tiny, perfectly-formed male child into his arms.

The boy stopped crying almost instantly.

Shashtah stared at the newborn.

Black hair still bloody from his mother's womb, dark eyes welling with tears of fright, bell-shaped mouth clamped firmly around his miniature right thumb in an apparent effort not to scream, the boy seemed a bit physically advanced for a newborn, but absolutely nothing indicated that the child was demon-spawned.

"I don't understand," Shashtah murmured as the blood from the bite on his neck slowly dribbled onto his shirt and mixed with the blood on the child. He could not find anything about the boy that would explain why three devils had tried to defend the baby any more than he could understand why one of Criton's elite guards had slain an unarmed woman and called the infant the Dark One's son.

"Nothing in war ever makes sense," sang an unexpected tenor in the elvish tongue.

Shashtah and Tkai glanced up to see an extremely tall and handsome elf taking off the magical cloak that had made him all but invisible against the trees at the edge of the clearing. His eyes, like Shashtah's, had no pupils nor whites. They were, however, solid violet instead of amber. His golden hair was cropped close around his ears and neck to fit easily under a helm. His pale features seemed young, but his regal bearing spoke of a field commander with decades, perhaps centuries, of experience fighting the evils of Cinnamar. The brilliant glint of priceless Galantite chainmail, as flexible as cloth but almost impossible to pierce, flashed from beneath his gold-trimmed, dark-blue tunic. An exquisite belt quiver, filled with what Shashtah assumed were extraordinarily lethal arrows, hung at his right hip, and a marvelous hunting bow was strapped firmly against his back. The elf's right hand rested nonchalantly on his sword belt, less than a heartbeat away from the pommel of a Galantite sword, the hilt and sheath of which were covered in magic runes so powerful that just looking at them made Shashtah's skin crawl. The elven warrior waved his left hand gracefully in the air and the flames in the two burning trees flickered out. "Are either of you going to tell me why I find a Dumnonian and his Dragon in the Great Woods, killing a member of the Kyondoca and his wife, stealing their child and burning my trees to the ground?" he asked in what was probably an extremely reasonable tone for him under the circumstances.

Shashtah, however, felt distinctly as if a death sentence had just been passed on him. He glanced at the bracers lying in the heap of ash then lowered his gaze to the body of the dead woman at his feet. No sign of the devils remained, and he instinctively knew that the elf was not going to accept Tkai's word that his preposterous story was true. His shoulders sagged. "No, lord. I can't even think of a bad reason to explain this," he replied in elvish, hoping that he would buy himself a little more time to think for at least knowing the warrior's tongue.

Tkai altered her humanform to a much younger version, stepped forward abruptly and dropped into a salaam. "Lord Juel."

The elf frowned. "Tkai?"

Shashtah glanced from Tkai to the elf. "You two know each other?"

Tkai ignored Shashtah as she straightened. "My Rider would like to throw himself on the mercy of the Elven King," she declared as she shifted to a slightly more elven form.

Shashtah flashed her another puzzled glance. :*I would?*:

:*Yes, you would,*.: Tkai replied without looking at him. She straightened and favored Juel with a suggestive smile that brought a blush to both Shashtah's and the elf's cheeks. "Please? For me?"

Slowly, Juel nodded. "For you." His eyes grew unfocused as if he were talking to someone silently.

Shashtah leaned closer to Tkai. "What's going on?" he whispered.

"Be still!" Tkai snapped. "And count yourself lucky that not everyone thinks of me as his great-great grandmother."

Farador, Elven King, shimmered into existence at Juel's side. The king wore a loose-fitting white silk shirt gathered at his wrists, green-dyed leather trousers, and a plain golden sash. Deerskin boots encased his feet and a flame-shaped brooch held his lightweight, forest-green cloak securely fastened at his right shoulder. A simple golden circlet was visible against his mane of oak-colored hair. A neatly trimmed, chestnut beard hugged his powerful jaw, all the more impressive since neither Dumnonians nor elves grew body or facial hair except for eyebrows. Compassion and wisdom struggled to contain the wicked sense of humor that danced in the Elven King's remarkable, glowing, solid-green eyes.

The simple fact that the Elven King carried absolutely nothing that looked remotely like a weapon froze Shashtah's soul. *The power he must have!*

Tkai bent in a deep salaam.

Shashtah followed her example as best he could with the Daethian child in his arms.

Farador's keen eyes took in the situation. "Do you want to tell me what happened?" he asked them in a heartbreakingly beautiful baritone that somehow managed to sound stern and playful at the same time.

No, Shashtah thought honestly, but he knew he had no choice.

Tkai rose and nudged Shashtah with her elbow, urging him to speak.

Shashtah shrugged his helplessness as he pulled himself erect, shifting the weight of the baby to his left arm and hoping that the elves would realize that he had just made it impossible for him to draw his scimitar instead of freeing what on anyone else would have been his sword hand. "I don't know where to begin."

A shrewd smile curled across Juel's grim lips as he spotted the gesture and shot a suspicious glance at Tkai. "At the beginning is customary."

Tkai shrugged her ignorance.

"Easy, lad," Farador crooned as if talking to a fine, spirited horse. He lay a quieting hand on Juel's arm. "Not everyone knows where the beginning is." He made his way across the clearing and knelt beside the pile of ash, taking care not to touch the bracers. He waved his hand over the warrior's remains and murmured the words to a spell. His right eyebrow arched in surprise as he looked up at Shashtah. "No soul?"

Shashtah's blush deepened. "I think I released it. At least I hope I did. I don't think the devils—"

"Devils?" Juel interrupted, slipping his rune-covered sword free of its sheath. "What devils?"

"Two of them flew through a warp just before you arrived." Shashtah quickly gestured at the spot at the edge of the clearing with his free hand as he wondered just how good a time the lethal elf had had with Tkai. "The other one flew through another warp in the air when my Dragon gave chase and attacked it."

Juel turned his worried gaze on Tkai. "Truth?"

Tkai nodded quickly. "You know I would not let him lie to you."

Farador rose from where he had been examining Davit's charred bow.

He scanned the ground for footprints as he crossed the clearing and knelt beside the woman's body. He pulled the shaft from her throat then placed the palm of his hand over the hole where the arrow had been. Green light danced from his fingertips, enveloping the corpse. His fingers began to tremble to the beat of a strong pulse.

Shashtah closed his eyes and added his silent prayer to the magic of the Elven King.

:*I told you to tell him that I had sent you,*: a familiar voice chided.

Shashtah snapped open his eyes and almost closed them again as rays of sheer white light stabbed into them.

"Gran'da!" Juel leapt at Shashtah, but the miniature sun that encased the tiny image of the Sun God threw him back.

Farador gasped as he blinked at the shining globe that hovered between him and the Dragonrider. "Brother?"

The glittering figure nodded. :*Yes.*:

Farador shook his head, denying the truth that hung in the air before him. "Impossible."

:*Not for a Prophet who is a Dragonheart,*: the Sun God smiled.

"A Prophet and a Dragonheart?" Farador stared past the light at Shashtah, seeing him as if for the first time. "Tkai has always been full of surprises."

Leot waved his hand, and the soul of the dead woman appeared at his side. :*Cease your efforts, Brother. This woman has endured enough for one lifetime by giving birth to my grandson. Do not ask more of her.*:

Farador immediately rose and stepped away from the corpse.

The green light vanished, and the pulse stilled.

Leot waved his hand again, and magical flames licked at the woman's mortal body, reducing it to ash. Then he kissed the woman's spirit and whispered, :*Fear not. Your husband's soul will be spared.*:

The figure of the woman bowed and vanished into the light of the deity.

Leot smiled at a private thought, then grew serious and turned his shining eyes back toward Farador. :*Have you found a way to stop my Dark Son?*:

Farador spread his hands apart in helplessness. "Criton thinks he has, but the White Wolf will not join with us. He fears the truth of what he is."

Leot nodded. :*I thought as much. That is why I have sent you a Dragonheart and let this child fall into your hands.*:

"We cannot seal the paths permanently without the White Wolf!" Farador protested.

:*Then use the Dragonheart to delay my Dark Son while you wait for the next Great Wizard to be born and trained,*: Leot instructed.

A flash of sorrow crossed the Farador's face. "You are asking me to sacrifice my daughter as I have already sacrificed my wife and son."

:*I know,*: Leot said as he stretched his image to human-size, reached out from the light and gripped his brother's hand.

Power such as Shashtah had never imagined flowed from the Sun God into the Elven King.

Farador's eyes glowed with a brilliant emerald light. "Tell Tira I love her!" he cried.

The image of an elven queen flickered in the light. :*Love Beyond Life*,: she called.

"Laedor!" Farador summoned.

The image of a painfully handsome elf appeared beside the queen.

"Da!" Juel shrieked.

:*I am safe,*: Laedor assured them. He turned his gaze on Farador. :*Take care of my son.*:

"Better than I could take care of mine," Farador promised grimly.

"No one needs to take care of me!" Juel swore.

Laedor grinned. :*I don't suppose they do.*:

:*Our time grows short,*: Leot warned. He stared at Farador. :*Use this Dragonheart and my grandson as you will. They are my gifts to you. I wish I could do more.*: The Sun God glanced at Shashtah then smiled at the Elven King. :*You might want to heal the Dragonheart before all of his blood leaks onto your leaves.*:

The Elven King reached out with his free hand and touched Shashtah without taking his eyes off Tira and Laedor.

A green, magical glow briefly surrounded Shashtah and the child.

Shashtah felt the wound in his neck heal. The blood and grime disappeared from him and the boy.

The Elven King lowered his hand, and the green light was gone.

Leot nodded at Farador. :*Someday, Brother. I promise. Someday.*: He released his grip on the Elven King.

Suddenly the orb of light vanished, taking the Sun God and the two elven spirits with it.

Shashtah legs buckled. He marveled that the Daethian child did not slip from his grasp as his knees hit the moss-covered ground.

Juel rushed forward and grabbed the suddenly weeping Elven King by the arms. "Gran'da?"

":*Dragonheart?*:" Tkai ventured both silently and aloud.

Shashtah picked himself up as he shifted the child to a safer position. "I'm all right." He gave the Elven King a worried glance. "I think."

Farador controlled himself. "I certainly hope so. Without the White Wolf, you are the only chance we have." He freed himself from Juel and dashed away his tears.

"Dragonheart and Elven King," Tkai intoned, "o'er the Dark Heart with Criton sing. Two-edged the spell, two-edged the pain, for Magic's sake some time to gain."

"'For Magic's sake,'" Juel echoed.

Farador nodded. "It takes time to create a Great Wizard." His glowing green eyes stared directly at Shashtah's soul. "Corin warned you of the risk?"

Shashtah managed to nod.

"I will not ask this of you, Dragonheart," Farador continued, "without first allowing you to try to succeed where my nephew and I both failed. Find the White Wolf and beg him to bring his power back to us."

Great. Now I'm supposed to find a Wizard who doesn't want to be found and convince him to do what the Elven King and the Lord of Daethia couldn't get him to do. Shashtah sighed and stared at the child who lay in his arms, snuggling against his breast. "What will I do with this one while I'm gone?" Taking the boy to the Northern Wastes with him was unthinkable, and Shashtah liked Kashon too much to ask him to look after the child while trying to train Tphah and fight a war.

Farador held out his hands to Shashtah. "May I see him?"

Shashtah placed the child in the Elven King's arms.

Farador stared at the tiny creature for a moment. "What is he called?"

Shashtah shrugged. "His parents never said his name."

"You name him then," ordered Farador.

Shashtah glanced at Tkai.

"My prophecies rarely include personal names," Tkai confessed unhelpfully.

Shashtah stared at the boy again. "Then let him be called 'Ally,' 'Quatar' in the Dumnonian tongue."

"Quatar it is, then," declared Farador. "May your prophecy of his worth be true."

"Would you protect him for me while I seek the White Wolf?" Shashtah blurted out.

Tkai stamped viciously on Shashtah's foot.

Shashtah bit his lower lip but remained silent.

Farador frowned. "You do not know what you ask. My magic is not attuned to Daethians as is Criton's." He shifted his glance to the bracers that still lay upon the ground. "Still—"

"Gran'da, you cannot seriously be thinking of asking an elf to raise a Daethian bastard of the Dark One!" Juel protested.

A dejected smile curled across Farador's lips as he raised his eyes and looked at Shashtah. "No. I was thinking of asking Adrial to care for an infant who has become the ward of my brother's Prophet." Sadness darkened his glowing green eyes. "If Criton ever weds her, she will not live to have the joy of raising a child of her own. Her heart will cease to beat the moment her baby is born, and that infant's heart will beat in time to the Dark One's."

Juel gaped at Farador. "Criton actually wed my aunt? Cinnamar will freeze over first! Criton has been avoiding anything that sounds remotely like a marriage vow for millennia!"

"Perhaps the Prophecy will not come true," Tkai observed, "if the Dark One has no heart to beat."

"You see it, too, then," Farador commented darkly.

"See what?" Shashtah asked, completely lost.

Farador tried to smile reassuringly and failed. "Find the White Wolf and convince him to return. If you can do that, you may yet change these glimpses of the future. But if you cannot, then you, Criton and I must work the spell against the Dark One. To do so, we must have his heart. That will be hard to come by, but only then can I be certain my daughter's child will live long enough to become a Great Wizard. Since I must protect the elves and Criton must protect the Daethians, only you will be free to obtain that heart. That will not be easy, even for my brother's Prophet."

"Harder than you think," Shashtah said as he stared at Tkai. "I have already placed the stone that contains the Dark One's heart in the hands of Corin's shade. To retrieve it I must Bond with another Dragon—"

"Which means you must break your Bond with Tkai," Juel finished for him.

"'Five years,'" Shashtah echoed Farador's words as he stared at Tkai. "You knew all along."

Tkai shrugged. "Nothing's ever certain. That's the nature of Prophecy. You might still prove everyone wrong by convincing the White Wolf to return to Daethia."

"Tphah," Shashtah whispered. "I thought I would not be Bonded to her when I worked the spell. If I am and if I am the sacrifice and if she has to share my pain—"

Tkai put her hand on his arm, suppressing his rising panic. "Easy, Dragonheart. As I've told Tphah a thousand times, you have to learn to control Prophecy so it won't control you. Do not second-guess the visions. If you do, you will go mad. The Future can alter just as the desert winds can reshape dunes. This detail apparently has changed. You may be Bonded when you work the spell. What seems to be one thing now may be something entirely different when the vision comes to pass. Do not be afraid. Accept the glimpses for what they are: a gift, a warning of what might be."

Shashtah nodded because she expected him to, but in his heart he felt far from comforted.

Farador gestured at the bracers. "Take those to Criton at Tor, and tell him of our plan. He may have knowledge that could aid you in finding the White Wolf or in convincing him to return."

"You have no such knowledge then?" Shashtah asked, slowly realizing that even though the Elven King could not touch the bracers for some strange reason he thought a Dragonheart could. *A Dragonrider return the bracers of a dead Dragonslayer to a living god in Tor. Right.*

Farador shook his head helplessly. "I'm afraid all I can tell you is that when you look at a winter-coated wolf and see a great black cat, the White Wolf will be nearby. But there are many winter-coated wolves in the Northern Wastes, and the armies of the Dark One have been looking for this specific wolf for a very long time. I wish you luck, Dragonheart." He glanced from Juel to the warp at the edge of the clearing in an unspoken order, then vanished, child and all.

Juel raised his sword and saluted Tkai. "A warrior's work is never done."

"Not in my lifetime," grinned Tkai. "If only you had been a Dumnonian!"

The memory of an old joke flashed in Juel's violet eyes. "Dumnonian or not, I could have had you for the asking, and you know it." He sighed. "My people needed me, your people needed you, and our need for each other was sacrificed in the name of this unholy War. Has it been worth it, Tkai?"

Tkai smiled softly at Shashtah. "I hope so." Her grin widened as her gaze returned to Juel, memorizing his every feature. "You will find happiness again, my love."

"Prophecy?" Juel asked, raising an eyebrow.

Tkai laughed. "No. Benefits of a long life. A very long life. Live forever, Elven Lord!"

Juel flashed her a lopsided grin. "'Is that a blessing or a curse?"

"Both," Tkai admitted. "Both."

Juel dropped in a deep salaam. He straightened and let out a deafening war cry, "For the Light!" He charged through the warp, closing it behind him.

Only then did Shashtah's night-sharp vision pick out a young girl crouched behind a bush at the clearing's edge. *Sands! Someone please tell me she hasn't been watching all of this!* "Do you need help, child?" he asked, switching to the Daethian language.

The girl stepped out from behind the bush, a puzzled expression on her grimy face. She wore a simple tunic, torn and muddied from romping through the woods, no shoes, and her right fist wielded a long stick like a make-believe sword. From the look of her slender body she could be no more than twelve or thirteen years old. With one eye on Shashtah, she picked her way across the clearing and reached for the dead warrior's armbands.

"They'll hurt you if your soul is not attuned to them," Shashtah warned.

Without any hesitation, the girl picked them up. "Mine is. They belonged to my father."

Shashtah felt his heart sink into his stomach like an unripe date. *This is not going well.*

The girl tried on one bracer, but the magical armor would not adhere to her skin the way it would have if the armbands had been placed on her by Lord Criton. Disappointment flooded across her face. "Papa was right: Women cannot be members of the Kyondoca." She glanced nervously at the spot where Juel had vanished in pursuit of the devils. "But the Kyondoca are the only Daethians who can hurt the dark thing that hurt Mama."

"The armbands will only work for awho is granted them by the leader of the Kyondoca," Shashtah said quickly, not completely sure he was telling the truth.

"But the Lord of Daethia is in Tor!" the girl protested.

Shashtah crossed the clearing in three strides and placed his hands on her shoulders. "A heartbeat away by dragonback."

:*WHAT?*: Tkai's voice thundered in his head.

:*I'm not leaving an orphan alone in the Great Woods at night!*: Shashtah smiled at the girl. "Have you ever ridden on a Dragon before?"

The girl looked shocked, then beamed. "You'll take me to Tor?"

"Of course," Shashtah assured the girl.

:*Are you sunstruck?*: Tkai asked.

:*Tkai—*: Shashtah stopped mid-thought as he turned and saw the look in his Dragon's eyes. :*Tkai,*: he thought quickly, :*don't fight with me on this. I can't leave her here, and I am supposed to take the armbands to Criton and ask him about the White Wolf. Criton is in Tor. The orphans of the Kyondoca are supposed to go to the temples in Tor. Tor seems like a perfectly reasonable place to take this girl since we have to go there anyway.*:

:You yourself suggested that the elves raise her brother,: Tkai glowered silently at her Rider.

:Half-brother, from what I gathered,: Shashtah corrected. :Spawn of the Dark One. He'd be dead in half a heartbeat if I took him to Tor. He's the grandson of my god. As such he belongs in the care of his uncle, Farador.:

The girl fidgeted, growing uneasy at the apparent silence of the adults.

"Ah!" Tkai exclaimed in dismay, forgetting to keep the conversation between just her and her Rider, though she did switch to the Dumnonian tongue. "You are going to be the death of me, Dragonheart!"

"Prophecy?" Shashtah asked viciously in the same language, annoyed at having to argue with his Dragon in front of a child.

"What do you think?" Tkai snapped.

"I think you should start acting like a proper Dragon instead of like your queen and take your dragonform when I ask you to!" Shashtah thundered.

Tkai abruptly took her dragonform.

Shashtah glanced at the terrified girl, took a deep breath, and did his best to smile encouragement he did not feel. "Don't be afraid," he said, returning to the girl's language. "I'm a new Rider, and she's a crotchety old Dragon. I'm still trying to train her. Did your father ever train horses or dogs?"

Apparently Shashtah's guess about the pastimes of the dead Kyondoca warrior was accurate because the girl nodded. "Sometimes it took him a while."

:So now I'm a horse?: Tkai fumed.

:No.: Shashtah did his best to keep his fury from showing on his face.

:A dog?: Tkai challenged.

:No!: Shashtah thought at her crossly. Why on Centuria did I ever think Bonding with the Leader of the Council of Ancients was a good idea? After spending his entire life wanting a Dragon, Shashtah found himself wondering if he should have remained a caravaneer.

"Can I give Papa's armbands to the Lord of Daethia?" the girl asked, this time ignoring the silence. "Maybe that will make him change his mind and he will give them to me some day."

"Huh?" Shashtah briefly tried to imagine the look that would be on

Criton's face when a half-grown girl asked to become a member of his all-male elite guard. "You can give them to him," he promised, fairly certain that that was where the matter was going to end.

"That almost makes up for the 'crotchety' comment," Tkai sniffed in the ear splitting tongue of the Bronze Dragons.

The girl winced at the sound.

:*Why can I understand your language now?*: Shashtah asked Tkai as he hauled himself and the girl onto his Dragon's back, remembering his father's comments in the Valley of Ancients. He had learned many languages at Garesh's insistence during his youth, but the speech of the Bronze Dragons had not been one of them. *Probably to keep me from understanding what they said when we ran into them,* he grumbled to himself.

:*Our language has always been in your heart,*: Tkai replied. :*Our Bond has released it.*:

Shashtah wrapped his right leg around the spike at the base of Tkai's neck, settled his feet into his Dragon's harness and perched the delighted girl on his right thigh. He gripped the child firmly with his right arm as he silently asked Tkai to rise.

The great Dragon leapt skyward.

The young girl gasped as the light of the rising moon glinted off the armbands that she clutched tightly in her fists. She took care to make sure they did not touch Tkai.

A chill washed over Shashtah's soul. :*We're going to Tor, agreed?*: he asked Tkai.

:*You'll find out,*: Tkai teased as she gave him an image of the capitol of Daethia as seen from the air.

Shashtah quickly recalled his sight of the legendary city on the one trip Garesh had made to trade with the barbarians of Rashtar. Their caravan had passed by the impenetrable fortress on its way to the only pass through the Dragon's Back Mountains. Shashtah had sulked for days when his father had refused to stop so they could see the remains of the School of Wizards, but now he realized how unwise it would have been for Garesh to venture into the greatest stronghold of the Daethian Dragonslayers.

The two images of the ancient fortress melded, and a heartbeat later Tkai carried them in a slow spiral toward the fields just beyond the massive walls of Tor.

Lord Criton

CHAPTER 9:

The Great Wizard

The true Light of Knowledge came to Centuria. Centuria was made through the Light, and the Light was Centuria, yet Centuria knew it not. But to all who received the Light, who believed in its truth, the Light gave power. Thus were the Wizards born, not of blood nor of the will of the flesh nor of the will of the Daethians, but of the Light.

—from *The Book of Corin,*
by Shane of Corin

TKAI LANDED IN A FALLOW FIELD within easy walking distance of the colossal gates of Tor, the only Daethian city besides Krillion to survive the War. Tor's battered buildings and crumbling walls were poor reflections of what had once been called the City of Corin, the home of the School of Wizards. The Great Causeway rose from the fields to the precarious perch where the city balanced atop an improbable hill that Corin had summoned from the earth by his magic. Or so the legend said. Shashtah had always meant to ask the Wizard about the truth of the ancient stories. Such mundane concerns, however, had completely vanished from his mind when he had finally stood in Corin's presence.

The night air felt heavy and damp against Shashtah's skin, and a chill gripped the land with a firmness that suggested a climate out of control. *Not unlike this War*, Shashtah mused as he helped the Daethian girl to the soft, freshly-plowed ground before dismounting himself. The pungent odor of the moist earth clogged his nose, making him feel as if he had suddenly developed a head cold. He successfully fought back a sneeze, but already his heart was aching for his desert. *Five years of this? I don't know if I have it in me . . .*

Tkai abruptly shifted to the shape of a Dumnonian queen in full regalia, complete with a white samite chador and exact replicas of the jewels from the Tribal Hoard that Makara had worn at their Bonding Feast.

Shashtah raised his right eyebrow as the girl they had rescued trudged through the field toward the causeway, oblivious to her elders. :*Does Makara know you do that?*:

:*Not unless you tell her.*: Tkai fell into step with him. :*It's past moonrise. The guards obviously saw a Dumnonian and a Dragon land. I thought it would be best to keep them guessing which was which as long as possible.*:

:*Guessing?*: Shashtah echoed, keeping one eye on the girl while he tried to read Tkai's features. :*The girl will tell them.*:

:*What does it take to make you think like a Dragonrider?*: Tkai scolded. She tucked her left hand in the crook of his right arm. :*Daethians place great value on appearance. It's the major weakness of their race. Your father knows that. That's why he is such a successful trader. I know he taught you that lesson. They cannot tell Dumnonians apart because we all look alike to them. Pretend you are my Dragon in humanform, and they will believe it.*:

Shashtah frowned. :*I have no cause to——*:

:*You have a Daethian child carrying the armbands of her rather dead father whom she saw you slay,*: Tkai reminded him. :*I have at least half a chance of convincing them to take you before Criton to let him judge you if they think I'm the Dumnonian queen. Somehow I think the Dragonslayers of Daethia will be less likely to kill a queen's Dragon than they will be to kill the insignificant Rider of a 'crotchety' old Dragon who was apparently senile enough to agree to Bond with him!*:

:*But Shaharadesh is King of Dumnonia!*: Shashtah protested.

Tkai pegged him an intimidating glare. :*Do you really think the Daethians either know or care?*:

Shashtah's shoulders sagged. :*This doesn't look good at all.*:

:*No better than it looked to Juel or the Elven King,*: Tkai said. :*Only I don't have any friends in high places in Tor. I'm hoping that, if I can get you an interview with Criton, his sense of filial loyalty will outweigh his good judgment and that he'll give you a break.*:

:*Otherwise he'll break me,*: Shashtah thought silently at her.

Tkai flashed him an unreadable look. :*Don't think he can't.*:

The girl reached the city gates well ahead of the Dumnonians and showed the guards the armbands.

Four members of the Kyondoca and one of their lieutenants were summoned at once. A third of the elite guard would be in battle on the Border by now. Another third would be on leave. But the last third would be within the walls of Tor, protecting the city and serving as Criton's bodyguards. Five of the warriors would be only a fraction of the number the Dumnonians would encounter before the night was through. Shashtah was certain of that.

:*But what if the girl tells them you're the Dragon?*: Shashtah ventured.

Tkai looked annoyed. :*She won't.*:

Shashtah stumbled on a stone. :*Prophecy?*:

:*Would you look at her?*: Tkai's exasperation was almost audible. :*She just saw her mother and father killed and the Elven King disappear with her brother. She hasn't shed a single tear. She's a Daethian yet she thought nothing about riding on a Dragon once she realized we could carry her to Tor. She hasn't thanked us or even looked at us since we landed. We have fulfilled our purpose and are of no further use to her. She has one thing and only one thing on her mind: Those bracers. She wants to get them to Criton and convince him to make them work for her.*:

As Shashtah reached the gates with Tkai he could tell by the looks on the Dragonslayers' faces that they had been tried, judged, sentenced and awaited execution. He came to a halt a few paces from the furious Daethians.

"Tkai of Dumnonia!" the apparent Dumnonian queen announced in Daethian.

Shashtah dutifully stood behind her and off to her side, where a proper Dragon should.

"We bring news of the death of a member of the Kyondoca. Take us to your Lord," Tkai commanded.

"I'll take those!" the lieutenant snapped as he tried to seize the bracers from the girl.

The child snatched her treasures away from him. "No! They were Papa's! I can only give them to the Lord of Daethia!"

Several hundred eternal heartbeats of arguments ensued during which Shashtah had the distinct feeling that the Daethian child was making more of an impression on the irate lieutenant than Tkai was. *Have mercy, Lord of Light! Have mercy!* His fervent prayer rang through his head over and over again, drowning out everything the girl, the Daethians and Tkai said.

Tkai gave him a worried glance.

Shashtah suspected that she was eavesdropping on his private thoughts again, and he bristled silently. He had absolutely no idea what he was doing as the Bond Partner of the Leader of the Council of Ancients, and Tkai seemed to have even less of an idea about what she was doing with him. Shashtah was of half a mind to leave the city while they still could, go back to Dumnonia and ask Shaharadesh to have a Dragonlord put them through the Training. The quest his deity had assigned him would only carry him further and further away from his precious desert, and he had serious doubts, in spite of Tkai's Prophecy, that he would live to return to Dumnonia. *If I even survive this night.*

Suddenly the lieutenant produced a leather thong and bound Shashtah's wrists together.

Shashtah stared at the flimsy strap, wondering why on Centuria the officer had put it on him.

:*The girl just told them you cut off her father's head,*: Tkai explained. :*What does it take to make you pay attention?*:

Shashtah glanced at the gleaming bracers on the warrior's forearms. :*I am paying attention!*: he lied. He met the lieutenant's furious gaze and decided to go quietly.

The Kyondoca led their prisoner none too gently through the mighty gates of Tor.

Tkai took the girl by the upper arm and escorted her after them.

The streets were all but deserted in the flickering light from the street lamps. The scent of incense from the temples along the outer walls draped around the city like a cloak. Shashtah did his best to step over the puddle-filled wheel-ruts in the cobblestone streets, but his desert boots were soon soaked. Citizens with haunted eyes fled from the growing shadows into the illusory safety of their homes and inns. Odors from leather, stews, woods, ales, produce, horses and dozens of other sources assaulted Shashtah's nose. This time he did sneeze, drawing glares from his escort. He shrugged apologetically and wiped his nose on his sleeve as best he could. A stray cat took one look at the somber party, hissed and fled into a crack in a stone wall. Shashtah said a brief prayer of thanks that the gutters were mercifully clean. The refuse that should have collected there had been miraculously swept away, presumably by one of Lord Criton's spells.

The guards marched their prisoner through the inner wall and into the palace their ruler had created out of the ruins of the School of Corin.

Shashtah couldn't help himself. He gaped.

The palace itself was as light as the streets were dark. Highly polished marble reflected the glitter of a thousand flames. Gold and silver traced intricate spells upon the walls. Priceless jewels sparkled on furniture and lintels. Wealth beyond reason shimmered over every surface. Everything seemed to dance with light.

Shashtah sensed his amber eyes darkening in response to the glare. He felt oddly embarrassed at the squishing sounds his wet boots made as he walked on the pristine, marble floors.

The Kyondoca led Shashtah, Tkai and the girl to the heart of the palace. Their ultimate destination, the Throne Room, was empty. An immense block of grey, black and white marble, shaped roughly like the couches in Dragonriders' tents, crouched like a thunderstorm atop a dais, which rose almost to Shashtah's height above the floor. Two rows of white marble colonnades ran the length of the enormous, rectangular room. They supported the jet-black ceiling, though Shashtah felt as if the entire structure was about to cave in on him. Smoke-grey marble glistened on the walls, and black, white and grey-flecked tiles covered the floor. Shashtah had the distinct impression he was surrounded by an architectural allegory as his captors led him through the massive ebony-set-with-ivory doors at the opposite end of the room from the throne. Having little knowledge of Daethian philosophy, however, he could not interpret what the builder was trying to tell him with this oddly dark room at the center of the light-filled palace.

The Kyondoca led their prisoner to a seemingly arbitrary spot before the dais, then turned to stand at attention in mirrored ranks on either side of the hall, one warrior between each set of columns. Their lieutenant stood directly behind Shashtah, preventing all hope of escape.

There, Shashtah waited, Tkai and the orphaned girl standing next to him, until Lord Criton appeared. Shashtah later speculated that he had been expecting someone more like the magic-loving Farador to be the Lord of Daethia. Accustomed to associating Tor with Corin and the legendary School of Wizards while presently fancying that he was standing on the very stones where the Great Wizards had studied, laughed, fought, and died, Shashtah could only gawk at the otherworldly warrior who strode into the hall through an almost invisible side door and flew up the six steps of the dais to the throne with a single beat of his white-feathered wings. Shashtah's jaw dropped even further as he realized the warrior was wearing nothing more than two golden anklets, a pair of golden bracers, and his sword and scabbard. His pale, unmarked skin matched the color of the white marble with bluish grey trails tracing what Shashtah suspected were his veins. Dumnonians were not body shy, but Daethians were, so Lord Criton's appearance in no way matched what Shashtah had anticipated.

Criton, Lord of Daethia, folded his wings behind him. Fury flashed across his face as he stared directly at Shashtah. His solid sky-blue eyes looked almost normal compared to the rest of him.

Shashtah stared back.

Those eyes were all that marked the deity as a relative of either Shashtah's god or the Elven King. No crown encircled his head: He did not need one. Like the elves and the Dumnonians, and decidedly unlike his Daethian guards, Criton's body grew no hair other than eyebrows and the luxuriant, golden-brown mane that cascaded from his head. Perfectly proportioned, Criton would have been the model of the ideal Daethian in his prime, if not for his coloring and the very disturbing wings that protruded from his back. The brilliant white feathers touched with highlights of blue that covered them seemed to glow, and Shashtah had never felt more transfixed by anything in his life.

Tkai tugged at Shashtah's sleeve.

Shashtah glanced at her and realized that she was not looking at Criton. Everyone in the room had dropped into deep bows, almost prostrating themselves on the floor. Shashtah made a belated salaam to the divine warrior, then rose. "Your father sends His greetings, Lord," he blurted out in Daethian.

Tkai's gasp of dismay washed through Shashtah's mind, although she made no audible sound.

Before Criton could respond, the girl ran forward.

The lieutenant chased after her. His grasping hands closed on empty air.

The girl clambered up the steps to the throne and held up her dead father's armbands. "I'm supposed to give these to you," she proclaimed, "so you can make them work for me."

Sudden anguish swept across Criton's face. He reached down and took the bracers from the girl. "Thank you for bringing these to me. You have done well." He glanced at the lieutenant, who finally succeeded in catching the youngster. "Take her to the temple of her choice." He straightened himself and stood, eyes closed, glittering tears running down his exquisite cheeks until the lieutenant had ushered the girl out of the room. Then Criton snapped open his eyes, howled in rage and crashed the dead man's bracers together.

A bolt of blue-white skyfire shot out of the bracers and caught Shashtah squarely in the chest. He flew backward. Every muscle in his body tensed. He tried to scream, but he could not open his mouth.

Tkai screamed for him.

The echo of her shout sent a wave of bright gold light crashing through

Shashtah's mind. Then, with a sickening splat, he slammed against the grey marble wall at the back of the Throne Room, and darkness claimed him.

Bright light split the blackness, engulfing Shashtah's soul. Everyone he had ever loved and lost stood ranged across an endless plain of Light. In the midst of them stood Leot, Lord of Light, Shashtah's god, holding open his arms to welcome the weary traveler home . . .

Well, that was what Shashtah had always been told would happen when he died. Waking up alone in a cold, grey prison cell, with its dimly glowing ceiling and damp stone floor and walls, paled by comparison.

At least Shashtah assumed it was a prison cell. He was lying on a cot next to a wall in a ten-by-ten room. His feet almost blocked his view of the door. His head pointed to where a window should have been. He studied the weak magical light that clung to the ceiling like dew on a field of grass. *Underground,* he decided.

:*WE'LL BE RIGHT THERE!*: Tkai's voice promised, nearly scaring Shashtah into the Afterlife.

:*Why am I not dead?*: Shashtah ventured when he could see straight again. He sat up, groaning, and cradled his throbbing head in his hands.

:*Criton will explain,*: Tkai answered.

:*What makes you think I want to see him?*: Shashtah demanded as he removed his keffiyeh and stuck it into his belt. He retied his leather thong around his head to keep his feather-cut hair carefully over the tips of his ears.

The cell door opened in response. A young man of about twenty-five strode into the cell. He was not completely unlike the deity in the Throne Room, except he was normally colored and did not have wings. A sky-blue kilt hung around his hips, concealing his manhood, a detail for which Shashtah felt absurdly grateful. The sight of Criton in all his glory was a bit more than he was prepared to deal with at the moment. *Or at any moment,* he mused.

"You look as if you are in one piece," Criton observed in ClearTalk. His solid blue eyes scanned his prisoner with a thoroughness that left Shashtah feeling naked. "Anything missing? I didn't mean to hit you so hard, but I had to teleport ashes from the fireplace in the dining hall to the floor of the Throne Room at the same time I transported you to this cell; I guess I cut it too close. I wouldn't have even tried it if you weren't a Dragonheart. I almost didn't believe my eyes, but I was pretty sure your Dragon wasn't the Queen of Dumnonia. I don't think you've had a Dumnonian queen for quite a while, but I'm never sure about things like that. Time runs so strangely in your world. I did remember, however, that two Dragons never Bond with each other. At least I don't think they do. Then again, I don't remember anyone telling me that another Dragonheart had become king. Or are you Bahakesh?" He glanced at Tkai's humanform as she slipped into the cell. "He looks all right, but I think he's still in shock."

Shashtah stared blankly at Criton, trying to readjust his image of the inhuman Lord of Daethia to fit the wingless, babbling warrior, who stood before him.

Tkai shut the cell door and settled onto the cot beside her Rider. "This is Shashtah, Rider of Tkai, not Bahakesh, Rider of Tchang." She smiled indulgently at the deity. She snaked a possessive arm around her still-muddled Rider. "This is Lord Criton's humanform," she explained to Shashtah.

"I'm not used to appearing wingless and dressed in Daethian garb," Criton continued defensively, "but your Dragon thought it would make you feel more comfortable while I questioned you."

Shashtah tried to imagine holding this or any conversation with the winged deity he had seen in the Throne Room—and failed. Even so, Criton was still the only one holding the conversation. Shashtah had no idea what words he should even try to get in edgewise. He gave a quick nod of thanks to the deity and turned to Tkai. "Our Bond—?"

"—is fine," Tkai finished for him. "I only felt a little concern when you hit the wall. Lord Criton really was trying to be gentle with you."

Shashtah shot Tkai a look that would have peeled the hide off a lesser Dragon. "'A little concern—!'"

Tkai ignored him and smiled again at the divine warrior. "He's fine. You did excellent work, sire."

Lord Criton practically preened at her praise.

"Why," Shashtah asked Tkai in Dumnonian as he tried to recover his nerve, "didn't the Kyondoca suspect a trick if our Bond didn't break?"

"I played along by pretending that it had," Tkai replied in the same language, a smug grin on her ancient face. "I collapsed, and Lord Criton had me carried to his quarters. He joined me as soon as he dismissed his guards and brought me here so he could question us together."

"He might have tried questioning us before he executed me," Shashtah groused. He rubbed the back of his neck, doing his best to forget that the deity was still there.

Criton did not seem to notice that he was being ignored.

Tkai did, though. She patted Shashtah gently on the knee and switched back to ClearTalk. "Lord Criton is still having trouble adjusting to the Daethian mode of thought. Things move a little too quickly for him in our world. Sometimes he overcompensates."

Criton crouched so his eyes were level with Shashtah's. "You don't understand what it is to be Mirari, to be confined to this flesh that can only reflect light, to be surrounded by beings who can die faster than it takes me to walk across this room in my normal realm."

"Then enlighten me," Shashtah suggested, his head still aching from the aftereffects of the magical bolt.

Tkai squawked in protest as Criton hit Shashtah with a second bolt of light.

Shashtah philosophically resigned himself to die, admitting with his last thought that he had asked for it. But another thought followed that one. And another. And another. Slowly he realized that the magical bolt contained nothing more lethal than knowledge. A lot of it. In fact, enough knowledge to send him reeling against the cell wall. Image blurred with image as he tried to absorb millennia of frustration and an eternity of reflection from the Lord of Daethia. Finally the physical light that bound him to Criton flickered out. Shashtah closed his eyes and took a deep breath, slowly becoming aware of the pressure of Tkai's arms around him. "I'm all right," he lied. He promptly shoved all of the new information to the back of his mind as she released him. He opened his eyes and stared warily at Criton. "Maybe," Shashtah suggested in what he hoped was a reasonable voice, "you don't need to move quite so fast with me. I am a Dumnonian, not a Daethian."

"Which is why I spared you in the first place," Criton grinned dangerously. "I'm curious: What, in the name of my Father's Light, possessed a Dragonrider to transport with his Bond Partner to the capitol of the Dragonslayers?"

Shashtah suddenly realized that he might yet be executed in earnest. He put his hand on Tkai's arm to still her response. "The Elven King told me to bring you the armbands of your dead warrior and to tell you that your father has sent me to help you with your plan."

"How did Davit die?" Criton asked slowly.

Shashtah took a deep breath and tightened his grip on Tkai. "Three devils attacked him in the Great Woods." As soon as he started to tell the tale, he thought it might be best to skip over most of the details. "Your father gave me the power to free Davit's soul so he would not be condemned to serve the forces of Darkness." Shashtah hoped Criton had not noticed his slight hesitation.

Criton was apparently worse at noticing things than Shashtah was. "Thank you for the Truth." He rose, arching his shoulders as if he were flexing invisible wings. "But as far as my plan is concerned, I need the White Wolf, not a Dragonheart."

Shashtah shrugged, relaxing his hold on Tkai as he sensed the immediate danger passing. "The Elven King told me that. He said I should try to find the White Wolf for you. He thinks that somehow I can talk him into coming back."

Criton laughed, a harsh sound, tinged with bitterness and despair. "My uncle, the Eternal Optimist!" He tossed his mane of golden hair. "I don't know how you could possibly succeed where both he and I have failed."

"The White Wolf won't be expecting me to come looking for him," Shashtah ventured. "I'm only a desert warrior with no real knowledge of magic beyond a few simple spells and no power except what your father grants to me. The White Wolf might be curious enough about what I am doing in the Northern Wastes to come find me. If he does, I have a message for him from Corin that just might bring him back to Tor."

"And if you can't find him or he still won't come?" Criton demanded.

Shashtah spread his hands in a gesture of helplessness. "Then I've been instructed to let you and Farador use me in the White Wolf's place."

Criton laughed again, barely concealing his hysteria. "You honestly think you will survive trying to cast that spell with me and my uncle?"

"No," Shashtah admitted. "That's why I will try to find the White Wolf first. I am not completely suicidal. Do you have any information that might help me?"

"Not much," Criton sighed. "All the Wizards of Corin died when the City fell, except for the White Wolf, and he fled before I arrived. That's how I became the first person to sit on the throne of Tor who didn't have to kill someone for it."

"'Kill someone for it'?" Shashtah echoed. He frowned at Tkai, wondering if he had heard correctly.

Tkai smiled gently. "The Great Wizard of Corin ascended the Daethian throne by winning a 'Duel of Mages,' not completely unlike the way Dumnonians duel to become Dragonlords."

"But we don't kill each other!" Shashtah protested.

"It was different for the Wizards. They were not Bonded, and they could not afford to leave a powerful opponent alive. Corin adapted their rite for us," Tkai explained as quickly as she could. "In a 'Duel of Mages' one Wizard stood on top of one mountain, and another stood on top of a second peak. Then both of them cast spells at each other."

"On peaks?" Shashtah echoed. "No one can stand on the peaks of the Dragon's Back Mountains." The Truth finally hit him, and he gasped. "That's how Corin died!"

Tkai's smile broadened with pride at his attempt to think. "So the legend says. He lost a Duel with another Wizard."

"Lost? How? Whom?" Shashtah sputtered.

"It doesn't matter," Tkai shrugged. "We needed Corin; Daethia did not. So he arranged to die."

"He arranged to die?" Shashtah repeated, wondering yet again why on Centuria his father had kept so many stories from him. Or, perhaps, how on Centuria his father had managed the feat since Shashtah knew he had been quite the unrepentant terror who slipped away practically every chance he got.

"The Wizards actually could stand on the peaks for a short time," Tkai continued patiently, trying to regain his attention, "just as you and I didn't die instantly when we accidentally transported to one." In a Duel of Mages each Wizard was allowed a Second, and battles were only two spells long, one for each of the major combatants and one for each of their Seconds. Whoever got their spells off first usually won, and their Seconds became their consorts. The losers tended to be extremely dead, if not from their opponent's spell, then from the lack of breathable air. This encouraged quick thinking among the Wizards and lightning defenses among their chosen partners."

Shashtah rubbed his forehead. "Did it ever occur to you that the White Wolf might be afraid to return because he thinks you will kill him?" he asked Criton.

"No," Criton declared in a voice that suggested he was not considering the possibility even now. "I would give him back the throne if he wanted it. I don't think he does. I suspect he is powerful enough to have killed *me* when I first arrived if he truly coveted the title of 'Great Wizard.' I do not believe that I am the reason he ran nor that I am the reason he has not returned. The only thing I have to do with this whole mess is that I'm stuck in it."

"We all are. Like a caravan in an unstable dune." Shashtah rose and paced the width of the tiny room, testing his muscles and reassuring himself that he really was still in one piece. He noted absently that his boots had dried, probably from Criton's magic rather than from the passage of time since the leather had not grown stiff. Thinking had never been his best skill, but he was apparently better at it than Criton, even if it did make his head hurt. "Is there anything else you can tell me that might help?"

"No." Criton brightened. "But there is something I can show you. Come with me." He turned like a warrior dancing out of the way of a sword thrust, opened the cell door and led them into the narrow hall.

Countless corridors and what seemed like a thousand stairs later, Criton ushered Shashtah and Tkai through an oaken door that was carved with the image of a tree, branches soaring into a sun-filled sky and roots plunging into the secret depths of the soil.

Everything in the room was arranged with the crystalline symmetry of a snowflake. Books, shelved according to size, lined the surface of the walls. A podium with an enormous spellbook lying open to a blank page was placed in the corner to the left of the door, and a splendid brazier was positioned in the corner to the right. A polished oak-framed mirror with gold fittings stood in the far right corner of the room. A massive black marble table, lined with bronze stools, dominated the center of the chamber. Beakers, tubes, and stoppered bottles of various powders and liquids lined silver-trimmed shelves that rose from the table, within easy reach of the edge. The faint scent of smoke hung about the brazier and mingled with the smell of leather and vellum that otherwise pervaded the room.

Shashtah stared wide-eyed at what had to be the inner sanctum of one of the most elusive Wizards ever to teach at the School of Corin. *The laboratory of the White Wolf!*

"Everything is just as the White Wolf left it." Criton nodded at the podium. "Even Shane's book."

Shashtah stepped forward, trying to get a better look at the legendary spellbook that had been written by the last Great Wizard of Corin. He surveyed the pristine laboratory again. Everything so neat, so clean— "No dust? After all this time?"

Criton closed the door. ""This room is part of a time warp. You see it as it looked the moment the White Wolf left. Seems like yesterday." He looked at Tkai. "Was it?"

Tkai shook her head. "No, Lord. It was millennia ago."

Criton nodded. "That's right." He turned until he was almost touching the ancient text. "What do you know about Shane's spellbook?"

Shashtah frowned. "Just what storytellers teach around campfires. Shane wrote it for the Great Wizard who would follow her. She knew that the next Great Wizard would be born long after her death and that no Wizards would be left at the School to teach the new one. Knowledge is Power for the Wizards, so the teachers told Shane everything they knew. She recorded the stories onto those pages. The Wizards scoured all of Centuria and everywhere else their magic could take them for the materials and the knowledge to make that book."

"And in their travels they accidentally opened the way for the Dark One to come to this world," Tkai sighed.

Criton nodded. "Close enough. Only the White Wolf knows the true story. What do you know about him?"

Shashtah's frown deepened as he tried to remember the wild tales told late at night in the taverns of Krillion. "A traitor, the legends say. A white-haired, young-faced giant of a man, quick to laugh, most-favored of the teachers at the School of Corin. He brought Shane to the School and trained her to be a Great Wizard. His close friend, Cobal, became Shane's consort. But when the war with the Dark One began, the much-loved teacher betrayed the Wizards of Corin and fled over the Pass to Rashtar in the form of a white wolf. The barbarians of Rashtar sheltered him and helped him escape into the Northern Wastes where he has been hunted ever since by the students of the Wizards of Corin and, some say, by the forces of the Dark One himself."

"Yes, yes." Criton waved his hand in annoyance. "But do you know who he is?" He stared at Shashtah as if he actually expected an answer.

"As Shane was dying," Shashtah said slowly, "she forbade anyone to ever speak his name again."

Criton waved aside that detail as well. "The druids of Rashtar have a similar taboo, but they remember the true name of the White Wolf. That's not what I meant. Why is it so hard for me to communicate in this world?"

Shashtah decided that this time Criton did not expect an answer and chose to remain silent.

Criton did not seem to notice. "Look around you. Do you know who this supposed traitor is?"

Shashtah hid a wince as he realized that Criton was back to expecting him to have an actual answer. He studied the lab. Every tome ever written on the subject of magic and on hundreds of other topics lined the walls. Copies of the spellbooks of all of the Wizards of Corin sat untouched, unopened since the School had fallen. Even Shane's spellbook still lay undisturbed on the podium where the White Wolf had left it. The collection was impressive even for a Wizard as renowned as the White Wolf. Shashtah felt the pieces of the puzzle fall slowly into place. "This isn't his collection. He was the librarian of the School of Wizards. He controlled their access to their spells."

Criton nodded slowly. "Yes." He sounded more as if the answer was only now occurring to him rather than like the teacher he had seemed to be only a heartbeat before. "Corin himself supposedly brought the White Wolf to the school and taught him the discipline of magic." Criton's voice fell into the sing-song pattern of someone repeating something he had been told many times. "Student eventually surpassed master, and everyone thought the White Wolf would be appointed Great Wizard by Corin. Instead, Corin created the 'Duel of Mages,' and the White Wolf withdrew to his lab. He outlived more Great Wizards than anyone can count, yet he never aged and never became a Great Wizard himself. He knew it all: every spell that every Wizard at the School ever learned. In the end he even knew everything Shane wrote in the spellbook she composed for the next Great Wizard. Yet knowing what he knew, having the power that he had, and seeing the forces of the Dark One marching on the School, he read one page in Shane's book, destroying that information forever, then took the form of a white wolf and disappeared. If any of the Wizards could have saved the City, he had the best chance. He may have had enough power to destroy the Dark One himself. But he took one look at my dark brother and ran away. Why?"

Shashtah could not think of a good answer to the question. He could not even think of a bad answer to the question. So he shot the question back at Criton. "Why?"

Criton closed his eyes and pressed his palms against them. "If I knew that, I would not be asking you." He lowered his hands, opened his eyes and stared at Shashtah. "This room was preserved for all eternity until someone with the powers of a Great Wizard and a heart that could have compassion for the Dark One as well as hate him opened the door from the other side. Shane couldn't do it and died trying, cursing the name of the White Wolf with her last breath. I succeeded where she failed, but I still do not know why the White Wolf ran. The Elven King is certain we could win this War if we could find the White Wolf and persuade him to fight on our side. But until we know his real name, we cannot bind him with our magic, and until we know why he ran, we cannot know what argument will make him return."

Shashtah glanced at Tkai and sighed. "Ever been to Rashtar?"

Tkai shook her head, looking puzzled at the apparent nonsequiter. "No. Why?"

Shashtah's shoulders slumped. "If the Rashtarians helped the White Wolf escape, they may know where to find him. Plus I can't think of any other reason my father would have taken our caravan over the Pass unless he wanted me to know what Rashtar looked like in case I had to go there someday."

"Ah." Tkai's eyes stared into the past. "Perhaps I did prophesy to Garesh that his son would visit the Rashtarians. I didn't mean for him to take you there."

Shashtah shrugged. "It was a profitable trip."

Criton looked more perplexed than ever. "What makes you think the High Druid will reveal one of the most closely guarded secrets of his religion to a Dumnonian when he will not share that truth with either me or the Elven King?"

"I'm a messenger from Corin to the White Wolf," Shashtah said. "For all I know the Druids of Rashtar have been guarding that secret for millennia, waiting for me to show up at their tent flaps and ask."

"Perhaps," Criton agreed. "We all seem to be doing a lot of waiting around here. You at least seem inclined to do something besides sit and watch the Dark One's forces repeatedly throw themselves at our borders."

"Caravaneers don't know how to sit still," Shashtah said.

"Always moving. Always changing." Criton shook his head as if to rid his thoughts of a nightmare. "I don't understand how you creatures put up with all the coming and going. There are days I just want to lock myself in this room and make all the chaos stop." He waved his hand at the mirror.

Suddenly the image of a crystalline Temple of the White Wolf appeared in the glass.

"This," Criton explained, "is the only working magic item the White Wolf left. The Elven King showed me how to use it. I ask the mirror to locate a specific place. When the image of that place appears in the mirror, a magical path is opened. You are looking at the Temple of the White Wolf in northern Rashtar, which the High Druid guards for the Wizard whom the barbarians worship as a god. The path is two-way, so whatever is there can come here if I leave it exposed. If you would question the High Druid, step through quickly. I must seal the path after you before my dark brother realizes it is open. May the Light of my Father go with you!"

Shashtah, absurdly grateful for finally being given the chance to escape, even if it was into a half-frozen wilderness, nodded his thanks for the blessing, motioned for Tkai to follow him, took a deep breath and stepped through the mirror.

Shashtah and the White Wolf

CHAPTER 10:

Northern Wastes

As to the time of your deliverance, you know well that the Day of the Light will come in the Darkness. That the Night shall become Day will not surprise you, for you are Children of the Light; you are not of the Night nor of the Darkness. So do not sleep as others do, but keep awake. Put on the breastplate of Light, and for a helmet don the hope of victory.

—from *Dumnonian Sermons of the Light,*
by Shane of Corin

SHASHTAH PULLED KASHON'S CLOAK tightly around his shoulders as he stood shivering before the Temple of the White Wolf. The deserts of Dumnonia could grow terribly cold at night, but that was a different kind of cold from the bone-chilling freeze that held Rashtar in its icy grasp nearly all year round. Shashtah was probably no farther north than the King's Camp in his homeland, but here the blades of grass snapped like glass beneath his desert boots and frost turned his blue-black hair almost grey. He removed his keffiyeh from his belt and tied it back into place with his leather thong in a futile attempt to keep the tips of his ears warm. He vaguely remembered his father outfitting the entire caravan in heavy furs for the one trip they had made through the Pass, and his aching body was mercilessly reminding him why. He wished fervently for a campfire, but Tkai had objected, fearing that the plant-worshiping druids might take offense. *Then at least they'd be here,* Shashtah groused to himself, not caring if his Dragon was eavesdropping yet again. He circled the curious structure that stood before him, trying to figure out how on Centuria one entered the strange temple.

The blue-white surfaces of the walls refracted the light from the waxing moon into a thousand illusions. Defiant, inscrutable, and perfectly squared on all sides, the crystalline structure stood sentinel at the very edge of the forests of Rashtar. No entrance or hoped-for shelter from the bitter cold presented itself to Shashtah's searching eyes.

"What is it made of?" Shashtah wondered aloud in Dumnonian. He startled, surprised to see his breath in the air.

:*Ice,*: came Tkai's reply.

Shashtah abruptly looked around for his Dragon.

A white she-wolf blinked up at him from where it stood at his left side.

"Do you think that's wise?" Shashtah chided half-heartedly, more interested in the patterns his breath was making in the night air than in what Tkai thought.

The wolf turned in a circle, trampling the brittle grass flat before lying down. :*It's warm. You're cold. You should try it.*:

Shashtah rolled his eyes skyward as he trudged around the temple once more. "Why build a temple without a door?" he puzzled, his brain feeling as sluggish as the half-frozen blood in his veins.

:*The White Wolf wouldn't need a door,*: Tkai offered. :*He doesn't come here.*:

"Then what are we doing here?" Shashtah roared his exasperation.

The wolf absently snapped at the frost from her own breath, ignoring the question.

Shashtah sat beside her, pressing greedily against her warmth as he stared at the glacial temple. His brain did not seem to work any better in the cold than it did in the heat. The object of a temple was to offer the worshipers a place where the presence of their deity could be felt. He thought about the greatest shrine of the Dumnonians, the Valley of Ancients, but Corin's Tomb had a door. The Mother dwelt in all living things so a humble tent was sufficient for Her temple, and a tent had a flap. But the worshipers of the White Wolf had a concerted interest in making sure that their deity was never found. Providing him with a true temple would be sunstruck at best, and the druids of Rashtar were not renowned for their stupidity.

Tkai nudged him with her nose. :*You could think more like a wolf if you were one.*:

Shashtah absently scratched her right ear. "Don't badger me. I'm terrible at magic. The Light only knows what would happen if I tried something as complicated as shapeshifting."

Tkai glanced around. :*Badger? Where? Badger would taste nice. I haven't eaten since last night.*:

Shashtah laughed. "Now you think about food? Go hunt if you want. There's bound to be something edible around here."

The she-wolf wagged her tail, licked his cheek and ran off, leaving him to stare once more at the block of ice.

Without her warmth, Shashtah quickly realized that he was going to turn into a frozen statue himself unless he did something to prevent that. He stood to reduce his contact with the frigid ground. The only living things he could see anywhere near him were trees. *At least they don't seem to be bothered by the cold.* He stared intently at the shifting patterns of light on the surface of the temple. The moonlight seemed to brighten into sunshine then fade to starlight. He was dimly aware that he had stopped shivering and silently thanked Kashon for the use of his cloak. The garment had stiffened with the cold until it felt like a second skin, protecting him from the frosty air. As his shaking ceased, he found his soul stretching skyward, delighting in the thrill of the open landscape after the confining halls of Tor. He also took absurd pleasure in having his feet planted firmly on solid ground after two days of soaring through the skies on unfamiliar dragonwings. He even forgot the hunger he had felt when Tkai had mentioned food.

As Shashtah watched the glittering cube, he began to feel as if he might never move again. Something deep within him did not care, as if he had finally found the peace he had sought so desperately throughout his restless life. He was intensely attracted to this place and imagined that he might spend the remainder of his life quite comfortably staring at—

A dark wolf chased a half-elvish woman with solid amber eyes, who was dressed as a Daethian, through a Rashtarian forest. Her heart hammered wildly as branches tore at her clothes and rocks seemed to spring out of nowhere to trip her. The hypnotic footfalls of the loping wolf echoed behind her, ever closer.

Shashtah tried to leap to save her, but he couldn't move. He seemed to overbalance and topple forward, yet he felt nothing . . .

The fallen tree in the woman's path had not been there a heartbeat before.

She tripped and sprawled forward. The fall drove the air from her lungs.

Then the wolf was upon her . . .

Shashtah felt something steadying him, supporting him, pulling him upright once more . . .

A barbarian wrapped in a white-wolf pelt paced in snow outside his tent. The screams of a woman in labor shattered the peace of the night. Muffled voices spoke words of encouragement and reassurance, but their tones were fearful.

A bloodcurdling scream brought silence to the camp.

The barbarian abruptly stopped pacing and stared at the tent.

Shashtah tried to lift his arms. He belatedly decided that they were already lifted. Light shone through his fingers. He tried to direct the healing beams at the tent . . .

Something that sounded more like a pup's yelp than a baby's cry rang through the night.

The tent flap opened, and a midwife handed a basket wrapped in a white wolf skin to the barbarian. "She's dead," the midwife said. "Tore his way out of her. Do yourself a favor. Don't look. Just get rid of it."

The barbarian nodded and trudged off into the snowy night, silent tears half-freezing on his bearded cheeks . . .

Slowly, it occurred to Shashtah that he was in the throes of the most powerful vision he had ever had. Information poured into him faster than he could process it just as when Criton had hit him with a similar spell. It was almost as if he were living someone else's life. Someone else's very, very long life . . .

Corin of Daethia sat across a campfire from a white-haired lad.

The youngster had a decidedly feral look in his silver eyes.

"Very good," Corin said. "That's good enough to fool all but the best."

The apprentice's face blurred, and the whites of his eyes vanished until only silver coloring that glowed oddly in the firelight filled the space where the Daethian eyes had been. "But the best will know," the boy growled.

"They won't care," Corin assured him.

The growl became a snarl. "Why not?"

"Because I'll tell them not to" came the matter-of-fact reply.

Shashtah tried to scream. "Don't lie to the boy!"

The sound of the North Wind whipping through tree branches drowned out Shashtah's cry.

The youngster wriggled his nose. "They'll care."

"Only if you do." The words were a challenge.

The boy bared his throat to the Wizard. "Teach me. I want to learn."

Image followed image. Some of it Shashtah recognized; most of it he didn't. And very, very little of it could he understand . . .

A young, white-haired giant with solid, silver-grey eyes strolled alone through the Great Woods in the dead of night as if nothing had a prayer of harming him. He settled beside a log and unpacked the bundle he had carried strapped to his back. He set up a brazier, started a small fire, and then began to sprinkle powders into it from the assortment of pouches he had strung around his belt. He chanted magical words that seemed almost visible in the night air.

Shashtah felt the words sweeping around him, caressing his skin, causing him to sway, calling him to follow them into the night . . .

A great black panther separated itself from the darkness and screamed at him.

The young man stopped chanting and focused on the panther.

The enormous black cat chuffed.

The Wizard started to chuckle. Then he threw back his head, white hair streaming down his back, and howled his amusement to the distant stars . . .

Faces flowed through Shashtah's mind. Names from ancient legends echoed in his heart. The story seemed to seep through his veins . . .

A young woman stormed across a desolate landscape. Volcanic rock jutted at awkward angles. Bolts of blue-white light flashed from the woman's hands—

A blast of skyfire narrowly missed Shashtah, discharging into the ground beside him and sending its power coursing through him—

The woman readied another bolt.

The white-haired youth appeared out of nowhere.

A stately, dark-haired Wizard intercepted the bolt with a shield of silvery magic, sending the destructive energy shimmering harmlessly into the sky.

The great black panther, nearly invisible against the volcanic rock, curled protectively around the younger Wizard's feet.

The sound of the white-haired giant's laughter cascaded over the rocks like the roar of a waterfall.

The woman's fury dissipated in the face of his mirth, and she went to him.

Books, countless books and scrolls, innumerable stories, baffling information in languages Shashtah did not understand, all of it mingled with strange faces and unfamiliar voices and flashes of incredible power. . .

"You are my son," whispered a sickly sweet voice. *"Born of my magic, if you destroy me, you will die as well."*

Shashtah shuddered violently. Evil laughter rang in his head, scattering all of the information like snowflakes in a blizzard. Everything that is, except for the knowledge of his own soul . . .

A she-wolf scrabbled at Shashtah's bark-covered back. A squirrel crawling quickly out of a knothole that felt uncomfortably like his left ear shocked Shashtah back into the present and into his own shape. "Tkai?" he asked the wolf as the squirrel chittered angrily on his shoulder.

Tkai shifted to her humanform and hugged him close. "Thank Corin!" she exclaimed in the language of the Bronze Dragons. "When I suggested that you shapeshift, I didn't mean for you to try when I wasn't around. And I told you to become a wolf, not a tree."

The squirrel hopped off his shoulder and transformed into a white-robed man with oak-colored hair. "Trust a dog to remember what tree wasn't in the forest when she left it," the man observed in ClearTalk.

"I wasn't a dog. I was a wolf," Tkai protested in the same tongue as she hugged Shashtah tighter. "I thought I'd lost you."

"What are you babbling about?" Shashtah asked, thoroughly confused.

Tkai laughed. "You might have tried to take dragonform to start with. That should at least come somewhat naturally to a Dumnonian. But a tree—?"

"A tree?" Shashtah asked. "Are you telling me I shapeshifted into a tree?"

Tkai nodded. "I knew you were something special!" she crowed with delight. "I had to find the High Druid before I could find you." She blushed. "Well, actually I had to remember you before I could find the High Druid, but then—"

"'Remember me?'" Shashtah echoed. "What day is this?" When his companions remained silent, he amended his request. "What year is this?"

"You don't want to know," the High Druid assured him. "Shapeshifting can be a bit disconcerting when you are first learning. You are an excellent student, though. The White Wolf must be pleased with you. He was not only able to teach you to shapeshift to a very difficult form very quickly, but he was also able to teach you how to hold that shape for a very long time."

Tkai beamed. "The druids all come to this temple to learn the art. Some of them stare at the walls for a decade before they learn. You're a natural. You even got the mind-disguise part right, and that's usually the hardest thing about shapeshifting for someone to learn."

"Mind-disguise?" Shashtah tried to get his sluggish brain to work.

The High Druid grinned. "You took the form of a tree, and you thought like a tree. That's what made it so hard to find you. If you had simply shaped your body but your brain was still thinking like a Dumnonian's, I could have found you in a heartbeat."

Finally something clicked in Shashtah's head, and he felt himself wake up. "That's how the White Wolf hides from the forces of the Dark One, isn't it," he stated. There was no question in his voice. "He shapes his thoughts to the patterns of a wolf. But his companion is not so skilled. The familiar can shape his body but not his mind. That's why the Elven King told me to look for a white wolf that looks like a big, black cat."

"'Panther' would be more accurate, but you have the general idea." The High Druid helped Shashtah to his feet.

"But that seems so easy!" Shashtah protested. "Why haven't the Dark One's forces been able to find him after all these centuries?"

The High Druid waved his hand, and the glittering surface of the crystalline temple revealed the image of another, far more massive temple in the Great Woods. "That is the Southern Temple. It was built near the site where the White Wolf originally called his familiar to him. The panther still prefers to hunt down there, and, whenever the Dark One's forces get too close in the north, the White Wolf sends the animal south as a decoy. That temple and the panther's hunting grounds are what the elves are actually defending in the Great Woods. The Dark One knows that if he could capture the familiar then the White Wolf, being a Wizard, would have no choice but to come for him."

"Sands," Shashtah sighed. "How am I supposed to find a shapeshifting panther that magically transports between the Northern Wastes and the Great Woods?"

Tkai slipped her right arm around his waist, warming him with her body as she drew him closer to the block of ice. "Think like a Dragonrider," she said for what seemed like the thousandth time. "We watch for the panther to return to the Southern Temple after a hunting trip. When he vanishes to rejoin his master in the north, you and I merge an image of the familiar stepping out of a warp and into snow as seen from the air. Then—"

"Tkai!" Shashtah shrieked. "You and I nearly got ourselves killed trying to transport without knowing exactly where we were going!"

Tkai released her hold on him and threw up her hands. "Do you have a better idea?"

"No." Shashtah sat down on the ground with a crunch and frowned at the temple of ice. "We never should have left Dumnonia without going through the Training. I can't think like a Dragon. You can't think like a Dumnonian. We can't work together to save our lives let alone save anyone else's life. Sand and Dragons I can handle. Snow and wolves? I don't know where to begin."

"That's where I can help," the High Druid smiled and pulled Shashtah to his feet. "The panther went south to hunt three days ago. He will have eaten his fill and miss his master soon. At that time he will go to the

Southern Temple. From there he will transport to his master's location in the Northern Wastes. Only for the very small amount of time it takes the panther to locate the White Wolf can anything else find the Wizard. At precisely that moment mount your Dragon, turn this ring, and wish for both of you to be in the Northern Wastes where the White Wolf's panther has just appeared." He removed a rather plain gold band from a pouch and held the unassuming object out to Shashtah.

"Wish?" Shashtah took the ring.

The High Druid nodded. "It's safer than the way you Dumnonians fly through warps. Just keep it simple, though. And use ClearTalk. Wishes have a nasty habit of going very wrong if you aren't extremely careful."

Shashtah had heard enough stories about deceptive djinn around his father's campfire to make the warning unnecessary. "I'll be careful." He slid the ring onto the smallest finger of his right hand and marveled as the unpretentious band blurred and hardened into metal again as it readjusted its size to form a perfect fit. His amber eyes, glittering with curiosity, met the High Druid's flinty stare.

"The White Wolf sleeps for a purpose," the High Druid said. "The Rashtarians have respected that and shielded him. But now the Balance tips so far in the Dark One's favor, I wonder whether we have shielded him too long. Good cannot exist without Evil, and both are needed to maintain the Balance." He watched to see that his words were understood. "If you truly wish to wake the White Wolf, I can give you the means to rouse him from his slumber."

"How?"

"You should ask 'what?'" the High Druid instructed. "Can you read magic script?"

Shashtah nodded.

"Quickly, then." The High Druid muttered something under his breath, squatted and traced some lines in the half-frozen earth.

Shashtah frowned at the letters. "Ai—"

"No!" the High Druid shrieked as he obliterated the single word with a brush of his hand and surged to his feet. "Don't say it! It's the true name of the White Wolf! His enemies could use it against him if they knew!"

Shashtah flushed. "I'm sorry. I didn't know. You might have warned me."

"And alert all the forces of the Dark One to what I was about to do?" the High Druid gasped, incredulous. "Were you born yesterday? We're fighting a war against a deity!"

Shashtah suddenly found a pine needle on the ground extremely interesting. He hoped that the High Druid would take the lowering of his eyes as a sign of submission even though barely-controlled fury lashed through him. *Are we? Are we fighting against a deity? Or are our gods simply powerful Wizards who have chosen to make Centuria their battleground?* Never in his life had Shashtah questioned the divinity of his own god or of the Dark One or of Lord Criton or of the Elven King. Never had he questioned the limits of their power. So why was he questioning all of those things now? The gods, the Miraculous Ones, the Mirari, seemed to be nothing more than a family of Wizards who were squabbling almost as badly as he was bickering with Tkai, and everyone else on Centuria had been paying for that quarrel with their blood and lives and souls for millennia. Had something in the visions on the temple walls so shaken his faith that he could no longer believe in the god who used him as a conduit for so many miracles? *No, I still believe in the Lord of Light. He is not walking around on Centuria like a mortal, and I cannot deny the miracles he works through me.* Yet was Criton right? Was the elusive White Wolf really more powerful than any of the Mirari? *What of the Mother? No, she is not one of the Mirari. She is older. Something much older. I still believe in her. But the others—* Was the problem that Centuria simply had too many Great Wizards wandering around, without any of them tied to Tor? Had the loss of the School that trained them brought the War to Centuria? Did training really matter that much? *Does that pine needle belong to my treeform?*

Tkai guffawed. "You are hopeless, Dragonheart!" She wrapped her arms around him, drawing him close beneath the feeble warmth of Kashon's cloak.

The High Druid's flinty blue eyes narrowed. "Dragonheart?" He seemed to look through Shashtah. "A sleeping Dragon. A sleeping Dragon who dreams."

"A sleeping Dragon," Tkai murmured as she listened to the pounding in Shashtah's chest, "to wake a sleeping wolf."

The High Druid frowned. "But what happens when the sleepers wake?"

Tkai shrugged. "I don't know. Yet I think I would rather have my Dragonheart preaching from well-considered waking thoughts than talking in his sleep."

The High Druid chuckled. "And so would I have my wolf." He gestured at the block of ice. "Watch for the time the panther returns to his master." With that he stepped into a tree as easily as a Dragon flying through a warp and vanished.

"If," Shashtah threatened in his most deadly voice as he pulled away from Tkai, "you don't stop eavesdropping on my private thoughts, talking about me to the greatest leaders on Centuria as if I'm not even here, and refusing to listen to what I tell you to do, I am going back to Dumnonia, even if I have to walk there, and put myself under Dragonlord Dameth's command for the Training!"

"Why Dameth?" Tkai asked, completely unruffled by his outburst.

"Because," Shashtah roared, "he trained Kashon, and I didn't hear Katrell disobeying *his* Rider!"

Tkai's humanform blurred as her anger got the better of her. "Kashon's a sunstruck nit, but perhaps you would do well to emulate him: He at least knows enough to respect a member of the Council of Ancients!"

"By all that's holy," Shashtah swore, no longer certain how much that really was, "I am your Rider! At least accord me the respect you would give a pocket rat! I didn't force this Bond on you. You offered yourself to me. Now, start acting like a proper Dragon, or I'll see to it that you spend the last five years of your life learning what those words mean!"

"Last year," Tkai corrected softly.

"What?" Shashtah grew still as her words shocked him out of his tirade.

"Last year." Tkai waved a negligent hand at the forest. "You were a tree for a long time. The High Druid warned you that you didn't want to know."

"No!" Shashtah protested. "No . . . " His voice faded in despair. "I had so much I needed to learn from you."

Tkai chuckled. "The Lord of Daethia hits you with the contents of several millennia of his memory after which you spend four years as a tree on the doorstep of the temple of the greatest teacher of the Wizards of Corin, and you fret about what you could have learned?" She took his hand in hers. "Dragonheart, you have learned far more than I could ever hope to teach you." She smiled softly. "What's the one spell Cobal knew how to do better than anyone else?"

"Shield," Shashtah replied abruptly, then frowned. "How did I—?"

"Who found the Mirari and gave your god a place to exile his rebellious son without destroying him?"

"Maelor." The name was out of Shashtah's mouth before he could think about what he was going to say. He gaped at Tkai.

Sadness tinged her smile. "Every day since he fled from the School the White Wolf has faced death. Every day he has risked the possibility that the Truth would die with him. The druids of Rashtar know pieces of what happened, but none of them has ever stared at the temple long enough to see the Truth. You did it, Dragonheart, just as my Prophecy told me you would. You gave the White Wolf more than four years to tell his tale. You know it all. It's not in your head." She placed her hand on his chest. "It's in your heart."

"I don't want to know about Wizards and gods and wolves and wars," Shashtah muttered. "I'm a simple desert warrior who just wants to ride a Dragon and stay alive. I want to know what you know."

Tkai spread her hands, palms up, and stared at him. "The Northern Wastes are just another kind of desert. Only colder. Have faith, Dragonheart. When you need to, you will always know what to do."

"But—" Shashtah's response was cut off as the image of an enormous black panther shimmered on the temple's wall.

Tkai quickly shifted to her dragonform. :*Hurry!*:

Shashtah scrambled onto her back and braced his feet securely in her harness. As the panther settled atop one of the twin altars of the Southern Temple and vanished through a warp, Shashtah twisted the magical ring. "I wish for myself and my Dragon, Tkai, to be flying above where the panther of the White Wolf has just appeared in the Northern Wastes," he said in ClearTalk.

The air took on an intense chill far colder than that of Rashtar. Great vistas of glistening glaciers spread out in all directions. Snow-blinding sunlight stabbed at Shashtah's desert-adapted eyes, and he shrieked in pain. :*I can't see! I don't know where the panther is!*:

:*Relax,*: Tkai advised him. :*The panther is nearby. Your eyes will adjust. Anyone who can look into the sun of Cinnamar at midday can handle the glare of the Northern Wastes.*: She circled downward and landed on something slippery. :*Now, get off, and shift—to wolfform this time—before we both freeze to death.*:

:*I can't*—: Shashtah felt something settle into place inside his head and realized that he actually did know how to do what Tkai commanded him to do. He slid from her back to the snowy ground. His legs grow thin and powerful as his boots vanished in favor of fur-insulated pads. As his arms changed to matching forelegs, he neglected to extend his ice-gripping claws before he slipped. He fell forward onto the ice, banging his sensitive muzzle against the unforgiving surface. :*Ouch!*:

:*Stop your whining,*: Tkai's voice laughed.

Shashtah's vision cleared as he looked through the eyes of his wolfform.

In the hollow Tkai's massive body had left in the snow stood a white she-wolf, wagging her tail.

:*Come on!*: Tkai bounded out of the hollow and raced after the swiftly-fleeing forms of two magnificent white wolves.

Shashtah growled, picked himself up and sprinted after her.

They ran for what seemed like forever, chasing each other into the vast whiteness of the Northern Wastes. Some half-remembered instinct that there was safety in numbers kept Shashtah pursuing the other wolves long after he had forgotten why a desert-loving nomad was plunging through snowdrifts that came up to his chest. The desolate beauty of the Northern Wastes carried some ever-present threat of danger to wolven eyes, but Shashtah's mind could feel only vaguely uneasy beneath the pleasure-seeking, present-bound mind of his wolfform.

Suddenly Shashtah yelped and threw himself backward into a snow bank as the vast maw of an ice-blue creature opened practically in his face.

The blast of heat from the creature's innards melted the surface of the snow around Shashtah and singed his pelt.

Certain he was about to be swallowed alive, Shashtah shifted abruptly to his true form and drew his scimitar.

Somewhere above him Tkai, once more in her true form, screeched "Eternal Death to the Dark One!" in the ancient language of the Bronze Dragons. Her talons fastened on the snow monster's white-veined dorsal fins and tried to pull the living nightmare away from her Rider.

Shashtah slammed his blade upward.

Light crackled along the edge of the scimitar, and the tip bit deep into the tender roof of the creature's mouth. Inexplicably the magical light flashed once and then flickered out.

Shashtah could drive the blade no further, and he dreaded that the minor cut would only anger the beast more.

Confirming Shashtah's fears, the monstrosity, part Dragon, part a lot of things he did not want to think about, and easily as big as Tkai, roared its fury and threw itself away from its prey with blinding speed.

Tkai lost her grip on the dorsal fins and slammed into an icy snowdrift with a squawk of pain.

Agony swept through Shashtah's mind as he sensed Tkai's left wing snap under her bulk. He tried to bring up his scimitar for another blow as the creature turned on him again, but he knew in his soul that the damage to Tkai had stunned him for too long.

The snow monster arched its neck, preparing to strike.

The movement revealed a giant warrior, battleaxe in hand, who was swinging down on the beast like a blacksmith pounding on an anvil.

Time seemed to freeze for Shashtah as his half-numbed brain tried valiantly to reconcile the confusing blur of images.

The warrior was a member of the Kyondoca, golden armbands glistening brighter than the snow. But the kilt he wore was white instead of black, as were his boots. He was impossibly tall by Dumnonian standards, far closer to the Elven King in height. Snarling wolves snatched at each other from the tips of the golden torc that encircled his throat. The pelt of a white wolf hung from his shoulders like a cape, complete with the head that served as a helmet. Most startling of all, a mane of snow-white hair framed a gaunt, chiseled face and two gleaming, solid silver eyes that peered out from the mask where the wolf's eyes had been. The warrior's rage exploded in a burst of sound and power and light as his battleaxe neatly sliced the snow creature in half. "NOOOOO!" he howled.

Shashtah stumbled backward, slipped and sat down hard in the snow, gawking as the warrior proceeded to chop the repulsive creature into bits.

A huge black panther snarled as it paced nervously just outside the range of the giant warrior's swing.

Tkai melted into her humanform. As she rose, her left arm hung, useless, at her side.

Shashtah, never taking his eyes off the warrior, held out his right hand to his injured Bond Partner.

Tkai stumbled through the snow toward him.

Shashtah's fingers closed firmly on her good arm and drew her into position behind him. Then he raised his scimitar in a salute to the white-coated warrior and said in a remarkably steady voice, "I bring greetings from Corin, Ailan." Having no idea what language the Wizard favored, he used ClearTalk.

The White Wolf looked up from the carnage he had wrought, bellowed in fury at the sound of his given name, and raised his battleaxe again.

Shashtah braced himself for the blow, shivering too violently from the soul-numbing cold to hold his blade steady.

Something about the ridiculous sight of a Dumnonian clad only in a light shirt, trousers and a woefully inadequate cloak sitting in a snow bank trying to defend himself and his injured Dragon with a wildly jerking and completely useless bit of metal stayed the Wizard's hand. He lowered his axe, threw back his head, and howled his amusement at the sky.

The panther immediately darted forward and purred as he rubbed his head against the White Wolf's leg.

Ailan reached down absently and scratched his beloved pet's ear. He released his grip on his battleaxe and waved his hand in the air as he muttered something under his breath.

The temperature around Shashtah and Tkai rose noticeably. Feeling at least half-thawed, Shashtah stood up, sheathed his scimitar and dropped into a salaam.

Tkai, cradling her broken arm, bent her head regally toward the Wizard.

"Come here, Dragon," Ailan ordered softly in Dumnonian. His voice was that of a man unused to speech.

Shashtah felt an uncharacteristic wave of uncertainty from Tkai as she stepped forward and knelt before the Wizard.

Ailan touched her broken arm.

Bones reshaped themselves into their unbroken forms, and Shashtah sensed the pain vanish from Tkai's thoughts.

"Thank you," Tkai whispered as she got to her feet.

A sardonic grin curled across Ailan's lips. "Don't thank me. Your Rider has paid dearly for my aid."

Shashtah, who had not noticed anything particularly different about himself now that the beast was dead and that he was feeling almost warm, frowned. He wondered if the White Wolf meant that he would face the Council for allowing harm to come to Tkai, but the Wizard had used the past tense. *Something has already happened . . .* "I don't understand."

Ailan shrugged. "Then you must not have cared much about your scimitar or cloak."

Shashtah glanced at his blade. Something deep within him sensed that the magic that had been present in the weapon was completely gone. He touched the brooch that held the cloak closed at his neck. *The cloak was magic? Kashon is going to kill me!* He met the White Wolf's gaze. "I have never been able to retain personal items for very long."

The Wizard laughed again, a harsh sound this time. "We seem to be kindred spirits on that count. What message does Corin send? Quickly! My use of power and your calling my name has already attracted the attention of the Dark One. I will not be able to trick his underlings for long."

"The message is short," Shashtah said. "I am to tell you that Corin says it is time to come home."

Unexpectedly the Wizard laughed a third time. "Home?" He glanced down at the panther at his side. "This is my home. Everyone I treasured died millennia ago."

"And still the Dark One sends his armies against all that's left of the world you loved," Shashtah heard his own voice proclaim. *I miss the days when I knew what would come out when I opened my mouth.*

Tkai shot her Rider a wary glance but remained silent.

Shashtah tried again and was pleasantly surprised to hear the words he intended to say. "We need you. We need someone to teach us how to work together. Lord Criton is having too much trouble with the way time flows in this world to keep track of what has already happened, never mind to figure out what is currently happening or to plan for what might happen. The Elven King's power is almost exhausted from trying to protect and preserve everyone who is hiding in and around the Great Woods. Dumnonia has Corin's spirit trapped in a tomb where he can do nothing more than send out strange orders or obscure Prophecies every time we send in a Pair for him to Bond. We need someone who has the power and the brains to pull us together. Unless you return—"

"If I return," the White Wolf snapped, "what little you have left will be lost."

"Corin thought you could help," Shashtah persisted, his voice sounding petulant.

"And what would you have me do?" the White Wolf snarled. "Render Shane's spellbook a useless stack of vellum the moment I cast my first spell in Daethia's defense? Or perhaps you would rather I collapsed the magical walls of the Elven Kingdom? Or would you prefer it if destroyed the enchantments on Corin's Tomb? Since Shane cursed me as she died, I can only cast a spell if I drain the most powerful magic around me that belongs to someone else. How much magic like that do you have that you are willing to spare?"

Shashtah felt his shoulders slump. "I don't know anything about that kind of magic. All I know is how to make a trade. If you will not help Lord Criton and the Elven King with the spell they need to cast, then I must return to Daethia and offer myself as a poor substitute in your place." He turned and started to trudge southward through the snow. He flinched as he left the warm spot and once again felt the bitter chill of the northern air.

"Please, Dragonheart," the White Wolf called. "Understand."

Shashtah stopped and stepped back into the area that had been warmed by the White Wolf's magic. "Understand what?"

Ailan stared at the bloody mess in the snow. "The price I pay to give you any hope of defeating the Dark One is to live a life alone. A very, very long life alone. If I return, you all will die."

"We are dying anyway," Shashtah countered.

The White Wolf's silver stare pierced Shashtah's soul. "I will not fight against the Dark One." He picked up his battle axe. "Nor will I help him fight against you."

Shashtah's head jerked up so fast his neck cracked. "That's how that spell on the door to your lab works."

Ailan nodded. "The Dark One and I will only destroy each other if we fight. All I can do is buy you the time you need to solve the problem on your own." He looked up as bands of magical light streamed across the sky. "Shane wrote her spellbook for the Great Wizard who would come after her. Someone named Miranda, 'Miracle Worker', a woman of Mirari blood. Criton must take Farador's daughter to wife. I know it will cost you all dearly, yet that path causes the least pain for those who can still fight. My return could easily cost you your souls."

The panther suddenly hissed as dark shadows began to appear in the ribbons of light.

The White Wolf stiffened. "I have stayed too long!"

Shashtah felt his heart quiver as the shadows resolved themselves into demons. "They fly by day!"

"Criton's magic is weakening more!" Tkai squawked.

"Flee!" the White Wolf ordered as he shifted to his wolfform.

The panther blurred into a mirror image of the White Wolf and fled in the opposite direction.

Tkai instinctively followed the panther's example and ran along another path. :*Help him, Dragonheart! The vision of the demons will be poor in the sunlight. They must not capture the White Wolf. Lead them away!*:

Shashtah abruptly dropped into wolfform and sprinted south.

Shashtah soon forgot where he was heading and why. He ate what prey crossed his path and slept when he needed to. The rest of the time he ran toward the power that tugged at his heart.

Snow drifts eventually gave way to solid ice and finally to frozen sand. The sand warmed, the ice vanished and Shashtah's wolfform became too hot. He shifted back into his true shape and glanced around him, searching for anything that might seem familiar.

All he saw was dunes and gassis and wadis and kavirs and the desolate and terribly beautiful landscape that he knew was Dumnonia. Where in Dumnonia, though, he had no idea. *How much time have I lost?* The thought cut through his mind like a sirocco.

Shashtah scanned the horizon with his darkened amber eyes. There were no Dumnonians, no Dragons, no caravans, nothing. He was completely and utterly alone, a feeling he had never thought to have again since—

Where is Tkai?! The terrifying question gripped Shashtah's heart. He still felt the glitter of their Bond, but it had grown very dim. :*Tkai?*: he called uncertainly.

A silent shriek of horror from the bowels of far-off Mount Cinnamar was the only response.

Shashtah and Peri

CHAPTER 11:

Broken Bond

No one shall be able to comfort the Rider who survives a broken Bond nor shall the sufferer drink from the cup of consolation. For such a being shall be a creature of sorrow and acquainted with grief until the Lord of Light shall reform the Bond in the Afterlife.

—from *The Dumnonian Code,*
by Corin of Daethia

TKAI'S MENTAL SCREAM tapped into an instinct hidden deep within Shashtah's heart. His clothes hardened into bronze scales. Massive leather wings sprouted from the powerful muscles in his shoulders. His mighty arms and legs grew even stronger, and razor-sharp talons curled from where his fingers and toes had been. He leapt into the air. The sharp crack of his tapering tail echoed the thunderclap of the downstroke of his wings. His long neck thrust his reptilian head into the wind. He opened his fanged jaws and bellowed more in fury than in surprise as he completed his shift to dragonform.

As soon as he had climbed a few dozen wingspans above the sand he called to mind the appalling silhouette of Mount Cinnamar. He knew every crest and gully by heart, having crawled over most of them at one time or another. With a roar of defiance he willed himself into the air above the mountain.

Briefly a second image blurred over his. As the two fused, Shashtah's lungs filled with the superheated air in the skies above the Dark One's prison. He pointed his snout toward the sand and dove. He landed near the opening he had used what seemed like only a few days before though it had been five years ago. He considered his options for a heartbeat, then shifted to batform and slipped inside.

Instinct and the pull of his Bond with Tkai drew him through the algae-covered corridors and into the depths of Mount Cinnamar. Demons and devils alike ignored him as he flew toward the source of Tkai's screams. Before he could reach her, the shrieks stopped. He clung to the ceiling a moment until a sense of steadily-growing discomfort replaced the sharp agony that had caused the screams. He dropped to the floor, shifted to ratform, and scurried along the tunnel until he came to a cell door.

The door creaked open, and he scuttled inside, narrowly avoiding the talonned feet that threatened to skewer him as something too massive and too unpleasant for his ratform to comprehend strode out into the hall. The door slammed shut, locking him inside.

Shashtah sniffed the air, scenting blood, urine, rotting flesh, decaying vegetation and a hundred other unpleasant smells. He sneezed, brushed his whiskers with his forepaw and scampered a few feet to the right of the door. He rose on his haunches and glanced around the cell.

The cell was enormous from a rat's point of view. At least he could not see the walls. He could, however, hear someone moaning somewhere in the darkness. He scurried across the cell floor until he found something that looked vaguely like a human-shaped lump. He blamed the strange proportions on his rat's-eye-view of the world and shifted back to his humanform. His heart froze when the proportions did not change. :*Tkai* ....: The name whispered through his mind like a lone falcon on a faint desert wind.

The Ancient Prophetess focused on him and screamed, unable to recognize him through her pain.

:*Hush!*: Shashtah cautioned as he sat cross-legged on the floor and tried to gather her head into his lap. :*It's me. Shashtah. I am here. You are not alone. I will help you. Just tell me what's wrong.*:

Tkai's hands flew to her grotesquely swollen belly as she screamed again.

Wave after wave of pain washed through Shashtah's mind. He pulled Tkai's writhing body into his powerful grasp. He positioned her so she faced away from him and held her arms tightly against the pain. :*Breathe! You have to breathe!*:

Tkai tried to breathe, but the effort was almost too much for her.

Why won't miracles happen when I want them to? Shashtah swore. :*What did this to you? Which devil? I'll slay it! I give you my—*:

:*The demons caught me after the rest of you ran,*: Tkai's voice whispered in his head, almost too far away to hear. :*They brought me to the Dark One. He experimented on me himself, taking shape after shape of dragon after dragon.*:

:*Stay with me, Tkai!*: Shashtah ordered. :*Talk to me! Tell me how to help you!*:

:*There's no helping me, Dragonheart,*: Tkai replied so softly he could barely make out the words. :*Help my son.*:

:*Your son?*: Shashtah hugged her close, burying his nose in her damp white hair. :*Where is he?*: He wondered absently what had happened to her veil.

:*He will be here soon,*: Tkai's voice tried to smile. :*Unfortunately Dragons usually lay eggs instead of give birth—*:

:*Give birth?*: Shashtah echoed. :*Just change to something that won't have trouble—*:

:*Don't you think I've thought of that?*: For that instant, as she argued with him, her mental voice sounded almost as loud as it once had. :*I wasn't carrying fertilized eggs when the Dark One mated with me! He trapped me in my humanform!*: Tkai wailed as another wave of pain hit her.

Shashtah felt her consciousness start to slip away from him. :*No! Tkai! Stay with me!*:

Tkai's mental shriek almost caused him to black out as her abdomen finally stretched beyond its limits and started to tear.

:*I need you,*: Shashtah said.

:*Save my son*.: Tkai's voice whispered, growing ever fainter. :*Dragonheart . . . !*:

The golden shimmer of their Bond flared. Millions of memories danced in the light, tracing their patterns in Shashtah's mind. Faces without names, places he had never seen, songs he heard long ago through dragonears, all of the sights, sounds, smells, tastes, and sensations of over a millennium of life echoed through him. His vision blurred, and his breath faltered as he tried to assimilate the information. The glittering knowledge stopped as suddenly as it had begun.

:Now you know everything I had to teach. Please, kill me!: Tkai begged. :Don't let me die like—: The tear in her skin widened, cutting short her thought.

Shashtah shook his head. :I'm already starting to forget!:

:We all forget,: Tkai lamented. :My life is over. Please. I'm too weak. End it for me, and save my son! Shaharadesh will want to kill him because he is a mutant. But the Dark One's magic can only change the physical body, not the soul.: She twisted and pulled away. She knelt before Shashtah, tears of pain and sorrow in her eyes. :Look at what he did to me, Dragonheart! He could destroy my body, but he could not change my soul! Not my soul!: She shuddered violently in utter agony. :KILL ME! LET ME GO!: The Ancient Dragon's voice screamed through Shashtah's mind.

Before Shashtah could think, he scrambled to his feet, drew his scimitar and slashed it through her rib cage, slicing her heart in two.

Tkai gasped. :Thank you, Dragonheart.: She smiled up at him. :You are the best Rider I have ever borne.: Then her amber eyes glazed over, and she lay still.

Shashtah staggered as if a thunderclap had struck inside him. He wrenched his scimitar out of Tkai's body. Blinding light flared behind his eyes, searing the inside of his skull. He doubled over, clutching his head between his fists, oblivious to the hilt of his scimitar. There was no escape from that light. It swirled through his mind like a sandstorm on a kavir. No rock offered him shelter. He found no tree to anchor him.

Shashtah had no way of knowing how long he knelt beside Tkai's corpse before he felt the tiny, blood-covered muzzle nudging at his neck.

The light finally vanished, leaving him lost in darkness and silence as he opened his eyes.

The putrid-green Hatchling, glistening with the blood of his mother's disemboweled body, regarded him with sparkling eyes and warbled his concern.

Shashtah scrabbled backward against the stone wall. Tkai was right. Shaharadesh would have killed the corruption on the spot. Shashtah raised his scimitar to strike, but the memory of Tkai's plea stayed his hand: Save my son! Shashtah dropped his weapon and took the Hatchling's head in his hands. "Oh, child! What has he done to you?"

"Peri!" the Hatchling squeaked in the tongue of the Bronze Dragons. "I am Peri!"

Shashtah winced. He glanced at where Tkai's body should have been.

Her corpse had vanished, but her son clung to him.

Claws on algae-covered flagstone sounded in the hall.

Shashtah swayed to his feet, hauling Peri up with him.

The Hatchling instinctively shifted into the form of a small boy with solid, moldy-green eyes so he would be easier to carry.

Shashtah wrapped Kashon's cloak tightly around them. As the key turned in the outer door he called to mind an image of Tkai's humanform and willed himself and Peri to be with her.

Another image briefly joined his own.

Shashtah found himself standing in the Valley of Ancients. Tkai's gutted body lay a few feet from him. Sorrow tearing at his heart, he reached down and touched the corpse. He smiled grimly as it reverted to its unmarred dragonform.

A hand with a Dragon-shaped ring caressed the line of the dead Prophetess's jaw. Flame leapt from fingertips, and Tkai's body crumbled into ash among the remains of her ancestors.

Suddenly Shashtah heard howls of pain and rage fill the desert air, grating against his raw psyche. He swayed dangerously. He closed his eyes and tried to stay erect as he clutched Tkai's son.

Peri held his breath but made no sound.

"Give me the mutant," Shaharadesh's disgusted voice ordered from somewhere in the vicinity of Shashtah's right elbow.

Shashtah shook his head in violent refusal. He instantly regretted the action. Pain lanced through his mind like a freshly forged Galantite sword sheering through ice. His humanform had not eaten solid food for longer than he could remember, and, with the lurch his stomach gave, he was glad. He briefly contemplated turning into a tree again but forced himself to maintain his true form for fear he might drop Tkai's son. The dragonboy with putrid green eyes. The repulsive product of the Dark One's magic that Shaharadesh wanted to kill. Shashtah tried to open his eyes, but, instead, shut them tighter against the blinding midday sun and the panel of unforgiving judges he knew lined the canyon walls.

"We will excuse your present disobedience," Makara observed generously in the ancient tongue of the Bronze Dragons, "since your Bond-Break is new. But the fact that you let the Dark One capture the Leader of our Council, our greatest Prophetess—"

"Makara, you knew Tkai as well as any of us. She let herself be captured. He couldn't have stopped her if he'd tried."

Shashtah gasped for air at the sound of Garesh's voice raised unexpectedly in his defense. *My father speaks for me . . .*

"You are not qualified to judge this one, Garesh," one of the other Ancients declared. "He is your son."

"There is no Dumnonian nor Dragon who is unrelated to any of us or one of our former Riders!" Garesh roared. "We sit on the Council precisely because we are the eldest and have ties to all!"

"The point is," another judge intoned, "that the Dragonheart was not around to try to stop Tkai."

Slowly the realization seeped through the wall of pain inside Shashtah's head that he was on trial for killing Tkai. Four judges had spoken. That left—

"He should have gone through the Training," another Ancient whined. "He would have known better than to risk a Bond-Break if he had."

"Isn't a Bond-Break punishment enough?" an Ancient Female argued.

"Besides, it's the king's fault for not forcing him to undergo the

Training before he left," an imperious male declared.

"My Rider could not have stopped a Dragonheart and a Prophetess, and you know it!" Makara snapped as the accusation veered too near Shaharadesh.

"Then kill the mutant," the final judge pronounced, "and call the Dragonheart atoned."

"No!" The scream tore from Shashtah's throat as he forced his eyes open. Nothing would come into focus. "Tkai's last wish was that her son should live!" He appealed to Shaharadesh. "I will raise him. He will be no burden to you. If by sparing his life I am committing an unpardonable sin, then let me bear the punishment for that. His soul is pure, even if his body is not. Tkai gave her life that he might be born. He is a Prophet, just like she was. I know it!" He angled his face skyward so it could be seen by the merciless Dragons who lined the edges of the cliffs. "How many Prophets do we have left? We cannot afford to kill another one!"

Shaharadesh closed his eyes against what must have been a violent protest from Makara. After several dozen heartbeats he opened his eyes and appealed to the Council. "Honored Ancients, the Dragonheart is fighting to save the life of a Dragon who holds no value to you, a life that was created at the expense of your Council Leader. I submit that the horrors he will encounter trying to raise this aberration will more than atone for allowing the creature to live. Further, I submit that the breaking of a Bond is no small thing to bear and that this pain and the dissension in your own ranks should be considered in connection with whatever punishment you choose." He leaned closer to Shashtah. "I'm sorry, Dragonheart," he whispered in Dumnonian. "All I can do is remind them of your point of view. I have no other power. Your fate is in their talons."

The Council of Ancients argued silently and briefly among themselves, then Garesh and the sympathetic female soared down to the valley floor and stared up at Makara in outright rebellion.

Makara motioned for Shaharadesh to step away from Shashtah.

The king complied.

"If," Makara ruled in the ancient language of the Bronze Dragons, "you can maintain your hold on the mutant, he may live."

"You feel true grief," the sympathetic female beside him affirmed.

"You make no excuse," a vaguely familiar Ancient Male intoned.

"You seek no mercy," another male declared.

A female judge shook her head with dismay. "You admit your error."

"You understand what is needed," Tlee agreed.

"You entrust yourself to us," Garesh concluded.

"It is decided," Makara informed him. "Your punishment, for allowing the Dark One to slay Tkai, Prophetess and Leader of the Council of Ancients, now begins." As she finished the sentence, she opened a scroll and began to read.

A wracking pain swept through Shashtah's soul. His grip on Tkai's son tightened as he convulsed.

Peri screamed. Then he seemed to sense what was wrong. He threw his tiny arms around Shashtah's neck, and pressed his lips close to the nomad's ear. "I am with you," he whispered. "Hold onto me as tightly as you need to. I am a Dragon. You cannot hurt me. Do not let go!"

Shashtah cackled insanely as he fancied he heard Tphah's voice. :*I am with you, Dragonheart. Have courage! My soul will help yours keep its shape.*:

:*No one will harm you physically, my son,*: Shashtah imagined Garesh's voice assuring him. :*You only need to fight the spell. I will protect you from everything else.*: He sensed that his father's dragonform had curled around him, shielding him as he would have protected a dragonegg.

Katrell's voice seemed to echo through Shashtah's head as well. :*Hold on to what you love. I will help you as you have helped me.*:

Shashtah sank to his knees but maintained his grip on Peri. The pain in his spirit fought with the pain in his head and, even with the support of the Dragons, the illusory torture eventually won. The darkness and loneliness he had felt at Tkai's death vanished in the wake of the all-consuming agony that raked at his heart more surely than Yapada's flail had ever flayed his back. He must have cried out, but sound had no meaning to him. His breath came in great, wracking sobs. Shashtah wanted nothing more than to just lie down and die, but he remained on his knees and did as the White Wolf had taught him at the temple in Rashtar. He kept control of his power and stayed in his true form, neither Dragon nor Dumnonian, somehow both.

An eternity later the pain stopped and friendly hands gently pried Peri from Shashtah's grasp. "It is over. I'll protect him until you are well," Kashon's voice promised.

Powerful, scale-covered arms hefted Shashtah's limp form.

Shashtah felt the unmistakable rush of air as a Dragon carried him into the sky. He dangled lifelessly from the creature's gentle talons. He had no idea which Dragon it was. His father, Katrell, Tphah, one of the others . . . he did not care. A Dragon was taking him back to the King's Camp. Probably to a Healer's Tent. His life was no longer in his control, and there was nothing he could do about it. Too exhausted to fight the darkness any longer, he gave up and mercifully blacked out.

When Shashtah regained consciousness, he was lying on a cot in a Healer's Tent, unable to move and having no real desire to try. Dark blue tapestries, devoid of decoration, were lowered in an attempt to keep out the blinding light of the sun. The tent was considerably smaller than those assigned to Riders, which probably explained why his was the only cot. He was still fully dressed, except for his keffiyeh. His thong had been retied tightly around his head, and he fancied that the thin strip of leather was all that was keeping his skull from flying apart.

Katrell sat on blue silk pillows near the foot of the cot, playing with Peri's humanform, while Kashon applied a cold compress—the missing keffiyeh dipped in water—to Shashtah's right temple.

"You sure you want to be awake?" Kashon asked. "I could ask a Healer for a potion to make you sleep, or I could cast a spell that would have the same effect."

The left corner of Shashtah's mouth twitched. "No magic. I've had too much magic. I want nothing to do with magic for the rest of my life." He sighed, knowing that the words were untrue the heartbeat they passed his lips. He could see the understanding and sympathy of one who really knew his pain in Kashon's eyes. "I'll stay awake for a while. At least this nightmare won't keep changing on me." He resettled himself on the cot. "How long have I been out?"

Kashon sponged Shashtah's forehead. "Only a few candlescars. You have the constitution of a Dragon, my friend."

Shashtah tried to laugh and decided it was a bad idea.

"Thirsty?" Kashon asked.

Shashtah made the mistake of trying to nod.

"Easy," Kashon murmured. He produced a wineskin from somewhere beneath the cot and propped Shashtah up enough to drink.

Shashtah coughed slightly in surprise as he recognized the taste of fruit juice.

Kashon smiled. "Did you really think the Healers would let me give you anything else?"

"At least it's not broth." Shashtah groaned as his friend laid him back onto the cot. "How's Peri?"

Kashon flashed a troubled look at the dragonboy, who had just won a round of a child's sign language game with Katrell. "Peri, Shashtah wants to know how you are."

Peri scrambled to his feet, rushed to the side of the cot and gripped Shashtah's arm. "Dragonheart! You saved me!"

Shashtah flinched at the too-loud outburst but managed to raise his hand and touch the child's cheek. "It is wise for you to stay in humanform until I am strong enough to defend you."

"He could shift to the form of a Bronze Dragon," Kashon suggested, "instead of—"

"No." Shashtah closed his eyes as everything began to swirl around him. "Everyone knows what he is." He found that having his eyes closed made his dizziness worse, and he opened them again. "I don't want people to mistake him for something he is not. Tphah—." He let the name of his prophesied future-Dragon hang in the air between them like an unasked question.

"She's outside," Kashon said softly. He smoothed Shashtah's hair away from his face. "I didn't know if you were ready to see her yet."

"I'm not," Shashtah said. "But I do want to know if she's all right."

"She's upset. All the Dragons are. So are their Riders." Kashon gripped his friend's shoulder, simply letting him feel his presence. "Shaharadesh had to call every Bonded Pair back from Mount Cinnamar where they'd transported to try to help you. You were in the Valley, facing the Council, before we realized what had happened. We still want to avenge our Prophetess, but the king is right: We have a better chance of doing that if we pay attention to defending the King's Camp and our own front line than if we all vanish into Mount Cinnamar like a troop of nit-witted mongooses down a thousand different snake holes."

Shashtah stared at the roof of the tent. "There's something I need to do." He focused on Kashon's troubled eyes. "I can't Bond with Tphah before then. I think I may be the weak link in the spell I must cast with Lord Criton and the Elven King against the Dark One. If I fall victim to the pain that we intend to visit upon him, I don't want Tphah to endure it, too. But Corin has the stone, and I can't think of any way to get it back except by Bonding again."

Kashon smiled grimly and held out his hand to Katrell.

Katrell gripped the proffered hand with visible distress that somehow failed to reassure either Dragon or Rider.

Shashtah swore. "I'm sorry. I didn't mean to—"

Kashon released Katrell and laid his fingers on Shashtah's breast, silencing him. "You can believe me when I say I understand."

Shashtah nodded and drew Peri closer in a partial embrace. "So Tphah is all right?"

Kashon grinned, trying to lighten his friend's mood. "'All right' doesn't really describe her. Superb? Stunning? Exquisite? What do you think, Katrell?"

Katrell actually blushed. "She grew up well," he offered practically.

Kashon gave an amused snort. "You can be more profuse than that in your praise, you nit! I promise I won't be jealous." He beamed at Shashtah. "The only Dragon I have ever Trained; the best I've ever seen," he declared. "She is truly worthy of you, Dra—" He caught himself. "Shashtah."

Shashtah's mouth twisted into a bitter grin. "But am I to be trusted with her?"

"I would trust you with Katrell's life," Kashon swore solemnly. "I already have."

Shashtah searched Kashon's face for a hint of humor. He found none. "Who am I to inspire such faith?"

Peri answered, "You are a Dragonheart. You understand both Dumnonians and Dragons."

"I don't understand anything." Shashtah met Kashon's gaze. "Is Tphah going to think I'm some kind of monster if I sleep a while longer before I see her? I don't want to cause her any distress."

Kashon pressed the damp keffiyeh to Shashtah's forehead once more. "Tphah wants whatever is best for you. I am sure sleep is much higher on the list of things the Healers want you to do right now than confronting her is." He adjusted the blanket that covered his friend.

Shashtah wondered why he needed a blanket in what should have been blistering heat. *Perhaps a Healer put a chilling spell around me to help my head.* He glanced at Kashon. *Or perhaps Kashon did?* he thought, suddenly remembering Kashon's offer to cast a sleeping spell. *I can only work a few simple spells, and even those I don't do well. But what about him? How much magic does he know?* Shashtah decided that his head hurt too much to try to answer the question. He closed his eyes. "Thank you."

"No thanks are necessary." Kashon disengaged Peri from Shashtah and handed the dragonboy back to Katrell. "This is just my turn to care for you." He placed Shashtah's arms gently on the cot, making sure that he never, even for a heartbeat, broke his contact with him.

Shashtah felt a silent prayer of gratitude whisper through him for Kashon's reassuring presence, and, a few unsteady breaths later, he drifted into a troubled sleep.

When Shashtah awoke again, he was alone with Katrell. "Where's Peri?"

Katrell held Shashtah's hand firmly as he sat beside him. "Kashon took him outside Camp so he could practice using his wings. He needs to exercise his dragonform or he will never fly. Kashon will make sure they are not seen."

"Why didn't you take him?" Shashtah asked.

Katrell smiled sadly. "I know more about Bond-Breaks than my Rider does." He laid the fingers of his free hand gently on Shashtah's forehead. "I know the pain never goes away completely, but is it any less?"

Shashtah smiled up at Katrell's worried amber eyes. "Don't fret so. I'm doomed to live, remember?"

Katrell took the damp keffiyeh and sponged the sweat from Shashtah's face and chest then pressed the moisture to his patient's lips. "I wish I could heal you the way you healed Kashon."

Shashtah pushed the cloth away from his face. "Please, don't be so upset," he begged. "I will heal in time."

"I haven't," Katrell confessed. "I've had so many Bond-Breaks I can barely think straight. I don't know why Kashon puts up with me." He glanced at the entrance to the tent.

"Kashon loves you," Shashtah assured him. "Besides, Tkai—" he choked on his dead Dragon's name—"always told me that Dumnonians don't depend on our heads. We depend on our hearts."

"That's probably why Bond-Breaks affect us differently," Katrell mused, "why it is easier for us to form another Bond than it is for a Dumnonian." He fell silent for a moment. "It is different this time, though. All the Dragons are more upset than usual. Those with Riders fear for their Bond Partners. Those without Riders fear for the surviving Council members and Tphah." He dropped his eyes to stare at a felt rug on the floor. "She's the only Prophetess we have left."

Shashtah wondered why Katrell seemed to want him to do something about that problem now. "Peri's alive," he offered.

"You know as well as I do that he is never going to be accepted as one of our own," Katrell countered. "If even I can figure that out, we have a serious problem. I have some trouble with him myself, but I make the effort to please you."

Shashtah smiled at Katrell's frankness. "You please me. You and Kashon both do. Very much."

Katrell glanced at the entrance again, frowning.

Shashtah followed his gaze. "Tphah?"

Katrell looked mortified. "I'm sorry! My Rider didn't want you to know. She's trying to be patient and obey your wish not to see her, but she's frightened and still very young by Dragon standards. I suggested that she go find a cave and sleep for a few rotations until you are well, but she won't listen to good dragonsense."

A soft smile curled across Shashtah's lips. "No, I don't imagine she will." He squeezed Katrell's hand. "That's what you are trying to tell me. You want me to see her."

"Kashon is going to be furious with me," Katrell fretted. "I shouldn't have said anything. I'm such a nit. Too many Bond-Breaks. Too many. I don't have the brains the Mother gave a sunstruck she-lizard." He glanced at the tent flap a third time. "Tphah . . . "

"Will you stop fussing and call her in?" Shashtah said with a conviction he did not feel.

Katrell heard the false tone and gave Shashtah a skeptical look. "You feel up to seeing an UnBonded Dragon who is madly in love with you and who is a close relative of the Dragon you just lost?"

"Of course I don't," Shashtah admitted, "but I don't want to cause her any more distress. The Council might not be as understanding as you and Kashon."

Katrell paled visibly and glanced at the tent flap yet again.

The flap covering the entrance trembled for a heartbeat, then a supple, young hand drew the fabric aside.

Shashtah took a deep breath and held it.

The Dumnonian maiden who glided into the tent bore scant resemblance to the gawky teenager he had left behind half a decade before. She stood perhaps two fingers shorter than he would if he had been able to stand. Silky black hair fell in great waves beneath her immaculate veil. Sculptured features surrounded a pair of glistening amber eyes that stared at the world with infinite wisdom. Her mischievous mouth parted slightly in surprise as she focused on him. She hovered beside the entrance, uncertain of her welcome, her white gown clinging suggestively to not-quite generous breasts and hips. A deep blush turned her flawless skin the color of burnished bronze.

Shashtah felt tension lance through Katrell at the mere sight of her. A single glance told him that if Tphah's desires had not been firmly fixed elsewhere Kashon might have had some serious competition for Katrell's affections. Shashtah's own gaze fastened on Tphah, devouring her. She might have taken her humanform from his deepest fantasies, so closely did she resemble his imaginary perfect Priestess of the Mother whom he had spent his life searching for and never found. "Sands!" Shashtah exclaimed, cursing at his own weakness. "Kashon has every right to be proud of you!"

A little smile of pleasure flitted across Tphah's inviting lips, vanishing as quickly as it had appeared. She lowered her eyes and stared dutifully at the rug. "Forgive me," she murmured in a voice that slipped through every defense Shashtah had tried to prepare and sent fire raging through his battered soul. "I have been told that you are doing as well as could be expected, but I had to see for myself. I'll go—"

"No!" Shashtah was as startled as Katrell at his protest.

Katrell quickly released his patient's hand and withdrew to the foot of the cot where he settled and let his fingers rest on Shashtah's boot.

Tphah raised her long-lashed eyes. "You don't have to be generous with me, Dragonheart. I behaved abominably toward you the last time we met."

"Come sit beside me," Shashtah ordered.

Tphah's eyes flashed with quickly-hidden delight as she slinked over to him and perched on the edge of his cot.

Katrell discretely removed his hand from Shashtah's leg and averted his eyes.

"Thank you for giving me those few precious years with—" Shashtah's voice cracked, and the sorrow and loneliness inside his head threatened to engulf him.

Katrell's hand instantly tightened around Shashtah's ankle.

Tphah gathered Shashtah into her arms and pressed him firmly to her breast. "Grieve for her, Dragonheart. We all do."

Lost and falling into darkness, Shashtah was only dimly aware of the great sobs that shook his body as Tphah's arms supported him and Katrell's hand provided him with an anchor against the emotional storm. Slowly the pain caused by the loss of Tkai lessened and a strange lethargy began to seep through Shashtah. He almost gave in to that insidious calm, but the firm presence of the Dragons drew him back to consciousness and an ache he suspected would never go away.

Tphah's exquisite hand brushed the tears from his cheeks.

Magical light flickered across Shashtah's eyes. His vision cleared, and fire of a different kind flared within him as he watched Tphah's rose-colored tongue lick the moisture from her fingers. With dismay Shashtah noted the despair that clouded Katrell's eyes. Before he could say anything Kashon burst in and dove for Katrell.

"What's wrong?" Kashon demanded.

Katrell released Shashtah and curled into his Rider's embrace. "I don't want to lose you, but I will someday, unless you lose me, and I don't want you to lose me and become like—" The incoherent babble stopped as he buried his face against Kashon's neck.

"Hush!" Kashon whispered. "Silly nit. Nothing's killed me yet. I may still defy the odds and live forever." His voice echoed with the emotion of a long, intimate dispute. He kissed Katrell firmly on the forehead.

Katrell, forgetting his dragonstrength in his need, twisted in Kashon's embrace, threw his Rider backward onto the pile of pillows, pinned him to the ground and pressed his mouth firmly against the startled but thrilled Dragonrider's lips.

Shashtah felt his soul shiver at the power of their Bond. He looked away—and made a small, inarticulate noise as his spotted Peri, who was standing just inside the tent flap, biting his lip to keep from crying out.

Tphah followed Shashtah's gaze and gasped as she saw the child. She held out a hand to him. "Peri! Come here!"

Peri ran to her and scrambled onto her lap, throwing his small arms around her slender neck.

Tphah balanced Peri in her right arm and keeping her left arm planted firmly across Shashtah's breast. She teasingly snapped at the dragonboy's nose with her perfect white teeth.

Peri giggled and relaxed into her embrace.

"Did you have fun using your wings?" Tphah asked.

Disappointment flooded Peri's features. "I didn't get very far off the ground."

Tphah favored him with a reassuring smile. "None of us do at your age. You'll learn."

Katrell and Kashon collected themselves, rose to their feet and stood, arm-in-arm, grinning sheepishly.

Tphah arched her eyebrow in mock disapproval. "Will you two nits take your antics outside? We have a patient who needs to rest."

Kashon suddenly sobered and looked abashed. "I'm sorry—"

Shashtah waved aside the apology. "It's my fault. I'm the one who upset the Dragons this time," he said with a bitter laugh.

Katrell's arm tightened possessively around his Bond Partner's waist, but Kashon's features were unreadable.

"Don't you think you can trust me with him," Tphah challenged her Trainers, "long enough for you two to go find a quiet dune somewhere and wrestle each other into submission?"

Kashon threw Shashtah a questioning glance, fully ready to shove aside his own needs and those of his Dragon at a single word from his exhausted friend.

"Go on," Shashtah said. "I won't crumble into ash and blow away while you're gone. Tphah and Peri can save me from any nightmares, and if anything comes up that they can't handle, I'm sure a Healer is only a shout away."

Delighted at the prospect of defending his hero, Peri crawled out of Tphah's lap and sprawled on top of Shashtah. "You won't need a Healer. I'll protect you!"

Tphah gave a low chuckle, then grasped Shashtah's left hand and pressed his fingers reverently to her lips. "So will I."

Kashon took Katrell by the elbow and escorted him outside. As soon as the flap closed behind them, Shashtah let his eyelids shut. Constantly aware of Peri's weight on his chest and Tphah's firm grip on his hand, he took a deep breath and willed himself to sleep.

The Spell

CHAPTER 12:

Walking Shadow

In the Darkness the Son of Darkness shall touch the Son of Light and reveal the Light in him.

—from *Dumnonian Proverbs,*
by Shane of Corin

NIGHTMARES HAUNTED SHASHTAH'S DREAMS, refusing to take shape. Black melted into white and white into black until everything smeared into a confusing shade of grey. Darkness shone like light, and sunbeams cast heavy shadows on the dreamscape of his abraded mind. Suddenly a man with the head of a white wolf squatted beside him, staring at his face with endless curiosity as the shade of Corin threw open the door of his Tomb and beckoned for someone to step inside.

Shashtah sat bolt upright, shrieking with voice and mind and heart.

Peri, in dragonform, stood on his haunches, balanced by his tail, agitated wings flapping, and the talons of his forepaws bared as he hissed like an asp.

Tphah crouched at the foot of the cot, her features blurring as if she could not decide whether to attack in human- or dragonform.

Completely oblivious to the two Dragons, the White Wolf stood and shook his head. "You shame me," he declared in Dumnonian.

Shashtah squinted against the pain in his skull, thankful that the Wizard was thoughtful enough to use his first language. "What are you doing here?"

Peri renewed his challenge, and Tphah contented herself with drawing her jambiya from her belt.

Ailan stared at Shashtah with all of the deadly intensity of a cornered wolf. "I told you, I fear contact with others because of Shane's curse. But this Camp sits atop the Dark One's heart, and you are the one who brought it here. My presence can cause no more harm than you already have."

Shashtah collapsed back onto the cot and closed his eyes. "I think I could have gone the rest of my life without anyone pointing that out."

Fingertips pressed against Shashtah's temples. Healing light flooded through him with a precision he had not thought possible, easing the ache in his soul and restoring his strength. Shashtah fancied that he saw the image of his god in that light, nodding his approval. Then the touch vanished.

Slowly Shashtah opened his eyes, wondering which of the magic items in Kashon's pack had just been rendered useless.

The White Wolf lay sprawled on the floor of the tent, struggling with Tphah as she tried, with all of the dragonstrength in her humanform, to thrust her jambiya through his heart.

"Tphah, no!" Shashtah sat up, swung his feet to the ground and stood, trying to pull her off his mysterious visitor.

The shock of Shashtah's touch more than the command in his voice caused Tphah to release her victim and turn to gape at him. "Impossible."

"Apparently not for the White Wolf," Shashtah observed wryly.

Peri dropped to all fours and whimpered his confusion.

Shashtah knelt beside the putrid-colored Hatchling and scratched the disgusting little beast under the chin. "Easy. I'm all right," he crooned.

Peri's left hind leg thumped a few times with pleasure, then he butted Shashtah affectionately with his head.

Shashtah almost fell over backward. "Easy!" he laughed. "I said I was all right, not that I was well."

Ailan rose and steadied Shashtah.

"Where's your cat?" Shashtah asked.

"Hunting," Ailan answered in a distracted voice as he glanced between Shashtah and Tphah. His mouth settled into a stubborn line. "You are out of your mind."

Shashtah's grin turned lopsided, and he settled back onto the cot, drawing Tphah down beside him. "Tell me something I don't know."

Ailan scowled. "Dragonheart or no, you are in no condition to Bond with another Partner yet."

Shashtah absently straightened Tphah's veil. "And I don't want to be Bonded if I turn out to be the victim of a magical backlash. But Corin has the Dark One's heart, and I don't have a better idea of how to get it back than by forming another Bond."

"I, however, do have a better idea," Ailan said. "If you insist on taking my place in this insane venture, the least I can do is fetch your stone." He waved his graceful hands in an intricate pattern, and the air began to shimmer around him. "Prepare to run." With that he was gone.

Shashtah frowned. "Prepare to—?"

Tphah grabbed Shashtah's face between her hands and kissed him soundly on the mouth.

Shashtah felt her power shock through him. He broke the kiss and gawked at her. *A Priestess of the Mother? A fully Trained Priestess of the Mother? At her age?*

Tphah blushed and released him. "I'm sorry. I swore I wouldn't—"

Shashtah grabbed her arm and held her slightly away from him, studying her closely. "You swore you wouldn't what?"

Tphah cringed.

Quickly Shashtah folded her into his arms. "Don't be afraid. I'm not angry. You just . . . surprised me." He spotted the dragonette behind her. "Peri, would you please shift to humanform and guard the tent flap? Tell anyone who asks that you're the Gate Keeper, and you can't let them in until Tphah tells you it's all right."

Peri, thrilled to have been given orders by the Dragonheart, shifted to the shape of a young boy. He raised his right fist to his left breast in the Dumnonian salute and rushed outside.

Shashtah stifled a laugh at the youngster's reaction, then turned his attention back to Tphah. He gently brushed her hair away from her face. "You have nothing to fear from me. I don't know what I was expecting. I knew you were a Prophetess, but I never dreamed—"

"You told me to be ready for you," Tphah said softly. "I did my best—"

Shashtah placed his fingers on her lips. He held her close.

Tphah cradled him in her arms as tentatively as she would have held a newly laid egg. "My poor Dragonheart!" She rested her chin on his shoulder. "I can't believe what they've done to you."

Shashtah laughed softly. "If the White Wolf has to manifest at my sickbed to remind me I'm alive, I'm in serious need of a refresher course on what it means to be a Dumnonian."

Tphah nuzzled against his neck. "And you think a Dragon can teach you that?"

"Not just any Dragon," Shashtah said. "Only you." His searching mouth found her lips again.

Tphah touched the headband she had given him. "The White Wolf may have repaired most of the damage from your Bond-Break, but the Council's magic—"

"He took care of that as well," Shashtah assured her. "I haven't felt half that much power and skill even from the Elven King. No wonder Criton wants him to help cast the spell against the Dark One instead of me." He cupped his hands along Tphah's jaw. "I'm about to risk a magical backlash that could put me under a spell like the Council's for all eternity. I'm terrified. This may be the only chance I have to be with you. I need your strength."

"I give you my love." Tphah reached up and, with very non-Dumnonian brashness, removed her veil.

Something about the gesture stirred Shashtah's memory, bringing back a sharp image of the priestess Tkai had sent to him as their Bonding Gift. He felt Tphah's power jolt through him again as her lips closed on his as they would have if they were doing the Mother's Dance. The touch of a Dragon's tail wrapping around his left leg made him gasp in shock. "It was you! She sent you! But—" Shashtah shook his head, perplexed. "It couldn't have been—. You—?"

"I'm a shapeshifter," Tphah reminded him. She stepped away from him and shimmered. "A virgin, if that's what you prefer—" she suggested, dropping into the image of the trader girl he had hurt so long ago, "or a fond memory," she shifted to the shape of the Priestess on his Bonding Night, "or anything else you desire," she teased, taking her usual humanform. She ran her fingers through his blue-black hair. "I can even take the shape of a lost love, if that would help."

"No," Shashtah whispered as he grabbed her hand and kissed it. "I never felt this way about—" He choked. "Has it always been you?"

Laughter danced in Tphah's eyes as she hugged him tightly. "We Prophetesses are very jealous about our Dragonhearts. The Mother's clergy let me know when you were in the mood." He felt her grow suddenly serious. Emotion blurred her dragon- and humanforms, and he felt her talons pierce his shirt and skin. "I've loved you from the first moment I saw you and knew you would one day be mine. I've loved you physically when I could, and when I couldn't my heart has always been with you, even if you can't feel or hear my soul. I swear to you that you never have been nor ever will be truly alone."

Shashtah could feel her passion washing over him as the storm of emotions she had unleashed roared through him. Tears of anger, tears of love, tears of pain flooded down his cheeks.

The violence of his emotion called to the Dragon in her, and she roared. Flesh turned to scale and scale to flesh unpredictably in response to his all-consuming need. Neither human nor Dragon, she twisted around him, letting him fill her with his despair and grief and pain.

Shashtah suddenly noticed the great claw-marks his own talons had left on her human skin. He tried to stammer an apology as he contritely resumed his humanform.

Tphah merely laughed and shifted to her half-dragonform. "You see why I didn't want a Dumnonian woman Dancing with a Dragonheart?" She thrust her muzzle at him and flicked her forked tongue briefly over his lips. She melted back into an unmarred version of her humanform and clasped his neck and lower back in her hands.

Shashtah felt the talon marks on his back disappear as she healed him.

"I will always be here for you," Tphah murmured. "You will return to me."

Ailan's warning suddenly echoed in Shashtah's head. "I'm supposed to be ready to run." He stole another kiss from Tphah. "Take care of Peri for me while I'm gone."

"Yes, sire!" Tphah laughed. She broke away from him and knelt. She selected an unrumpled keffiyeh from Kashon's pack and rose again. She untied Shashtah's leather headband, arranged the keffiyeh on his head and tied it into place with the thong. Tphah stepped back slightly and gave him an appraising look. "Really, now!" she scolded. "You don't even have a scimitar!"

Shashtah belatedly recalled his rust-covered scimitar lying on the floor of the cell where Tkai had died. His thoughts swerved swiftly away from the painful image.

Tphah kissed him and gently wrapped him in her loving arms. "Don't worry. Your strength does not lie in a weapon." She placed her hand against his chest. "It lies within your heart."

Shashtah buried his face in her hair and was still holding her when Ailan appeared just inside the tent flap.

The White Wolf grabbed Shashtah and pulled him away from Tphah. "You Dumnonians have never had any concept of time!" He thrust the black stone with the Dark One's heart into Shashtah's left hand.

"Get it over with!" Tphah hissed with unexpected vehemence.

Ailan grabbed Shashtah's upper arm and made an elaborate gesture with his free hand.

Suddenly the two star-crossed warriors were standing in the Great Woods near the Elven Kingdom's gates.

Shashtah stared nervously at the gem in his hand. "It still works. Why isn't its magic drained? Where are you getting the power from?" Shashtah asked as soon as he caught his breath.

A half-smile curl across Ailan's lips. He dipped his hand into his belt pouch and drew out several simple pieces of polished stone. Only one of the stones shimmered with the light of a powerful magic aura. "I paid a visit to Krillion before I came to you. The Crown Prince of the Krills guaranteed that these gems would definitely be the most powerful magic items in my vicinity, and the fact that they came from the Krills ensured that they belonged to someone else. He must've been as good as his word."

"I've always found Treigo to be an extremely honorable thief," Shashtah concurred. He peered at the pieces of rock. "I wonder what they were."

Without answering the question, Ailan pocketed the still-glowing stone and let the others fall to the forest floor. Then he dropped into the form of a white wolf and fled into the woods.

"Millennia in hiding, and you can't even say 'Hello!'" Farador's voice boomed.

Shashtah turned and hastily bent into a deep salaam, still holding the pulsing black gem in his left hand. He straightened and studied the Elven King, his unasked question glittering in his eyes.

Farador seemed to read his mind. "No, I would not trap him and force him to take your place even if you did tell me his real name. Nor will I force you to take the place that he should fill. Criton thinks like that. Not me. Are you truly willing to sacrifice yourself?"

"Yes," Shashtah hissed.

"Then come." Farador grabbed Shashtah's shoulder, uttered the words to a spell and smiled with grim satisfaction as they arrived safely inside Criton's private quarters.

A large desk dominated the sparsely furnished room. An intricately carved stool rather than a chair stood behind it. Shashtah's gaze settled on a single scroll case, the only object on the desk's pristine surface. Across the room, a slit of a window looked out on the battlements of Tor.

Farador approached the desk, picked up the case and angled it so Shashtah could see the telltale mark that matched the symbol he had seen on the punishment scroll the night the Council judged Kashon. "Set the Dark One's heart on the desk."

Shashtah obeyed, placing the stone in front of Farador. "Where's Lord Criton?"

Farador set the case in the center of the desk and nodded at the window. "He's coming."

Shashtah glanced through the slit and saw Criton, astride a winged white stallion, land on the palace battlements. Solid silver eyes flashed on either side of the exquisite creature's noble head. Stories told on seemingly endless treks through the desert by caravan whispered through Shashtah's mind. Some claimed that Criton had brought the miraculous steed with him from the homeland of the Mirari. Others swore that the half-bird, half-horse mutant had been forged in the bowels of Mount Cinnamar by the Dark One's magic and had been stolen by the Kyondoca as a gift for their winged Lord. Staring at the beast and recalling with a shudder the disgusting runt of a Dragon that was Tkai's son, Shashtah could not bring himself to believe that the Dark One's magic had ever created anything so breathtakingly beautiful.

Criton dismounted and touched the stallion lightly on the nose in an intimate gesture that sent a shiver through Shashtah's soul.

The beast nuzzled him, then nickered and leapt into the air.

Criton watched the stallion soar back to his favored perch, high in the Dragon's Back Mountains. The Lord of Daethia turned, folded his own wings behind his back, bowed his head and vanished.

Criton reappeared across the desk from Shashtah, between the Elven King and the wooden stool.

Shashtah marveled at how Criton's bare skin was almost the same shade of white as his wings. He tried to remember the first time he had seen the deity in the Throne Room, but he could not recall if Criton had always looked quite so pale.

Criton acknowledged Farador's presence with a nod. He took no notice of Shashtah, but he did address the Elven King in ClearTalk, probably as a concession to the Dumnonian's presence. "This is madness. We need the White Wolf."

Farador regarded his nephew with determination. "We don't have the White Wolf. We have a Dragonheart."

Criton gestured impatiently at Shashtah. "He'll never survive the backlash. At least the White Wolf has Mirari blood."

"The Dragonheart has proven he can survive this spell," Farador snapped. "That's more than either you or I can say." He turned his gaze on Shashtah, the respect of a comrade in suffering flashing in his forest-colored eyes. "I have waited centuries to demand justice for the deaths of my wife and son. Juel is old enough to rule if I prove too weak."

Criton ruffled his feathers. "What if my brother proves too weak? I will not have the Dark One destroyed for what he has become. Don't you remember what he was?"

"I do not command any type of magic that is capable of destroying him!" Shashtah declared, a little surprised to hear the venom in his own voice. "I ask only that the Dark One be made to suffer until he understands the anguish he has caused. If I have to suffer with him for him to see his actions through his victims' eyes, then so be it!" He held his right hand over the throbbing black stone.

Farador held his right hand above the Dragonheart's. "So be it!"

Criton hesitated, then thrust his right hand into position above the Elven King's. "So be it."

At a glance from Farador, Shashtah opened the scroll case with his left hand.

The ancient vellum unfurled before them. A golden border framed Shane's violent scrawl. Magical letters shimmered on the page, glistening with the reddish-black glow of rubies mixed with demonblood.

Shashtah, only dimly aware that Farador's and Criton's voices chanted the words of power with him, began to read the magic script: "I command you, Serak . . ."

The words vanished from the page as quickly as the trio recited them.

The heart of the Dark One flashed wildly beneath their hands.

Shashtah found himself saying the words, almost without thinking about them. "Pain as you've wrought, so must you feel . . ."

The stone beneath their hands seemed to convulse.

The words flowed on, much more complicated than the scroll the Dumnonian's used. "—and consign you to—"

The stone flared with the pure absence of light.

Shashtah's voice nearly faltered as image after image of Tkai's humanform being raped by dragon after dragon, scaly hides shining obscenely in all the hues of the rainbow, rose before him, blotting out the final words to the spell. The sound of a sword being drawn echoed through his soul, and he repeated the last words from his memory of when they had been read against himself and Kashon. Carefully, he left out the syllables that would signify "until dawn."

When Shashtah could see straight again, the scroll was blank. He dropped the page and glanced at Farador, who was staring at him with intent concern.

Then Criton screamed.

Shashtah reacted first. He vaulted over the desk and grabbed the winged warrior by the waist, trying to keep him from falling and damaging his wings. His desert boots had almost no traction on the stone floor. He could barely brace himself, let alone Criton. He slipped.

Criton sprawled backward.

Farador threw a spell at his nephew.

Criton's wings vanished.

Shashtah clenched his teeth as Criton's weight sent them both crashing onto the stone. He managed to break the writhing deity's fall.

Criton shrieked again.

This time the winged horse echoed his cry. The beast fought to force his way through the slit in the wall.

Shashtah gawked at Farador. "He was Bonded?"

The Elven King's head inclined slightly.

Shashtah stifled an outburst about the stupidity of supposedly divine beings and disentangled himself from Criton. He surged to his feet and rushed around the desk to the window.

The winged stallion screeched in pain and terror as he scrabbled with his silver hooves against the impervious stone wall.

Unable to reach the horse from inside the room, Shashtah warped to the other side of the wall and shifted form. "Calm down!" he shouted as much to himself as to the stallion in a language he did not know he knew. "Your Partner needs you!"

Blood-flecked froth at the corners of the winged stallion's mouth, the beast turned his wild, unseeing eyes on Shashtah.

A little stunned, Shashtah realized that he had instinctively taken his dragonform and was backwinging to hold himself in place near the distraught flying horse. "Let him know that you are with him and that you will always be with him no matter what!" The language felt odd in his reptilian mouth, and he wondered whether the winged horse could understand him at all.

The stallion bucked in the air. He wheeled away from Shashtah and flapped violently to attain a higher altitude. The magnificent creature neighed a challenge.

Shashtah executed a rather concise barrel-roll and stared directly into the stallion's terrified eyes. "Stay with him! Let him know that he will hurt, but he will live, no matter what!"

The stallion reared midair, whinnied and stamped his fury on an unseen cloud.

"Dragonheart!" Farador's voice called from Criton's study. "Below you!"

Shashtah landed on the battlements. His fear shocked him into his humanform just before a deadly magical bolt from one of the Kyondoca's bracers sliced through the air where his dragonform had been. *Dragonslayers*, Shashtah reminded himself. He forced himself to concentrate and warped his surroundings until he was standing beside Criton. He heard Farador come up behind him.

Criton exhaled sharply as he tried to handle the unexpected reality of his pain.

"I didn't dream—" Farador cut himself off mid-thought.

Shashtah swiftly knelt beside Criton and put his left hand on the deity's heaving breast.

Light flashed from Shashtah's fingertips and flooded through Criton.

:*I give you the strength to endure, my son,*: the voice of sun god echoed in Shashtah's ears, :*until the Great Wizard can allow you to rest.*:

The light vanished, and Shashtah fancied that Criton's labored breathing eased.

The Elven Lord, Juel, threw open the study door and strode into the room. A glitteringly beautiful maiden who could only be the Elven Princess, Adrial, followed him, a dark-haired Daethian boy holding her hand.

Adrial made a small sound, released the boy's hand and rushed to Criton. She sank to her knees beside him and pulled his head into her lap.

Juel locked stares with Farador, as if they were communicating silently.

The boy simply stood there, staring in shock at Criton's writhing body.

Shashtah gave a squawk of dismay as none of the other adults paid any attention to the child. He rose and hefted the boy into his arms. "Quatar?" he asked, hoping to distract the youngster. He used his body to block the child's view of Criton's agony.

"What are you?" Quatar asked in elvish. He lifted the folds of Shashtah's keffiyeh and peered intently at his ears. "You're not an elf," he declared, dropping the headcloth back into place. "Your ears aren't pointy enough."

Shashtah half-smiled at Quatar's imperious tone. "I'm a Dumnonian," he replied also in elvish. He had no idea if the boy had learned any other tongue.

Quatar's eyes widened. "A Dragonrider? Where's your Dragon?"

Shashtah's face darkened as Quatar glanced around the study in search of the Dragon he would not find. "She died fighting the Dark One."

The clatter of boots sounded in the hall outside the study.

Farador's grip on Shashtah's upper arm was the only warning he had before a warp formed around them.

The sheer walls of the Valley of Ancients suddenly towered above them in the midday sun.

Farador squinted against the light. "Adrial will nurse my nephew, and Juel will look after Tor until Criton can control it again. I must return to my kingdom before anyone realizes that the entire Royal Family has stepped out for an afternoon of War without so much as a bodyguard." He spread his hands apart as if he were bestowing an offering. "Quatar, do you want to return to the Great Woods with me, or stay here with the Dragonheart and learn about Dragons?"

Quatar glanced up at the cliff tops as the Council of Ancients settled into their places. Glee instead of terror swept across his face. "Can I ride one of those Dragons?"

Shashtah turned an indignant splutter into something that sounded remotely like a laugh. "If you prove yourself worthy, and if one will have you. My blood is your water," he said, formally accepting Quatar into his household. *I'm not a Rider anymore. I have no water to give him. No tent,*

no food, no supplies, no money . . . Garesh is right. I must have been raiding a
candy stall in Krillion the day the Lord of Light passed out brains.

"My brother's Light be with you." Farador inclined his head toward
Shaharadesh, who sat astride Makara above Corin's Tomb.

Shaharadesh returned the Elven King's acknowledgement.

With an elegant flourish of his hand, Farador vanished.

Quatar's hands swiftly covered his ears as the Councilors started
shouting at each other in their Ancient tongue.

Shashtah winced, wishing he could follow the boy's example without
dropping him.

"He brings a Dragonslayer to our sacred Valley!" Makara charged over
the ringing in Shashtah's ears.

"The Elven King brought the Dragonslayer!" Garesh countered.
"How was the Dragonheart supposed to stop him?"

"He defies our Traditions!" an Ancient Female protested.

"How can he defy what he does not know?" Tlee mused.

Another Female Councilor sniffed. "He is too powerful. He must be
Bonded to a Dragon who can control him!"

"He just had a Bond-Break," one of the Male Councilors reasoned.
"He needs time to heal before he can Bond again."

"'Neither Dragon nor Dumnonian. Somehow both,'" another Male
recited. "Dragons can Bond more than once, often immediately after a
Bond-Break. Katrell has proven that time and again."

"The Dragonheart might be able to do it," the sympathetic male who
had arrested Kashon agreed. "Perhaps as a Dragon to a Rider this time?
The Prophetess may not see him Bonded to another Dragon because he is
Bonded to a Rider until it is time for him to Bond with her."

"Tkai always said never to second guess the visions." Garesh warned.
"What say you, Prophet?" he asked Shashtah. "Do you see yourself
Bonded to a Rider or a Dragon?"

Shashtah set Quatar down and stepped away from the excited rather
than frightened boy. He spread his hands in supplication. "My entire life
my heart has told me that I'm the Rider not the Dragon." *Tphah's not old*
enough, but I have to Bond. Quatar and Peri aren't going to survive in

Dumnonia if I don't. "I formally ask that you allow me to Bond with a Dumnonian Bronze."

Shaharadesh narrowed his eyes to mere slits at the sound of the words to the ancient tradition. "So be it."

Garesh and the Council abruptly bugled their summons to the desert skies.

Once again the unBonded Dragons of Dumnonia appeared above the Valley and settled onto the canyon's rim and the rolling dunes behind Shashtah.

Unlike the first time when Shashtah could not choose, this time he could see himself with no other Dragon than the Stripling Prophetess he knew was not among his potential Bond Partners. *Tphah's going to kill me.*

Shaharadesh raised his hands, demanding silence. "A Rider presents himself! A very worthy one. A Dragonheart. A Prophet of the Lord of Light. The former Rider of our Council Leader and Prophetess Tkai. I give to you Shashtah Dragonheart! Is there one among you who will consent to Bond with him?"

Kashon, with Peri and Tphah in formation off Katrell's wingtips, burst into the sky above the Valley, immediately silencing any response the Dragons had prepared to make.

Peri landed near Quatar and shifted to humanform. "You don't look like a Dumnonian. What are you?" he asked, oblivious to the commotion around him.

"I'm the Elven Ward!" Quatar declared importantly.

Peri cocked his head. "You don't look like an elf."

Shashtah's attention turned from the boys to Tphah as she alighted gracefully on the ashy sand beside him.

Without looking at Shashtah, Tphah snaked her head toward the Tomb and roared, "He is mine!"

Shashtah studied Shaharadesh carefully, but his king's stony features could have matched Garesh's at a bargaining table. *Will he keep his word? Will he Bond me to Tphah now that she is our last Prophetess?*

Katrell set down behind Shashtah, extended his wings and thundered something completely unintelligible.

Shashtah gave Katrell a worried glance. *I have no idea what language that is. I've never heard anything like it before. Does Shaharadesh speak it? Can he understand him?*

Kashon leapt to the ground and rushed to Shashtah's side. "Why do you call the other Dragons?" he shouted at his king. "You promised Tphah you would Bond the Dragonheart to her!"

Shashtah blinked at Kashon. *I can get away with addressing the Council because I am a Prophet and a Dragonheart, but even I don't talk to them like that!*

Shaharadesh, confronted by a Dumnonian instead of a Dragon, snapped, "The Prophetess is too young!"

Tphah ruffled her scales. "You swore you would Bond him to me whether I was old enough or not so long as I was fully Trained!"

"She is fully Trained!" Kashon bellowed.

Shaharadesh gave a mocking laugh. "How would you know? She is the first Stripling who's ever been assigned to you!"

Shashtah frowned. *What did Tphah say when I first Bonded with Tkai and I spoke to Shaharadesh like that? That I was acting like an "overprotective Dragon who outranks the king," that my brains were scrambled with hers.* He ventured another wary glance at Katrell.

The glint of madness lashed through Katrell's eyes.

O Lord of Light! Kashon's not the one who's talking. It's Katrell! Shashtah drew a sharp breath. *The Bonding Feast! I made their Bond the way mine was with Tkai, but it wasn't supposed to be like that! It was supposed to be different! I didn't repair their Bond; I scrambled their brains!*

Katrell cried his distress in the foreign tongue once again.

Kashon grabbed his head.

Tphah glanced from Katrell to Shashtah, then made a decision. Faster than skyfire she threw herself at Katrell. Her shoulder connected with his breast plates.

Katrell folded his wings protectively around Tphah as her weight carried him onto his side.

"Stop fighting, you two!" Kashon's hands curled into fists.

Katrell's reaction to Tphah in the Healer's Tent flashed through Shashtah's mind.

Kashon shook violently, and his fingernails dug into his palms so hard that they nearly drew blood.

Shashtah seized Kashon by the shoulders. "They're not fighting! She's treating his dragonform the same way you treat his humanform. Watch."

Tphah put her muzzle next to Katrell's ear. She hissed softly in the same foreign language he had used.

Katrell responded with a low, hypnotic moan.

Tphah flicked her forked tongue across Katrell's nostrils. She breathed a puff of her scent at him.

Slowly, Katrell relaxed and sanity returned to his eyes.

Kashon stopped shaking. "I don't understand."

Shahstah touched Kashon's temple with his left hand. Light flickered softly from his fingers, restoring their Bond to the way Corin had created it. "You couldn't control Katrell while your brains were scrambled with his, so he taught Tphah to control him instead. He trained her to be his dragonform's mate."

Katrell collapsed into his humanform.

Tphah melted in unison with him, embracing and being embraced by Katrell.

Kashon stifled a small sound.

Katrell heard the noise and disentangled himself from Tphah. He focused on Kashon like a lion spotting an addax.

Shashtah released his friend and danced out of the way as Katrell tackled Kashon.

The Pair sprawled onto the ashy sand between Shashtah and the boys.

Katrell pinned Kashon efficiently to the ground. "For someone who is so smart, you can be a real nit sometimes."

Kashon glanced quickly from Tphah to Shashtah and then refocused on Katrell. His lips formed into a perfect, soundless "Oh!"

Katrell smiled impishly. "Let's get the Prophet and the Prophetess Bonded so she can worry about him and you can go back to worrying about me." He rose, helped Kashon to his feet, and turned to face Shaharadesh. "It does not matter how many Striplings my Rider has trained!" he thundered. "What matters is how many Dragons I have trained. Tphah is a fully trained Dragon and Priestess of the Mother, and you will Bond her with the Dragonheart!"

"The Dragonheart is going to Bond with her?" Quatar piped up, unintentionally reminding everyone that he was there. "Isn't she a bit small? I want to Bond with one of the big Dragons!"

Peri shushed Quatar, but the Council had once again noticed him.

An Ancient Female cracked her whip-like tail in annoyance. "The mutant and the Dragonslayer—"

"Will not be harmed!" Garesh bellowed. "The Dragonheart has bought the life of the mutant with his pain, and the Elven King has entrusted us with his Ward. Neither of them will be touched!"

"Tphah is our only Prophetess," an Ancient Male sniffed. "We cannot let her risk herself until another Prophet is Hatched!"

"Tkai's son is a Prophet!" Tphah shouted as she pointed at Peri. "So is he!" She pointed again.

Shashtah felt as if she were aiming straight through his heart.

"He stands above as Dragons sing," Peri chanted, "for Dragonheart the Dragonking!"

Quatar took a closer look at Peri. He grinned, thoroughly enchanted by the odd dragonboy.

The world around Shashtah blurred into an image of hundreds of Dragons filling the Valley. He snapped his eyes shut, trying to make the vision go away, but it only got worse. The number of Dragons multiplied, and their Riders joined them. He opened his eyes again, but the double vision remained. *Is it my Prophecy? Or a Dragon's?*

"The Dragonheart shall not have the Prophetess!" Makara declared.

Garesh scowled at Makara. "It is not your decision to make. If Tphah says my son is her Rider, then my son is her Rider. We would be sunstruck to contradict her!" He shifted his glare from Makara to Shaharadesh. "Tphah!"

A female Councilor repeated his cry. "Tphah!"

Somewhat unwisely, Kashon and Katrell took up the call and were echoed by Quatar and Peri.

Three more of the Ancients, including Dameth's Dragon, Tlee, screamed at Shaharadesh. "Tphah!"

Abruptly the Dragonriders of Dumnonia filled the air above the Valley as they had in Shashtah's vision. Bonded Dragons and Riders added their calls to the growing cacophony.

Makara roared her frustration and reluctantly bared her throat to Garesh.

Shaharadesh thrust his fist into the air, displaying the ring that marked him as king.

The shouts ceased.

"The Dragons have spoken!" Shaharadesh proclaimed. "I choose the Prophetess Tphah as the Bond Partner for Shashtah Dragonheart!"

In the time it took Kashon to disengage himself from Katrell and propel Shashtah and Tphah through the crowd and present them at the door to Corin's Tomb, Shaharadesh managed to talk Makara into carrying him to the canyon floor.

Shashtah stared warily at his king.

Shaharadesh smiled inscrutably at Shashtah. "I'm not dead yet," he said as he slid from Makara's back and climbed the steps to Corin's Tomb, "and this time you will go through the Training."

Shashtah felt like an errant Hatchling beneath his monarch's gaze. "Yes, sire." He turned to Tphah.

The Prophetess locked eyes with him. "Are you ready, Dragonheart?"

Shashtah nodded. "I am ready." He faced Shaharadesh. "Create the Bond."

"Shashtah Dragonheart," the king intoned, returning to the Council's formal speech, "do you intend for me to Bond you soul-to-soul, heart-to-heart, with the Dragon Prophetess Tphah, until Death or Judgment severs that Bond?"

Shashtah stared confidently into his king's eyes. "I do."

"Will you," Shaharadesh continued, "care for her needs before your own in both her dragon- and her humanform?"

"I will," Shashtah swore with all his heart.

"Will you submit without protest to the Judgment of the Council if, for any reason—be it your fault or no—she comes to harm?"

Shashtah's soul shuddered at remembered pain, but his voice held firm as he declared, "I will."

Shaharadesh nodded, acknowledging the oath, and then turned to the Prophetess. "Will you, Tphah, give up your freedom and do the bidding of this warrior, serving him to the best of your ability with body, mind and soul?"

Tphah beamed at Shashtah. "I will, sire. I've never wanted anything else."

Shaharadesh suppressed a smile at the youthful outburst as he continued. "Will you give up all wealth to him that he might purchase what he needs to care for you?" He watched the Prophetess closely.

"I will," Tphah swore solemnly. "He is the only thing of true value to me."

The king held Tphah's gaze. "Will you guard yourself against harm so that your Rider will never have to face the Council on account of you?"

Tphah let out a squawk that sounded almost exactly like the Bronze Dragon cry of distress. She stared in horror at Shashtah. "I will try, Dragonheart!" she screeched. "I will try so hard! But one day I will fail! I don't know how far in the future it is, but one day I will fail!"

"One day I will fail!" The words of Shashtah's dead Prophetess reverberated in Tphah's cry of distress. Shashtah quickly gathered Tphah into his arms. "Will I survive?"

Tphah nodded. "Yes."

Shashtah smiled. "And you'll be there to comfort me?"

"Yes!" Tphah swore fervently.

Shashtah kissed Tphah's forehead. "Then let us be Bonded. We have no idea how far in the future our Prophecy allows us to see, and sometimes futures change." He released her and turned toward his king. "Create the Bond."

Shaharadesh reached out and drew Shashtah into an embrace.

Shashtah closed his eyes and wrapped his arms around his king as he had done what seemed like days before rather than half a decade ago. His soul once again lay bare before Shaharadesh's probing mind.

Shaharadesh released Shashtah, then turned to embrace Tphah.

Shashtah felt himself shivering violently at the familiar loneliness flooding through him at the absence of his king's touch. His heart ached as the same haunted look spread across Tphah's face.

Shaharadesh released her. "Do not touch," the king intoned, "until the magic of Corin instructs you to do so." He turned and cast the spell that opened the doors to the tomb. "If you will be Bonded, enter herein. "

"What's in there?" Tphah whispered as Shashtah fought the urge to gather her into his arms and assure her that everything would be all right.

"Our test," Shashtah's voice shrugged in a chilling imitation of Tkai's words to him. "The Challenge of Corin's Tomb is different every time, designed to form a Bond between a specific Pair."

"So said Tkai," warned Shaharadesh.

Shashtah hastily offered his apology with a salaam, then focused on Tphah. At her nod he took a deep breath and stepped through the doors with her.

First Flight

CHAPTER 13:

Second Chance

For the formation of a Bond is a vital and dynamic magic, sharper than any two-edged sword, piercing and joining soul and lifeforce, thoughts and the essence of the heart. Before the Dragonking no Dumnonian nor Dragon shall be concealed; but all are opened and laid bare to the eyes of he who helps create the Bond.

—from *The Dumnonian Code,*
by Corin of Daethia

SHASHTAH SENSED THAT SOMETHING was wrong the heartbeat the doors of Corin's Tomb slammed shut, locking them inside. His desert-adapted eyes strained at the darkness, once again unable to make out ceiling, floors, walls or even the Dragon at his right side. *It's different for every Pair,* Tkai's words haunted him. Yet, exactly as the first time he had entered the Tomb, he could not hear himself breathe and the same foul odor assailed his nostrils. More disturbing, though, was the realization that he could not feel Corin's magic pulsing in the air. "Something's not right," he said experimentally and was more disconcerted than surprised when his voice made no sound. Stony fear encased his heart as he realized that unlike Tkai, Tphah had never been through the Bonding Ritual before and had no idea what to expect. *I have to warn her!*

With deft fingers he rapidly unfastened his belt buckle and slid the leather strap from around his hips. As he had done with Tkai, he made a slip knot out of the belt and drew it snugly about his right wrist. Gently, he flicked the free end of the belt toward the spot where Tphah should be.

A firm hand gripped the other end of the strap and gave a tug that nearly pulled him off his feet.

Shashtah's sense of uneasiness deepened. Either Tphah was terrified out of her mind or the person on the other end of the belt was not the Prophetess.

Shashtah tugged carefully, inching his way toward the wall just as he had done with Tkai. He reached out with his left hand, expecting the glassy surface of the lava tube and felt the score marks of a pickaxe on the rock.

Shashtah drew back his hand so fast, he overbalanced and fell into the pit in the floor. His left forearm once again slammed flat against the ledge that protruded from the wall and his right arm slapped down hard on the edge. Rough cut stone caught his shirt but did not tear it. His mind began to race. *Is this what Tkai meant? Is this what's different?* But something deep inside him knew that the Ancient Prophetess had never foreseen whatever it was that Shashtah sensed was now amiss. The soles of his desert boots found a purchase against the sides of the pit, and he hauled himself easily onto the ledge beside the wall.

The belt trembled as if someone were laughing on the other end.

As it had before, the ledge on which Shashtah lay began to move toward the center of the tunnel.

Shashtah scrambled to his feet and stumbled to the far side of the pit, dragging whatever was on the other end of his belt after him.

Lord of Light! The prayer ripped through Shashtah, setting his blood on fire in the very corridor where he had almost fallen asleep during his Bonding with Tkai. Nightmares rather than dreams of peace and lethargy whispered through his mind. *The magic of Darkness blinds me! The fear of thine enemies confounds my senses and hides thy Truth from my searching eyes! Lend me thy brilliance that I might see!*

Instantaneously an orb of light bloomed from the fingertips of Shashtah's left hand.

The yellow-toothed grin of the Demonlord Yapada flashed back at him from the other end of the leather strap.

Shashtah screamed, yanked the belt from the Demonlord's paw, and fled. The travel-worn soles of his soft leather boots pounded against stone. His pulse hammered wildly in his ears. The stench around him increased, choking his lungs with foul air as he careened down one corridor after another, into the heart of Corin's Tomb.

The light in Shashtah's hand seemed to show him the way, glowing brighter when he took the correct path through the maze and dimming as he approached a dead end.

Shashtah almost sighed with relief when he saw a massive bearskin draped over what could only be an enormous harp. He moved the skin enough to let him squeeze past the strings, then let it fall back into place.

Magical grease covered the surface of the chute beyond the harp, sending Shashtah sliding at a manic pace away from the Demonlord. Suddenly he was in midair. With a shout of glee he felt his body elongate and his clothes harden into scales as his massive wings unfurled and caught the air. ":*Tphah!:*" he shrieked silently and aloud.

:*Dragonheart!:* came the answering scream, setting up a familiar, tingling sensation along the inside of Shashtah's skull.

Shashtah's light revealed the dim outlines of the absolutely enormous cavern surrounding him. He looked down.

Tphah's humanform, stretched between two demons, stared up at him.

Behind her Yapada howled with delight and raised his flail.

NO! Shashtah's soul screamed as he backwinged in place near the ceiling of the cavern. *I will not lose another Dragon!* He had no idea how Yapada had managed to get ahead of him or how the demons had captured Tphah, but he had no time to waste on such Daethian thoughts. He threw his light at the deadly flail, causing the dreaded object to grow to match the size of the fearful image in his nightmares.

Yapada howled in rage as he overbalanced and fell, pulled down by the weight of his own weapon.

With a mighty clap of wings Shashtah sent his dragonform plummeting toward the furious Demonlord. Talons extended, wings folded tightly against his bronze-covered sides, Shashtah swooped close to the dimly glowing cavern floor, raking his claws across his enemy's unprotected chest.

Yapada howled in pain.

Shashtah extended his wings and landed inelegantly near Tphah. He bowed his head in prayer as he shifted to his humanform. As he saw the desecration of Corin's Tomb, the defiled coffin, the signs of a warp leading to the very heart of Mount Cinnamar torn in the sacred walls, his furious roar resounded through the cavern.

Sunbeams suddenly filled the space that had never seen the light of day.

The demons holding Tphah shrieked in terror, then crumbled into tiny piles of ash.

The deadly flail resumed its normal size.

Yapada grabbed his weapon, gibbered a curse Shashtah could not understand, and fled toward the warp.

Shashtah charged after him.

Yapada yowled and dove headlong back into the prison of the Dark One.

:Dragonheart!: Tphah's voice screamed in Shashtah's mind as he leapt through the wall.

Shashtah sprawled forward, tripping over something he could not see. His eyes tried to make out his surroundings in the sudden darkness.

"How nice of you to visit me," an achingly beautiful baritone, filled with more pain than Shashtah could imagine, commented drily. "You even have the sense to prostrate yourself before me! Father picks his Prophets well."

Clawed hands grasped Shashtah's wrists and hauled him to his feet. Tentacles wrapped around his ankles, spread-eagling him in the darkness. Talons shredded the cloak and shirt from his back, raking long furrows in his scar-toughened skin.

:Tphah!: Shashtah's reeling mind shrieked.

The baritone mimicked the cry. "Tphah!" The voice chuckled viciously in the darkness. "I almost hope the Dragon bitch comes. I could rape her in front of you the way I raped that other feeble excuse of a Prophetess. Why Bonding with you Dumnonians makes Dragons so frail, I'll never understand. You, however, I am told are extremely resilient."

"Serak!" Shashtah bellowed.

The spiked balls and chains of Yapada's deadly flail whistled through the blackness.

Shashtah convulsed as the devil-forged metal struck his exposed skin.

A hand quickly pressed against his breast and soft lips closed over his mouth to swallow his scream.

Shashtah's soul writhed in horror.

The lips reluctantly pulled away from his face as the sting of the initial blow diminished. The sigh of a man feeling a cool zephyr on a merciless hot day hissed near Shashtah's left ear. "How delightful to be able to take from you what you have given me. Pity I have no heart to keep you alive this time. Again!"

The flail whirred down on Shashtah's back with a viciousness that almost sent the Dragonrider and the unseen demons crashing to the floor.

Try as he might Shashtah could not stifle the scream that the hungry lips once again covered his to receive. *Lord of Light, don't let me die in the Darkness!* The prayer mingled with his mental cry.

Light suddenly shimmered along his skin, casting an eerie blue-white glow on the faces of the demons that held him.

Yapada's fangs flashed beneath his yellow eyes.

Shashtah gaped in horrified awe at the palpable absence of light that was the Dark One.

Serak grabbed Shashtah's head with one hand and placed his other hand on his prisoner's breast. "As you destroyed my heart, so I shall destroy yours! Again!"

Yapada obediently raised his flail and brought it down on Shashtah's lacerated back.

The vile darkness smashed his lips against Shashtah's mouth and sucked at his pain.

Shashtah tried to retch, but the pressure of the hand seeking to crack his breastbone and reach his wildly pounding heart prevented the acid in his empty stomach from rising. Near the end of his sanity, he felt his true essence begin to fade as he endured yet another blow from Yapada's wicked flail. Suddenly the image of Tphah blurring between her human- and dragonforms and his own half-dragonform leaving talon marks on her human skin slithered through his mind. The fire in his heart flared and shocked through him.

The Dark One bent his mouth once more to absorb Shashtah's expected scream.

Instead, Shashtah's form blurred, and dragonjaws, parted slightly for precise aim, met the startled deity's gaping mouth. A bolt of magical light crackled from Shashtah's throat and into the open maw of the Dark One.

Serak yelped and fell to the floor.

The wrath in Shashtah's heart changed him into his full dragonform. He did not care. He threw the distracted demons against opposite walls of the dark chamber with an appalling crash! With a mighty leap and a thrust of his powerful wings he half jumped, half flew back through the warp that led to Corin's tomb.

Corin's shade, shimmering with a blue-white light, abruptly cast a spell, and the warp hardened once more into solid stone.

Still half mad with pain, Shashtah reared on his haunches, spread his wings and roared. :*Tphah!*:

:*First*,: Tphah's voice roared back, causing their Bond to glitter inside his head, almost blinding him, :*you leave me standing in the dark! Then I almost get myself killed falling into a pit! Then I have to chase you like some insane will-o'-the-wisp down corridor after corridor with that overgrown tunnel rat loping along behind you! Then you don't have the courtesy to move that stupid harp out of my way or at least warn me about the grease—*:

:*Where are you?*: Shashtah demanded.

"Look up," Corin suggested with a bemused grin.

Shashtah tilted his head backward.

Tphah's dragonform in all its glory sailed to the cavern floor and landed a wingspan away from him, showering him with sand. On purpose.

Shashtah lunged at her, some draconic instinct making him close his jaws tightly around her throat just beneath her chin.

Tphah flapped wildly, trying to get away.

Shashtah held her firmly, his fangs only a dragonhide away from taking her life, as he furled his wings safely out of the way. He waited just long enough for her to fold her wings securely against her sides, then rolled her onto her back.

Tphah scraped at his impervious hide with her glistening talons, shrieking her indignation at the cavern walls.

Shashtah used his powerful arms and legs to restrain her, twining his tail around hers.

Tphah struggled to free herself from him, but he held her tightly with all of the strength that he had left. Her squawk melted into a halfhearted protest and passionate glee sparkled in her glistening amber eyes as the Mother's Blessing washed over her dragonform sending wave after wave of pleasure surging through their Bond.

Shashtah gasped, relaxing his jaws and freeing her neck.

With a wicked gleam in her eyes, Tphah closed her fangs around his suddenly unprotected throat. :*Let's see how you like it!*:

When Shashtah's dragonform stopped convulsing with pleasure and the shimmer in their Bond had diminished enough for him to see straight again, he decided that he liked it just fine.

Corin's laugh startled them both back into their humanforms.

They prostrated themselves in front of him in profuse apology.

"Tphah, would you do something about his back?" Corin asked. "He's bleeding all over my tomb."

Tphah gasped in dismay and scrambled to her knees beside Shashtah's prone form. She placed one of her hands firmly on his buttocks and the other at the back of his skull. She bowed her head. Healing light flickered between her hands, washed over Shashtah's damaged back and made him whole.

When the light flickered out, Shashtah twisted slightly so that his head was in her lap as he stared up at her concerned eyes. "I guess you did learn a few things while I was away. Why didn't you follow me into Mount Cinnamar?"

Tphah brushed the sand from his face. "I knew you would survive, and presenting the Dark One with the last Prophetess of the Bronze Dragons like the main course at a Bonding Feast seemed unlikely to help." She bent down as if to kiss him. Just before their lips made contact she rose abruptly, dumping him unceremoniously onto the sand. "But don't you dare run off like that on me ever again!" She caught sight of Corin's shade and dropped into a deep salaam. "Forgive us."

Corin smiled benignly as Shashtah picked himself up off the ground and belatedly mimicked Tphah. "Forgive you? You two are the most entertaining Pair who have been sent to me in a long time." He stared thoughtfully at where the warp between his tomb and Cinnamar had been. "Criton's spells are weakening faster since he became the victim of the backlash. His magic will soon fail." With a wave of his spectral hands he restored his sepulcher to its unviolated appearance.

Shashtah drew himself erect and slipped his left arm possessively around Tphah's waist, pulling her close to him. He reached up and smiled as he straightened what he recognized belatedly recognized as the coin-decorated headdress of a Dumnonian matron that adorned her head. "Thank you for creating our Bond. I am eternally grateful to you for that."

"That?" Corin's shade sniffed in disgust, a wicked sense of humor gleaming in his long-dead eyes. "That hardly took any magic at all! I'm surprised you two weren't already hearing each other think. How about a real challenge next time?"

Shashtah looked deep into Tphah's eyes, seeing the Dragon in her soul. "No next time for me. This is the last time I intend to saddle a Dragon with a daydreaming—."

Tphah stopped his protest with her kiss, the pressure of her loving lips softening his memory of the Dark One's obscene mouth. "My Dragonheart." She stepped away from him and shifted to her dragonform, complete with harness.

Shashtah, suddenly feeling like a child in a Krillion candy stall, half-climbed, half-vaulted onto her back.

Tphah shifted her shape beneath him as his leg wrapped around the last spike on her neckridge, adjusting her size to fit him perfectly. :*Hold on!*: she instructed as she leapt into the air with a happy roar.

Corin's shade watched as Tphah's great wings carried them higher and higher above the cavern floor.

Shashtah relaxed his grip as he felt the upward motion press him firmly against her back. Beneath the thunderous clap of dragonwings he heard Tphah's thoughts ring in his head.

:*You will never be alone*,: Tphah promised, :*and I will never drop you*.:

Shashtah laughed. *So much for arranged marriages,* he mused.

:*What?*: Tphah's mental voice squealed with delight as she executed a barrel roll.

:*I was remembering the time I flew on Katrell*,: Shashtah explained, reminding his heart to beat.

:*No one will ever Bond with me but you!*: Tphah declared as she somersaulted in the air and swooped back toward the floor.

:*Prophecy?*: Shashtah teased, absurdly proud of himself for not feeling quite as queasy as he had when riding Tkai. A deep sadness tinged his delight in his new Dragon as he remembered the Dragon he had lost.

:*We will always miss her*,: Tphah's voice whispered gently through his mind. :*But she would want us to celebrate*.: She reinforced the suggestion with an image of the Valley of Ancients, walls lined with the massive members of the Council and most of the living Dragons and Riders in Dumnonia anxiously awaiting their return.

Shashtah snorted. :*Optimist!*: He gave her his own image of the Valley, Kashon's worried face scanning the empty sky as Katrell tried valiantly to distract Quatar and Peri.

The images merged, and Tphah's wings clapped loudly in the open air. Sunlight glittered off her burnished hide, and pride in herself and her Rider glistened in her amber eyes as she bugled her triumphant cry to the desert winds.

The Dumnonians and their Dragons barely noticed them as Tphah landed in the circle of space that had formed around Kashon. Their silence sizzled in the desert air.

There had always been a distance between Kashon and the people around him, but this was somehow different.

Shashtah leapt from Tphah's back and raced to his friend. "What's wrong?"

"Nothing I can't handle now that you're safely Bonded to Tphah," Kashon snapped with uncharacteristic vehemence.

Tphah quickly shifted to her humanform and took Quatar and Peri from Katrell, gathering them protectively under her arms.

"The sunstruck fool plans to challenge a Dragonlord for command of a century so he can accept you and Tphah under him for the Training." Katrell's disapproving voice crackled like skyfire as he joined them in the center of the circle.

Shashtah glanced from Katrell to Kashon. "Is that wise?"

"Probably not," Kashon growled. "But if I fail, Katrell and I can take Peri into exile with us and you can stay here with Tphah."

"Exile?" Shashtah echoed.

Kashon dropped his voice even lower. "You bought Peri his life, not a place in our society. Adding a Dragonslayer to your household only makes everything worse. None of the Dragonlords think you can raise the boys and function as a Dragonrider at the same time. You will have to leave Dumnonia if you insist on keeping them with you."

"But the Council isn't going to banish our last living Prophetess!" Shashtah protested.

Katrell and Kashon both reflexively reached out and laid their hands on Shashtah's arms, as if they were ready to restrain him.

"Tphah would stay here," Shaharadesh said as he separated himself from the crowd.

"And you would go into exile without her," Makara added, taking her place at Shaharadesh's side.

Shashtah closed his eyes against what he thought was a headache. He belatedly recognized the straining of his new Bond with Tphah as she tried to control her distress. He opened his eyes and stared at her, standing there with Peri and Quatar in her arms, glittering in the midday sun. *My new Prophetess or my dead Prophetess's son.*

Kashon tightened his grip on Shashtah's arm. "It's an impossible choice, and everyone knows that. There is nothing you can do, but I can do something. Either I win and take you under my command or I lose and you stay here with Tphah while I take the boys and go into exile with them and Katrell. I am not going to let you risk another Bond-Break!"

"Nor I!" Garesh boomed from where he had returned to his perch on the canyon wall.

Several of the other Council members echoed Garesh's support.

Shashtah frowned at Kashon. Some of Tkai's memories of a younger version of his friend drifted through his mind. "How could you do that, after all you have endured over so many years in order to stay here?"

Kashon kept his eyes on the Dragonlords, refusing to meet Shashtah's gaze. "Because the answer to our problems isn't always found in our desert. You taught me that."

Makara stepped forward, pointing at the boys. "There is another way. Execute the mutant and the Dragonslayer. Then all the true Dragons and their Riders can stay."

"Peri is too a true Dragon!" Quatar contradicted the Dragonqueen and was rapidly silenced by Tphah.

Peri looked trustingly at Shashtah.

"We cannot have this kind of discord!" Kashon insisted. "If I win, our problem is solved. If I lose, there are many here who will neither miss me nor the problems I take with me."

Shashtah's eyes widened as he heard the double meaning in Kashon's words. Peri and Quatar weren't the only problems. Katrell was also one. *Is he planning to throw the fight so he can take Katrell to safety outside of Dumnonia?* Shashtah felt the calculations tumble through his mind as quickly as if he were trading with the Crown Prince of the Krills. *No. Both he and Katrell are too invested in Tphah. They will not abandon her, and they will not allow her to be separated from them. She is too valuable to Katrell. Kashon plans to win. But how?* "I stand with you in the Valley of Ancients." Shashtah clasped Kashon's hand as he quoted from *The Book of Light*.

"I have no fear," Kashon replied.

Shashtah released him and smiled his resignation at Katrell. "I'm sorry. Your Rider is correct: This is the only way." He joined Tphah at the edge of the circle and took Peri from her, hefting the dragonboy into his arms.

Tphah took her place at her Rider's side and lifted Quatar, creating almost an exact mirror image of Shashtah's stance. She turned her anxious eyes on her Trainers.

Shaharadesh took his frustration out on Kashon. "Dragonrider Kashon, is it your intention to challenge a Dragonlord for command of a century?" he snarled.

"It is," Kashon said solemnly and loud enough for there to be no mistake.

"By tradition," Shaharadesh spat, "you will fight for yourself with your Dragon acting as your Second." He turned on Katrell. "You may intervene if at any time you fear for your Rider's life." He clearly expected Katrell to do so before the fight even started. "The moment you enter the fight, the judgment will go against your Rider. Is that understood?"

Visibly flustered, Katrell nodded. "Understood."

Kashon, with a reassuring smile, smoothly guided Katrell into position. "I believe in you," he whispered. "Believe in me."

Shashtah took a deep breath and held it. *Katrell has to stay out of the fight for Kashon's plan to work.* Shashtah glanced at the grim faces in the crowd. Kashon was the only one who seemed to have any confidence in Katrell's ability to remain in control.

"If the judgment goes against you," Shaharadesh droned, calling Kashon's attention back to him, "you may resume a post under the command of any Dragonlord who will have you. If you cannot bring yourself to do this, or if no one will accept you, you must withdraw beyond the borders of Dumnonia and stay there until your Bond breaks. Do you understand?"

Kashon nodded. "I understand."

"Whom do you Challenge?" Shaharadesh indicated the nine Dragonlords who stood at the edge of the circle.

Shashtah studied the officers. Two of the male Dragonlords looked annoyed. Corban looked as if Kassandra had just stepped on his foot. Most of the rest looked heartsick. Only Dameth, Kashon's own Dragonlord, looked smug.

"You!" Kashon stabbed his finger at the corpulent figure of the aging Dragonlord. "I challenge Dameth, Dragonlord of Dumnonia!"

Dameth's face hardened with glee. "I accept, and, as is my right, I choose to have my Dragon, Tlee of the House of Tchang, member of the Council of Ancients, fight for me while I act as his Second."

Kashon shrugged as if he had expected nothing less, but Katrell noticeably paled.

"So be it!" Shaharadesh declared, stepping to one side of the circle, escorting Makara with him.

Shashtah fought to remember what the humanform of the Ancient Dragon looked like as the enormous male leapt from his place on the rim and glided toward the Valley floor.

:*He looks like anything he wants to!*: Tphah despaired. :*He's a shapeshifter, remember?*:

Tlee shifted to his humanform. He looked much like Katrell only taller and more muscular. Everything about him practically screamed "Dragon Warrior." He may have been descended from Tchang, but the Dragonprophet's skill at foretelling the future had completely skipped over the Councilor. Instead, he appeared to be as perfectly designed for war as Garesh was for trading. Tlee, the grimmest expression Shashtah had ever seen on anyone's face, stepped into the circle and saluted Kashon.

Dameth took his place as Tlee's Second but seemed to pay more attention to the Dragon-shaped ring that shone on his left hand than to the impending fight.

Shashtah swallowed his heart back into his chest as Kashon returned Tlee's salute. :*Hope you like spending your leave in Daethia,*: Shashtah commented silently to Tphah.

Tphah's desperately-suppressed chuckle unexpectedly set up a glitter in their Bond. :*I see his plan! Have a little faith in your friends, Dragonheart! Kashon might not stand a chance against most of the Dragonlords, but he has spent almost every day since he Bonded wrestling with a Dragon. Do you think he always lets Katrell come out on top?*:

Shashtah felt a blush spread over his cheeks at her crude but accurate remark. :*Dameth is a fool and too prejudiced to see that in his choice of champion he has already lost the fight!*: He held his breath as Shaharadesh signaled for the challenge to begin. Shashtah watched the two fighters subtly shifting their weight, reminding their muscles to subdue rather than kill. Causing a death in a challenge fight, by Corin's Law, would result in the execution of both Dragon and Rider. Neither party wanted to risk that.

Kashon and Tlee circled each other, feinting, testing for habits and weaknesses.

Tlee closed first, grabbing Kashon by both arms, heaving him into the air, and throwing him toward the sand.

Kashon arched his back, landed on his feet and hands and sprang into a fighting position once more.

Tlee raised an eyebrow in surprise and began to circle his opponent more cautiously.

Kashon darted in and out like an asp. On his third strike he managed to trip Tlee.

Tlee sat down hard, but swiveled and was back on his feet faster than an eye could blink.

Tphah pressed close to Shashtah. Her reassuring presence and confidence in Kashon flowed into his mind.

He's her teacher, Shashtah reminded himself. *She thinks he can do anything.*

Quatar indecorously urged Kashon on, while Peri clutched tightly to Shashtah's neck, apparently hoping he could help the Dragonheart hold him tightly enough to save him again.

Katrell, every muscle in his body poised to spring to the rescue if a mishap should befall his Rider, watched Tlee close on Kashon again.

Dameth, in contrast, seemed more immediately concerned about a speck of dirt under one of his too-long fingernails than about his Dragon.

This time Tlee stood with his legs apart as he prepared to gather his opponent into a constricting hug.

Kashon abruptly slipped feet first between Tlee's legs, twisted, clasped his opponent's ankles and tugged, overbalancing him.

Tlee fell inelegantly onto his face in the sand.

Kashon twisted again, caught Tlee between his own extraordinarily powerful legs and flipped the flailing Councilor onto his back.

"Told you," Tphah murmured in Shashtah's ear.

Kashon straddled Tlee and tried to force his shoulders toward the sand. Dismay swept over Kashon's face as he suddenly realized that, for all his effort, he simply did not have the brute strength it would take to pin Tlee and force him into submission.

Katrell fidgeted as Tlee grabbed Kashon, pulled him to his chest and started to squeeze.

:*Stay put!*: Shashtah ordered silently, even though he knew Katrell could not hear his thoughts. :*Kashon can do this. He will be all right. Tlee will not endanger his life. You know he won't. Dameth might have risked Breaking your Bond, but Tlee never will! He will not kill Kashon! Stay put!*:

Kashon's hands, trapped inside the crooks of Tlee's elbows, prevented the Councilor from forcing all of the air from his lungs. He suddenly exhaled.

Tlee's hold loosened by a fraction of a sword's edge.

Kashon's hands dove for Tlee's throat as he swung his legs onto either side of the Councilor's hips.

Tlee blurred unpredictably between his dragon- and humanforms as Kashon dug his fingers deeply into his throat, imitating the draconic lovemaking hold. His instincts hopelessly confused, Tlee gripped Kashon's shoulders with his talons, drawing blood.

Katrell whimpered but held still.

At the sight of the blood Tlee immediately relaxed and bared his throat in submission.

Dameth gave a strangled scream.

"The match goes to Kashon, Dragonlord of Dumnonia!" Shaharadesh declared.

Kashon instantly released Tlee and bounded to his feet. Disoriented, he glanced around until he found Katrell. He charged. He leapt into the air, his legs wrapping neatly around his Dragon's hips, hands gripping each side of the beloved head, and lips planting an ecstatic kiss on Katrell's relieved smile as the dragonman caught him in his powerful arms.

"Why you unholy—!" Dameth drew his jambiya and charged at Kashon's bleeding back.

Shashtah dropped Peri and dove at the former Dragonlord.

Shaharadesh saw the problem just as Shashtah's hand closed on Dameth's cloak. "No!"

Katrell spun automatically, shielding his cherished Rider with his own body.

Shashtah's weight on the cloak overbalanced Dameth just enough so that the blade of the jambiya only ripped Katrell's shirt.

Tlee, horror lining his features, staggered to his feet. "You would kill a Rider?"

Dameth wheeled in fury, brandishing the jambiya only a handspan from Shashtah's throat, as Katrell lowered Kashon to the ground. "Abomination!"

Tphah released Quatar.

The boy spun into a fighting stance between Peri and Dameth with the skill of a much older warrior.

"FREEZE!" Tphah thundered in her dragonvoice.

Dameth froze.

Shashtah placed his hand over Dameth's heart to push him away. Light leapt from his fingertips.

Tlee screeched his distress and dropped to his knees, clutching his head.

Dameth collapsed, letting his jambiya fall from his hand so he could grasp his own head.

Horror swept through Shashtah like a sandstorm. "What happened?" He slid onto the sand beside the Councilor and grabbed him by the shoulders. "What did I do?"

"You Broke their Bond!" Kashon whispered in awe.

Light flashed from Shashtah's fingers yet again, this time enveloping Tlee.

Shashtah snatched his hands away from the Councilor. "No! No! I don't have that power! I'm not the king!"

"Maybe I'm not the king," Shaharadesh observed quietly.

Shashtah looked at his fingers and silently screamed. *Dragonheart. Prophet. King? While Shaharadesh is still alive?*

"You didn't harm me, Dragonheart," Tlee insisted. "You freed me." He rose, walked over to Dameth and kicked the jambiya out of his former Rider's reach. "Get out of my sight!" he spat in ClearTalk.

Dameth looked up at Tlee in pain and shock. Unable to face the Councilor's fury, he staggered to his feet and stumbled away.

The crowd parted to let Dameth pass.

"Bond magic," Shaharadesh marveled. "And not even a Trained Rider yet."

"I couldn't—" Shashtah's mind refused to form a complete thought. "I wouldn't—"

Kashon helped Shashtah rise. "Calm down," he said quietly.

Light flashed from Shashtah's hands again, this time healing Kashon.

"I can't control it!" Shashtah shrieked.

"Look at me." Kashon grabbed Shashtah's shoulders. "It's not your power to control. It's your god's. The Dumnonians know that. The Dragons know that. You are not a danger to us. You are a gift."

Shashtah kept staring at his hands. "It just—! I didn't mean to—!"

Kahson tried again. "We all saw what happened. You didn't hurt Tlee. You helped him. Just as you've helped me."

Tlee strode over to Shashtah, a worried look on his face. "Is the Dragonheart all right?"

"I think his mind is snapping," Kashon replied in a somewhat conversational tone. "It may have been too soon for him to Bond again." He glanced from Shashtah to Tphah, who was indeed holding her temples as if her newly formed Bond was about the break. "Get over here, you nit," he called to her. "You've seen me do this thousands of times with Katrell."

Tphah hurried to Shashtah's side. She took him from Kashon and embraced him. Bronze wings sprouted from her back. She pulled Shashtah close and folded her wings around him, blocking out the world. "Listen to me, Dragonheart," she whispered as she leaned her forehead against his. "It is just as you Prophesied. That's all. You told me to be ready, and I am. I am not going to lose you."

"How much damage can I do before they banish me?" Shashtah heard the horror in his voice.

Tphah kissed his temple. "It's not damage, Dragonheart," she whispered in his ear. "It is change. Change we should have made long ago. It is not your will. It is the will of your god. You are simply his instrument in this world. I am with you, and I will not let them separate you from me. You no longer have to bear the burden alone. Take strength from me."

Tphah's lips closed on his. She welded her soul to his in ways even their Bond had not made possible.

A member of the House of Tchang. A Prophetess. A too-young Priestess of the Mother. The thoughts tumbled through Shashtah's head. *She's not just a Dragon. What on Centuria is she?*

:*I AM YOURS!*: Tphah's voice resounded in his head.

The power drove all fears from Shashtah's heart. His head cleared until all that remained was the certainty of his love for his beautiful Prophetess.

Tphah broke the kiss, and her wings disappeared as she took her fully humanform once more. "Fear not," she assured Shaharadesh. "You are still king. The Dragonheart is only what he is."

Shaharadesh nodded his acknowledgement of the Prophetess's words. "Then Shashtah Dragonheart, I assign you to the century of Kashon, Dragonlord of Dumnonia."

Shashtah sank backward unabashedly into Tphah's possessive embrace as she hugged him from behind. He looked at Kashon. "What time do we report for duty, sir?"

Kashon stifled a slightly hysterical laugh and reached for Katrell's eager hand. "*Tah!*"

Shashtah groaned in dismay as he translated the word. "Dawn."

Kashon leaned closer and lowered his voice. "The Training begins with learning how to spend a week, safely, under your Dragon's wing. And believe me, after tonight, you aren't going to want to move."

Shashtah shifted his weight so he stood on his own feet, but he still felt Tphah's touch on his body and mind. He raised his fist to his chest in the proper salute to his Dragonlord.

Katrell beamed proudly at Kashon.

Shaharadesh tugged at his beardless chin. "Now I have to figure out where I'm going to scavenge enough food for a double feast. Unless you have another miracle planned . . ." He let his voice trail off half-hopefully as he stared at Shashtah.

Shashtah spread his hands in genuine regret. "Unfortunately I don't have the slightest control over such mundane things as miracles."

Shaharadesh's laugh held no rancor. "I didn't think it would hurt to ask. Makara!"

From the speed with which Makara shifted to her dragonform, Shashtah suspected that the king's shout had been mental as well as physical.

Katrell convulsively gripped Kashon's arm.

Kashon, his grin never wavering, patted Katrell's hand.

Shaharadesh hauled himself onto Makara's back and settled firmly into his seat.

Makara launched herself into the air. With a rush of sand and wind, the Dragonqueen rose high above the Valley.

As soon as the royal pair flew through a warp Quatar and Peri charged at Shashtah. They crashed into his knees.

Katrell and Kashon reached out their hands to steady Shashtah as his searching fingers latched onto the scruffs of the necks of his two overzealous charges.

Tphah hastily picked up Peri, and Shashtah hoisted Quatar onto his right hip.

Quatar threw his small, but powerful, arms around Shashtah's neck. "I'm going to be a Dragonrider just like you when I grow up!" he exclaimed in Dumnonian.

Shashtah laughed silently at himself. *I should have known the elves would teach him my language.*

"And I'm going to be his Dragon!" Peri proclaimed.

Shashtah held out his left hand for Peri.

Tphah released the dragonboy.

Shashtah lifted Peri onto his left hip. "For now will you both simply be my fosterlings?"

The boys promptly smacked their heads together in their eagerness to hug him.

"Ow!" Quatar yelped, rubbing his forehead.

Peri stopped rubbing his own bump and reached out to touch his foster brother's. "I'll have Tphah show me how to heal you the way she heals the Dragonheart."

Tphah chuckled and laid her hands on the boys' heads. Light flickered briefly over their injuries at her touch. "There. Now pay attention to what's going on around you so you can take better care of each other. Just because my Rider has sand for brains doesn't mean his fosterlings have to follow his example!"

Shashtah's laugh was cut short as he noticed Garesh standing on the opposite side of the rapidly-filling circle. The Ancient Councilor beamed with pride as he met his son's gaze. "Father . . . " Shashtah whispered. Then the Dumnonians and their Dragons surged around the newly Bonded Pair and their Dragonlord, offering congratulations, and Shashtah lost sight of Garesh's face in the crowd.

Shashtah and Tphah

CHAPTER 14:

True Friends

A friend loves for all seasons, and a sibling is born for adversity.

—from *Dumnonian Proverbs*,
by Shane of Corin

SHASHTAH, ONCE MORE BEDECKED in a simple white aba and keffiyeh, lounged at left end of the head table, doing his best to appear relaxed. This time the clothes had been procured for him by Tphah's seductive wheedling rather than Tkai's vicious glare, and they fit him much better. He quickly suppressed the sadness that welled within him at the thought of his dead Dragon, not wanting to upset his new Bond Partner. A slight smile curled across his lips at the memory of the appalled look on the tailor's face when Shashtah had refused the traditional agal and insisted on wearing the carved leather thong Tphah had given him so long ago in what seemed like another life. *Am I destined to break every tradition Dumnonia has ever had?* He felt Tphah send a wave of pleasure through their Bond from where she was sitting at the other end of the table. She was happier than he had ever thought she could be, and that should have been all that mattered to him. His smiled faded as his gaze fell on Kashon, and he sighed.

Kashon sat between Shashtah and Shaharadesh, fidgeting with the ring shaped like a Bronze Dragon that now adorned the third finger on his left hand. Whether he was upset that Makara was making another attempt to enlist Katrell's services for the evening or at something else, Shashtah could not tell. The Dragons sat at the other end of the table, well out of his sight. :Is Katrell all right?: Shashtah ventured as he braced himself to receive a reprimand for speaking silently to his Dragon in the presence of others.

Instead of the sharp retort he had become accustomed to with Tkai, Tphah's chuckle shimmered through his head, sending a feeling of warmth and wellbeing through him. :Katrell's making mad, passionate love to me. Makara's turning copper with jealousy!:

Unsure whether to believe her since he was not experiencing any of the discomfort Kashon and Shaharadesh suffered while Katrell and Makara were mating, Shashtah tried to lean out over the table to peer discretely at the Dragons, but the detritus from the feast that littered his plate prevented him from getting a clear view. Everyone had been able to eat his or her fill with food to spare. This celebration was no paltry feast from scavenging Dragons or otherworldly bounty from an overgenerous god. They had all gorged themselves disgracefully on the unexpected plenty Shaharadesh himself had managed to conjure for the celebration. Fresh-baked bread, crocks of butter, candy from the best stalls in Krillion, wheels of white and yellow cheese, herb-roasted chickens, luxuriant dates, sweet figs, smoked fish, wild fowl stuffed with rice, bowls of honey, great skins of fermented mare's milk, pitchers of camel and goat milk, two whole roasted haunches of mutton, and piles of nuts, olives, and raisins had laden the center table and spilled out of the enormous tent that was woefully inadequate to hold the number of Dragons and Riders who were in Camp for the Bonding of their last Prophetess. Dumnonian maidens and youths slipped unobtrusively through the crowd, filling empty goblets with fine red wine and offering small cups of strong, dark qaffah to those who had tired of the alcohol. The question of where the caravan and its timely trader, who bore an all-too-marked resemblance to the Elven Lord, had arrived from still tugged at Shashtah's mind, but he was determined to enjoy the feast in spite of Kashon's nerves. Kashon had already warned him that he would pay for his indulgence with his hide at dawn. Shashtah smiled to himself, rejoicing in the friendship of a comrade who would treat him just like everyone else. He was neither monstrosity nor Prophet to Kashon. Simply another Dragonrider . . .

Shashtah glanced around for his boys and spotted them at the rear of the tent with the elf whose caravan had supplied the feast. Shashtah's trader's curiosity finally got the better of him. He leaned close to Kashon's ear and murmured, "With your leave."

Kashon favored him with an understanding smile. "Go."

Shashtah threaded his way to the back of the tent, exchanging a private word with each reveler he met on his way. He did not know their names nor recognize their faces, nor even remember if they were a Dragon or a Dumnonian. But they did not seem to mind. He was there among them, and he took the time to notice them. Hand after hand silently reached out to touch his robes as he passed through the exuberant crowd.

Shashtah felt curiously exhausted when he finally reached the tiny group that was his goal. "I see you've found a friend, Quatar," he observed in elvish as he dropped in a salaam to the trader.

The elf's arms were enormously powerful beneath his simple desert robes, and his head, as he returned Shashtah's greeting, inclined with the fluid, choreographed movement of royalty long used to command.

Shashtah hid a grin of self-satisfaction at his discovery of the ruse. "My personal thanks for this bounty and for attending to my obligations." He placed his hand lightly on Quatar's head.

Quatar beamed up at him with delight. "Dragonheart!" The boy's dark hair blended well enough with that of the Dumnonians, and years of living beneath the desert sun would eventually turn his pale skin the appropriate shade of bronze. But his intelligent, deep brown, all-too-Daethian eyes would make Quatar an outcast among Shashtah's people as surely as Peri was an outcast among Dragons.

"He doesn't like to be called that," Peri reminded Quatar.

Shashtah tousled Peri's hair with genuine affection for the putrid little runt he knew hid beneath the shapeshifted skin. "I think I'm stuck with the name whether I want it or not." *At least they will have someone to play with while I'm earning those scars and callouses Kashon has been raving about.* He glanced at the head table, noting that Tphah was indeed cavorting shamelessly with Katrell in her efforts to keep him out of Makara's clutches. Shashtah turned his grimace into a smile. "Fortunate for Shaharadesh that you rode into Camp," he observed. "So few caravans survive the trip from the Great Woods anymore. What on Centuria was my king able to trade you for such bounty?"

The elf-in-trader's clothing flushed at the unwanted attention. "Garesh mentioned that the Galantites of Mount Paradin need several dunes worth of sand for their mining operations."

Shashtah threw back his head and roared with laughter. "I wish I could have seen Shaharadesh's face when he heard that!"

The disguised elf smiled. "He was indeed . . . perplexed."

Shashtah returned Juel's grin. "How in the name of the Light were you able to get away from Tor?"

"The Kyondoca are extremely efficient, and my aunt is paying attention to no one except Criton. I doubt anyone has noticed that I'm gone." Juel snaked his arm absently around Peri.

"Plus you had an uncontrollable urge to see Tkai's son," Shashtah observed.

Juel shrugged. "Do you blame me?"

"No," Shashtah said. "Thank you for enabling my king to supply a worthy feast. I do not deserve such generosity from you."

"Oh, but you do!" Juel lowered his solid violet eyes, suddenly ashamed. "I should have been as generous for your first Bonding Feast, but I was angry with Tkai and jealous of you when Gran'da told me you two had Bonded." He looked at Shashtah, his features melting just for an instant into those of his true form as his emotions blurred his ability to control his magic. The deep hurt of a lost love cast shadows within his violet eyes. "Forgive me, Dragonheart. We owe you so much for helping Gran'da and my uncle buy this delay." Juel's features hardened into the shape of the disguise once more.

Shashtah favored the Elven Lord with an understanding smile. "Tkai would be pleased."

Tphah rose, hauled Katrell to his feet, and whirled him away from the head table. The Dragons joined the other revelers in a festive dance.

Makara's face darkened with frustration, and she made a move to go after them.

Shaharadesh put a restraining hand on the Dragonqueen's arm.

Makara continued to scowl at Tphah and Katrell, but she settled once more beside the king.

Kashon looked both relieved and abandoned at Katrell's escape. His keffiyeh draped just enough that Shahardesh could not see his own haunted look reflected in his newest Dragonlord's eyes.

Shashtah contemplated for a moment about how much the two Dumnonians looked alike, then smiled at himself. *It's hard for two Dumnonians not to look alike. Isn't that the point? To keep enemies from guessing who is who? Still,* he sighed, *clothes, no matter how awkward, always seem to look better on Kashon.*

"Enchanting," Juel murmured as he watched Tphah and Katrell twirl like dervishes as they danced their way through the crowd. "Lovers?"

"Hmm," Shashtah grunted. "But not each other's." He intercepted the dancing Dragons, preventing them from crashing into his two young charges and the elf. "Must you carry on like a couple of overgrown pigeons?"

Katrell blushed, his bronze skin glistening with perspiration from his dancing. He glanced at Kashon who was staring wistfully at him.

"I will not allow any of my friends to be unhappy tonight!" Tphah declared. She laughed as she planted a kiss on Shashtah's lips and acknowledged Quatar and Peri with a nod. She reached down and grasped Juel's hand. "That includes you, Elven Lord," she murmured in elvish. Her voice was almost too soft to hear. "A greater love has been saved for you than the one you have lost. That's a Prophecy."

Juel favored her with a sad smile. "Thank you for your gift, Prophetess. Forgive me if I cannot take your words to heart just yet."

Shashtah noted that Juel's free hand never stopped caressing Peri as if the boy were a beloved pet. He crouched until he was at eyelevel with Peri. "Tphah and I have to do a lot of boring political stuff. Would you like to spend tonight with this trader and learn how caravaneers live?"

Peri stared up at Juel, wide-eyed. "Could I?"

"Me, too?" Quatar asked promptly.

Juel smiled his thanks at Shashtah. "Come on. You can help me put the camels to bed for the night." He rose and escorted the children outside.

Shashtah stood up and watched them go.

"That was sweet," Tphah said softly.

Shashtah sighed. "This War is going to tear Juel away from Peri as surely as it tore him from Tkai."

Tphah nodded. "He will always be a good friend, but a distant one."

Shashtah slipped his arm around her waist and turned her so that she could see the head table where Makara, Shaharadesh and Kashon were all looking as if they had each lost their only friend. "One of us has to rescue Kashon while the other cheers up our grim majesties."

"It's my fault," Katrell sighed, sending Shashtah and Tphah, who had forgotten he was there, jumping halfway out of their skins. "You two need to enjoy tonight more than Kashon and I do. I'll stop torturing everyone by delaying the inevitable. Thank you for trying, Tphah." He lowered his eyes. "I'm sorry things have to change between us tomorrow."

Shashtah clapped Katrell on the shoulder. "I want you to be harder on us than you've ever imagined anyone could be," he declared, an irrepressible gleam twinkling in his eyes, "and then I want you to remember how you treated us when Tphah's Prophecy comes true about me becoming king some day!"

Katrell shot a rueful glance toward Kashon. "My Rider has done everything he can to stay away from our king, and now he's stuck on display next to him. I'm not convinced this was a good plan."

"Since when do Dumnonians plan?" Tphah shrugged.

Shashtah's face brightened at a sudden idea. He tapped Katrell on his arm. "Go back to your tent, and wait for Kashon. I think I can guarantee he'll be with you shortly."

Katrell looked puzzled but bared his throat slightly and ducked outside.

Tphah studied Shashtah's face. "What are you up to?"

"Probably too much," Shashtah murmured. "Could you find my

father and suggest to him that as the Council Leader he should spend some time with Makara, sorting out their new relationship?"

Tphah raised her eyebrow in curiosity, but nodded and set off to locate Garesh.

Shashtah swiftly made his way through the crowd to Kashon's side. He sank onto the elaborately embroidered pillows beside his friend. "Lord Kashon?" he asked, receiving a resigned smile from his friend. He went on without waiting for permission to speak. "Your Dragon wishes me to tell you that he is waiting for you in your tent: He needs to go over the plans for our Training, and he wants to inform you of your other responsibilities as Dragonlord."

Kashon's forced smile widened into a genuine grin. "Don't think I'm going to go easy on you if you do me enough favors."

"By this time tomorrow I fully expect you to be making my life utterly miserable," Shashtah confirmed. "So take advantage of my largess while I'm still feeling charitable."

"As you command, Dra—" Kashon grinned and corrected himself. "Shashtah." He leapt to his feet in a swirl of robes and took his leave of Shaharadesh with a salaam.

Shaharadesh shifted so Kashon's traditional parting met his back.

Shashtah held his breath, but Kashon simply straightened and left the head table without another word. Shashtah watched the crowd part before Kashon as he strode outside. Shashtah popped a date into his mouth as he spotted Tphah deep in conversation with Garesh.

Shaharadesh followed Shashtah's gaze as the onetime trader took his leave of Tphah and wound his way to the head table.

Garesh, looking hardly a day over fifty, bent in a salaam before Makara, took the Dragonqueen's hand in his own and kissed it reverently.

Over the laughter of the crowd, Shashtah could not hear what his father was saying, but he had heard the honeyed spiel directed at his mother often enough that he was not surprised when Makara made her apologies to Shaharadesh and followed Garesh outside. Shashtah raised his wine cup and toasted his king. "A spectacular feast, majesty."

Shaharadesh stared down at his barely-touched plate. "Take care of her for me when I'm gone, Dragonheart. She's not all bad."

"She's not bad at all from a Dragon's point of view," Shashtah responded. "She adores someone who is only going to be around long enough for her to blink a few times, and she has no idea how to deal with that. No wonder Lord Criton is so frustrated with us! We're like trying to stop a star from falling out of the night-darkened sky!"

Shaharadesh sipped slowly at his wine, then stared at Shashtah. "Not you, Dragonheart. There's too much Dragon blood in you for you to die too soon. I'm afraid you are doomed to live."

"Doomed to stand around long enough for Lord Criton to figure out what a Dumnonian looks like anyway," Shashtah said.

"A pity Tkai didn't curse us all to live forever as she did the Elven Lord," the king mused, too far gone in his wine to notice his tactless reference to Shashtah's dead Dragon.

Shashtah felt the light in his heart drive the darkness from his breast. "The bodies die, sire," he proclaimed. "But the souls live on. All that is good in us cannot be lost. I will not accept that! We're like metal in a forge, trying over and over until we work out our impurities and show our worth forever and ever, like the sun."

Shaharadesh suppressed a smile. "And then what, Dragonheart?"

"And then," Shashtah declared, feeling the words rise from his burning heart and blaze out of his mouth, "then we shall join with all the loved ones we have lost and add our own brilliance to the eternal glory of the Light!"

Shaharadesh stared thoughtfully into his cup for a moment. "Do you really believe that?"

Shashtah paused for a moment, then gave his king a decisive nod. "With all my heart."

Shaharadesh raised his goblet in a toast to Shashtah. "May you be right, Dragonheart. A man could ignite a nation with such a dream." He downed his wine. "But beware of nomads with a vision: They tend to conquer the world. You may not want to rule that much." He smiled and waved Shashtah away. "Go on! I'm not so fragile that I need a nursemaid. Makara will return soon enough. Go enjoy Tphah while you can."

Shashtah took leave of his king and pushed his way through the crowd until he found Tphah among the revelers.

Tphah daintily danced away from a male Dragonlord who had claimed her as a partner and whirled into Shashtah's arms.

"Now," Shashtah murmured, "if I can just get you to pull a maneuver like that in midair . . . "

"Until you've fasted for a week as punishment for one imagined fault after another, I doubt either Kashon or Katrell will let us try!" Tphah laughed.

"I'm glad you're going to enjoy this," Shashtah growled as he danced a few steps with her, then took her hand firmly in his and pulled her out into the blessedly cool night air.

Tphah slipped her arm around his waist as they strolled toward the edge of the King's Camp.

Shashtah gazed at the black velvet sky, dotted with countless stars. "It almost seems a shame to spend a night like this inside a tent."

"I should warn you," Tphah murmured, "the Trainee's tent we've been assigned is a good deal smaller than Kashon's. It could prove embarrassing if we let our dragonforms get the better of us, and I won't guarantee that either of us will have the energy for such amusements for a long time after tonight."

Shashtah hugged her close with his left arm. "The offer is tempting, but I really should get some sleep. It's been a hard rotation."

"More like a hard five years," Tphah chuckled softly.

They paused at the edge of the King's Camp, slowly filling their lungs with the clean scent of the desert wind.

:*The Dark One will never know from which way that wind comes nor which way it will blow,*: Shashtah thought grimly.

:*Prophecy?*: Tphah grinned as she shifted to her dragonform and carved a nest in the side of a sand dune.

Shashtah happily crawled into the cradle she made for him out of her forearms. :*Possibly.*:

Tphah folded her wings tightly behind her back and laid her armored head on the still warm sand. :*Pleasant dreams, Dragonheart,*: she wished him as she closed her glittering eyes. :*Pleasant dreams.*:

:*You, too, Tphah,*: Shashtah's mind whispered as he drifted safely off to sleep in his Prophetess's loving arms.

Acknowledgements

I created the world of Centuria well over a quarter of a century ago when I was at Alhambra High School in Mr. Craig Heney's Creative Writing class. My friend, Dave Rangel, had recently shoved the works of J.R.R. Tolkien into my hands and then introduced me to the game of Dungeons & Dragons (D&D). I wrote the first novel of what would become *The Wizards of Corin* series in Mr. Heney's class. At the time, Dave drew illustrations of many of my characters, which helped me visualize them and the world in which they lived. So many thanks to Craig Heney and Dave Rangel for starting me on this journey.

I continued to develop the world of Centuria while playing D&D games with members of The Third Foundation, the science fiction and fantasy club at Occidental College (yes, I did attend at the same time as President Obama. No, I don't remember him. I got the room below his on the floor in Haines Hall the year after he lived in that dorm). Eventually Third Foundationers convinced me to write more of the stories down. Hence, I owe a big shout-out to The Third Foundation for encouraging me to continue along this path.

The Dragonlords of Dumnonia series is a spinoff from *The Wizards of Corin*, which I began penning in Scriptorium 101, the writing group that met in my home for many, many years when I lived on the Westside of L.A. I truly appreciate all of the support, comments, critiques, discussions, and time they volunteered to help me take the D&D games we played in Dumnonia and turn them into these stories.

I am tremendously grateful for the support and advice of Dr. Ken Atchity, who was my Creative Writing professor at Occidental College and who is now helping me publish my books through Story Merchant Books.

A huge thank you to my illustrator, Laura Cameron! We first worked as a team in the 1990s when I was publishing stories in Mercedes Lackey fanzines. Laura has always had a knack for taking what was in my head and putting it into drawings. I greatly admire her skill and thoroughly enjoy working with her.

As to everyone else who has been part of the process of taking *Dragon Heart* from creation to novel, you have my deepest gratitude. A thousand apologies if I have failed to mention you by name. Know that I am eternally grateful to you all.

Dear Reader,

As a storyteller, I am honored that you have chosen to spend your time dreaming my tale with me. As I mentioned above, there are many more of the Dragonlords of Dumnonia and Wizards of Corin books yet to be published. I chose to start with Dragon Heart because my short story Dragonprophet won an award in an online magazine many years ago, but, as the other books come out, I hope you will return to spend time with old friends and to make new acquaintances as you follow their adventures in their magical world. Please take the time to tell others about *Dragon Heart*, be that by word of mouth or by writing a review on Amazon.com or elsewhere on the Internet or in print.

May the Light be with you! Or, as Shashtah would say, "Eternal Death to the Dark One!"

Linda A. Malcor

About the Author

Dr. Linda A. Malcor is a folklorist and comparative mythologist who specializes in the traditions of King Arthur. She is the co-author, with C. Scott Littleton, of *From Scythia to Camelot*, a nonfiction work that has been translated into several languages. She served as the researcher for the movie *King Arthur* (2004), which was inspired by her publications. She has written many articles, short stories, and other works of fiction and nonfiction. She lives in Southern California, where she is known in fan circles as Herald-Mage Adept Danya Winterborn, co-president of the Mercedes Lackey fanclub Queen's Own (yes, she really can do stage magic!). She is an ordained elder in the Presbyterian Church (USA), through which she has engaged in many human rights activities. Her particular passion is LGBT issues, though she has recently become an advocate for Freedom of Expression in the Middle East.